PENGUIN CLASSICS

TITUS ANDRONICUS

T. J. B. SPENCER, sometime Director of the Shakespeare Institute of the University of Birmingham, was the founding editor of the New Penguin Shakespeare, for which he edited both Romeo and Juliet and Hamlet.

STANLEY WELLS is Honorary President of the Shakespeare Birthplace Trust, Emeritus Professor of Shakespeare Studies at the University of Birmingham, and General Editor of the Oxford Shakespeare. His many books include Shakespeare: For All Time, Shakespeare & Co., Shakespeare, Sex, and Love and Great Shakespeare Actors.

SONIA MASSAI is Professor of Shakespeare Studies in the English Department at King's College London. She has published widely on the history of the transmission of Shakespeare on the stage and on the page. Her publications include her book, *Shakespeare and the Rise of the Editor* (2007); collections of essays on *Shakespeare and Textual Studies* (2015) and *World-Wide Shakespeares: Local Appropriations in Film and Performance* (2005); and critical editions of *The Paratexts in English Printed Drama to* 1642 (2014) and John Ford's *Tis Pity She's a Whore* (2011).

JACQUES BERTHOUD was Head of the Department of English at the University of York between 1980 and 1997, and later Emeritus Professor. He wrote on a wide range of subjects, including Shakespeare and the South African writer Uys Krige, and was a specialist in Joseph Conrad.

WILLIAM SHAKESPEARE

Titus Andronicus

Edited by
SONIA MASSAI
and with an Introduction and Commentary by
JACQUES BERTHOUD

PENGUIN BOOKS

PENGUIN CLASSICS

UK | USA | Canada | Ireland | Australia
India | New Zealand | South Africa

Penguin Books is part of the Penguin Random House group of companies
whose addresses can be found at global.penguinrandomhouse.com.

This edition first published in Penguin Books 2001
Reissued in the Penguin Shakespeare series 2005
Reissued in Penguin Classics 2015

009

Set in PostScript Monotype Fournier
Typeset by Palimpsest Book Production Limited, Falkirk, Stirlingshire
Printed in Great Britain by Clays Ltd, Elcograf S.p.A.

ISBN: 978-0-141-39632-3

www.greenpenguin.co.uk

CONTENTS

GENERAL INTRODUCTION

Every play by Shakespeare is unique. This is part of his greatness. A restless and indefatigable experimenter, he moved with a rare amalgamation of artistic integrity and dedicated professionalism from one kind of drama to another. Never shackled by convention, he offered his actors the alternation between serious and comic modes from play to play, and often also within the plays themselves, that the repertory system within which he worked demanded, and which provided an invaluable stimulus to his imagination. Introductions to individual works in this series attempt to define their individuality. But there are common factors that underpin Shakespeare's career.

Nothing in his heredity offers clues to the origins of his genius. His upbringing in Stratford-upon-Avon, where he was born in 1564, was unexceptional. His mother, born Mary Arden, came from a prosperous farming family. Her father chose her as his executor over her eight sisters and his four stepchildren when she was only in her late teens, which suggests that she was of more than average practical ability. Her husband John, a glover, apparently unable to write, was nevertheless a capable businessman and loyal townsfellow, who seems to have fallen on relatively hard times in later life. He would have been brought up as a Catholic, and may have retained Catholic sympathies, but his son subscribed publicly to Anglicanism throughout his life.

The most important formative influence on Shakespeare was his school. As the son of an alderman who became bailiff (or mayor) in 1568, he had the right to attend the town's grammar school. Here he would have received an education grounded in classical rhetoric and oratory, studying authors such as Ovid, Cicero and Quintilian, and would have been required to read, speak, write and even think in Latin from his early years. This classical education permeates Shakespeare's work from the beginning to the end of his career. It is apparent in the self-conscious classicism of plays of the early 1590s such as the tragedy of *Titus Andronicus*, *The Comedy of Errors*, and the narrative poems *Venus and Adonis* (1592–3) and *The Rape of Lucrece* (1593–4), and is still evident in his latest plays, informing the dream visions of *Pericles* and *Cymbeline* and the masque in *The Tempest*, written between 1607 and 1611. It inflects his literary style throughout his career. In his earliest writings the verse, based on the ten-syllabled, five-beat iambic pentameter, is highly patterned. Rhetorical devices deriving from classical literature, such as alliteration and antithesis, extended similes and elaborate wordplay, abound. Often, as in *Love's Labour's Lost* and *A Midsummer Night's Dream*, he uses rhyming patterns associated with lyric poetry, each line self-contained in sense, the prose as well as the verse employing elaborate figures of speech. Writing at a time of linguistic ferment, Shakespeare frequently imports Latinisms into English, coining words such as abstemious, addiction, incarnadine and adjunct. He was also heavily influenced by the eloquent translations of the Bible in both the Bishops' and the Geneva versions. As his experience grows, his verse and prose become more supple, the patterning less apparent, more ready to accommodate the rhythms of ordinary speech, more colloquial in diction, as in the speeches of the Nurse in *Romeo and Juliet*, the characterful prose of Falstaff and Hamlet's soliloquies. The effect is of increasing psychological realism, reaching its greatest heights in *Hamlet*, *Othello*, *King Lear*, *Macbeth* and *Antony and Cleopatra*. Gradually he discovered ways of adapting the regular beat of the pentameter to make it an infinitely flexible instrument for matching thought with feeling. Towards the end of his career, in plays such as *The Winter's Tale*, *Cymbeline* and *The Tempest*, he adopts a more highly mannered style, in keeping with the more overtly symbolical and emblematical mode in which he is writing.

So far as we know, Shakespeare lived in Stratford till after his marriage to Anne Hathaway, eight years his senior, in 1582. They had three children: a daughter, Susanna, born in 1583 within six months of their marriage, and twins, Hamnet and Judith, born in 1585. The next seven years of Shakespeare's life are virtually a blank. Theories that he may have been, for instance, a schoolmaster, or a lawyer, or a soldier, or a sailor, lack evidence to support them. The first reference to him in print, in Robert Greene's pamphlet *Greene's Groatsworth of Wit* of 1592, parodies a line from *Henry VI, Part III*, implying that Shakespeare was already an established playwright. It seems likely that at some unknown point after the birth of his twins he joined a theatre company and gained experience as both actor and writer in the provinces and London. The London theatres closed because of plague in 1593 and 1594; and during these years, perhaps recognizing the need for an alternative career, he wrote and published the narrative poems *Venus and Adonis* and *The Rape of Lucrece*. These are the only works we can be certain that Shakespeare himself was responsible for putting into print. Each bears the author's dedication to Henry Wriothesley, Earl of Southampton (1573–1624), the second in warmer terms than the first. Southampton, younger than Shakespeare by ten years, is the only person to whom he personally dedicated works. The Earl may have been a close friend, perhaps even the beautiful and adored young man whom Shakespeare celebrates in his *Sonnets*.

The resumption of playing after the plague years saw the founding of the Lord Chamberlain's Men, a company to which Shakespeare was to belong for the rest of his career, as actor, shareholder and playwright. No other dramatist of the period had so stable a relationship with a single company. Shakespeare knew the actors for whom he was writing and the conditions in which they performed. The permanent company was made up of around twelve to fourteen players, but one actor often played more than one role in a play and additional actors were hired as needed. Led by the tragedian Richard Burbage (1568–1619) and, initially, the comic actor Will Kemp (d. 1603), they rapidly achieved a high reputation, and when King James I succeeded Queen Elizabeth I in 1603 they were renamed as the King's Men. All the women's parts were played by boys; there is no evidence that any female role was ever played by a male actor over the age of about eighteen. Shakespeare had enough confidence in his boys to write for them long and demanding roles such as Rosalind (who, like other heroines of the romantic comedies, is disguised as a boy for much of the action) in *As You Like It*, Lady Macbeth and Cleopatra. But there are far more fathers than mothers, sons than daughters, in his plays, few if any of which require more than the company's normal complement of three or four boys.

The company played primarily in London's public playhouses – there were almost none that we know of in the rest of the country – initially in the Theatre, built in Shoreditch in 1576, and from 1599 in the Globe, on Bankside. These were wooden, more or less circular structures, open to the air, with a thrust stage surmounted by a canopy and jutting into the area where spectators who paid one penny stood, and surrounded by galleries where it was possible to be seated on payment of an additional penny. Though properties such as cauldrons, stocks, artificial trees or beds could indicate locality, there was no representational scenery. Sound effects such as flourishes of trumpets, music both martial and amorous, and accompaniments to songs were provided by the company's musicians. Actors entered through doors in the back wall of the stage. Above it was a balconied area that could represent the walls of a town (as in *King John*), or a castle (as in *Richard II*), and indeed a balcony (as in *Romeo and Juliet*). In 1609 the company also acquired the use of the Blackfriars, a smaller, indoor theatre to which admission was more expensive, and which permitted the use of more spectacular stage effects such as the descent of Jupiter on an eagle in *Cymbeline* and of goddesses in *The Tempest*. And they would frequently perform before the court in royal residences and, on their regular tours into the provinces, in non-theatrical spaces such as inns, guildhalls and the great halls of country houses.

Early in his career Shakespeare may have worked in collaboration, perhaps with Thomas Nashe (1567–*c*. 1601) in *Henry VI, Part I* and with George Peele (1556–96) in *Titus Andronicus*. And towards the end he collaborated with George Wilkins (*fl.* 1604–8) in *Pericles*, and with his younger colleagues Thomas Middleton (1580–1627), in *Timon of Athens*, and John Fletcher (1579–1625), in *Henry VIII*, *The Two Noble Kinsmen* and the lost play *Cardenio*. Shakespeare's output dwindled in his last years, and he died in 1616 in Stratford, where he owned a fine house, New Place, and much land. His only son had died at the age of eleven, in 1596, and his last descendant died in 1670. New Place was destroyed in the eighteenth century but the other Stratford houses associated with his life are maintained and displayed to the public by the Shakespeare Birthplace Trust.

One of the most remarkable features of Shakespeare's plays is their intellectual and emotional scope. They span a great range from the lightest of comedies, such as *The Two Gentlemen of Verona* and *The Comedy of Errors*, to the profoundest of tragedies, such as *King Lear* and *Macbeth*. He maintained an output of around two plays a year, ringing the changes between comic and serious. All his comedies have serious elements: Shylock, in *The Merchant of Venice*, almost reaches tragic dimensions, and *Measure for Measure* is profoundly serious in its examination of moral problems. Equally, none of his tragedies is without humour: Hamlet is as witty as any of his comic heroes, *Macbeth* has its Porter, and *King Lear* its Fool. His greatest comic character, Falstaff, inhabits the history plays and *Henry V* ends with a marriage, while *Henry VI, Part III*, *Richard II* and *Richard III* culminate in the tragic deaths of their protagonists.

Although in performance Shakespeare's characters can give the impression of a superabundant reality, he is not a naturalistic dramatist. None of his plays is explicitly set in his own time. The action of few of them (except for the English histories) is set even partly in England (exceptions are *The Merry Wives of Windsor* and the Induction to *The Taming of the Shrew*). Italy is his favoured location. Most of his principal story-lines derive from printed writings; but the structuring and translation of these narratives into dramatic terms is Shakespeare's own, and he invents much additional material. Most of the plays contain elements of myth and legend, and many derive from ancient or more recent history or from romantic tales of ancient times and faraway places. All reflect his reading, often in close detail.

Holinshed's *Chronicles* (1577, revised 1587), a great compendium of English, Scottish and Irish history, provided material for his English history plays. The *Lives of the Noble Grecians and Romans* by the Greek writer Plutarch, finely translated into English from the French by Sir Thomas North in 1579, provided much of the narrative material, and also a mass of verbal detail, for his plays about Roman history. Some plays are closely based on shorter individual works: *As You Like It*, for instance, on the novel *Rosalynde* (1590) by his near-contemporary Thomas Lodge (1558–1625), *The Winter's Tale* on *Pandosto* (1588) by his old rival Robert Greene (1558–92) and *Othello* on a story by the Italian Giraldi Cinthio (1504–73). And the language of his plays is permeated by the Bible, the Book of Common Prayer and the proverbial sayings of his day.

Shakespeare was popular with his contemporaries, but his commitment to the theatre and to the plays in performance is demonstrated by the fact that only about half of his plays appeared in print in his lifetime, in slim paperback volumes known as quartos, so called because they were made from printers' sheets folded twice to form four leaves (eight pages). None of them shows any sign that he was involved in their publication. For him, performance was the primary means of publication. The most frequently reprinted of his works were the non-dramatic poems – the erotic *Venus and Adonis* and the more moralistic *The Rape of Lucrece*. The *Sonnets*, which appeared in 1609, under his name but possibly without his consent, were less successful, perhaps because the vogue for sonnet sequences, which peaked in the 1590s, had passed by then. They were not reprinted until 1640, and then only in garbled form along with poems by other writers. Happily, in 1623, seven years after he died, his colleagues John Heminges

(1556–1630) and Henry Condell (d. 1627) published his collected plays, including eighteen that had not previously appeared in print, in the first Folio, whose name derives from the fact that the printers' sheets were folded only once to produce two leaves (four pages). Some of the quarto editions are badly printed, and the fact that some plays exist in two, or even three, early versions creates problems for editors. These are discussed in the Account of the Text in each volume of this series.

Shakespeare's plays continued in the repertoire until the Puritans closed the theatres in 1642. When performances resumed after the Restoration of the monarchy in 1660 many of the plays were not to the taste of the times, especially because their mingling of genres and failure to meet the requirements of poetic justice offended against the dictates of neoclassicism. Some, such as *The Tempest* (changed by John Dryden and William Davenant in 1667 to suit contemporary taste), *King Lear* (to which Nahum Tate gave a happy ending in 1681) and *Richard III* (heavily adapted by Colley Cibber in 1700 as a vehicle for his own talents), were extensively rewritten; others fell into neglect. Slowly they regained their place in the repertoire, and they continued to be reprinted, but it was not until the great actor David Garrick (1717–79) organized a spectacular jubilee in Stratford in 1769 that Shakespeare began to be regarded as a transcendental genius. Garrick's idolatry prefigured the enthusiasm of critics such as Samuel Taylor Coleridge (1772–1834) and William Hazlitt (1778–1830). Gradually Shakespeare's reputation spread abroad, to Germany, America, France and to other European countries.

During the nineteenth century, though the plays were generally still performed in heavily adapted or abbreviated versions, a large body of scholarship and criticism began to amass. Partly as a result of a general swing in education away from the teaching of Greek and Roman texts and towards literature written in English, Shakespeare became the object of intensive study in schools and universities. In the theatre, important turning points were the work in England of two theatre directors, William Poel (1852–1934) and his disciple Harley Granville-Barker (1877–1946), who showed that the application of knowledge, some of it newly acquired, of early staging conditions to performance of the plays could render the original texts viable in terms of the modern theatre. During the twentieth century appreciation of Shakespeare's work, encouraged by the availability of audio, film and video versions of the plays, spread around the world to such an extent that he can now be claimed as a global author.

The influence of Shakespeare's works permeates the English language. Phrases from his plays and poems – 'a tower of strength', 'green-eyed jealousy', 'a foregone conclusion' – are on the lips of people who may never have read him. They have inspired composers of songs, orchestral music and operas; painters and sculptors; poets, novelists and film-makers. Allusions to him appear in pop songs, in advertisements and in television shows. Some of his characters – Romeo and Juliet, Falstaff, Shylock and Hamlet – have acquired mythic status. He is valued for his humanity, his psychological insight, his wit and humour, his lyricism, his mastery of language, his ability to excite, surprise, move and, in the widest sense of the word, entertain audiences. He is the greatest of poets, but he is essentially a dramatic poet. Though his plays have much to offer to readers, they exist fully only in performance. In these volumes we offer individual introductions, notes on language and on specific points of the text, suggestions for further reading and information about how each work has been edited. In addition we include accounts of the ways in which successive generations of interpreters and audiences have responded to challenges and rewards offered by the plays. The Penguin Shakespeare series aspires to remove obstacles to understanding and to make pleasurable the reading of the work of the man who has done more than most to make us understand what it is to be human.

Stanley Wells

THE CHRONOLOGY OF
SHAKESPEARE'S WORKS

A few of Shakespeare's writings can be fairly precisely dated. An allusion to the Earl of Essex in the chorus to Act V of *Henry V*, for instance, could only have been written in 1599. But for many of the plays we have only vague information, such as the date of publication, which may have occurred long after composition, the date of a performance, which may not have been the first, or a list in Francis Meres's book *Palladis Tamia*, published in 1598, which tells us only that the plays listed there must have been written by that year. The chronology of the early plays is particularly difficult to establish. Not everyone would agree that the first part of *Henry VI* was written after the third, for instance, or *Romeo and Juliet* before *A Midsummer Night's Dream*. The following table is based on the 'Canon and Chronology' section in *William Shakespeare: A Textual Companion*, by Stanley Wells and Gary Taylor, with John Jowett and William Montgomery (1987), where more detailed information and discussion may be found.

The Two Gentlemen of Verona	1590–91
The Taming of the Shrew	1590–91
Henry VI, Part II	1591
Henry VI, Part III	1591
Henry VI, Part I (perhaps with Thomas Nashe)	1592
Titus Andronicus (perhaps with George Peele)	1592
Richard III	1592–3

Venus and Adonis (poem)　　　　　　　　　　1592–3
The Rape of Lucrece (poem)　　　　　　　　　1593–4
The Comedy of Errors　　　　　　　　　　　1594
Love's Labour's Lost　　　　　　　　　　　1594–5
Edward III (authorship uncertain, not included
　　in this series)　　not later than 1595 (printed in 1596)
Richard II　　　　　　　　　　　　　　　1595
Romeo and Juliet　　　　　　　　　　　　1595
A Midsummer Night's Dream　　　　　　　　1595
King John　　　　　　　　　　　　　　　1596
The Merchant of Venice　　　　　　　　　　1596–7
Henry IV, Part I　　　　　　　　　　　　1596–7
The Merry Wives of Windsor　　　　　　　　1597–8
Henry IV, Part II　　　　　　　　　　　　1597–8
Much Ado About Nothing　　　　　　　　　1598
Henry V　　　　　　　　　　　　　　　1598–9
Julius Caesar　　　　　　　　　　　　　1599
As You Like It　　　　　　　　　　　　1599–1600
Hamlet　　　　　　　　　　　　　　1600–1601
Twelfth Night　　　　　　　　　　　　1600–1601
'The Phoenix and the Turtle' (poem)　　　　　by 1601
Troilus and Cressida　　　　　　　　　　　1602
The Sonnets (poems)　　　　　　1593–1603 and later
Measure for Measure　　　　　　　　　　1603
A Lover's Complaint (poem)　　　　　　　　1603–4
Sir Thomas More (in part, not included in this
　　series)　　　　　　　　　　　　　　1603–4
Othello　　　　　　　　　　　　　　　1603–4
All's Well That Ends Well　　　　　　　　1604–5
Timon of Athens (with Thomas Middleton)　　1605
King Lear　　　　　　　　　　　　　　1605–6
Macbeth (revised by Middleton)　　　　　　1606
Antony and Cleopatra　　　　　　　　　　1606
Pericles (with George Wilkins)　　　　　　　1607

INTRODUCTION

I

It has taken nearly four hundred years for Shakespeare's first tragedy to recover its original credit. That it made an overwhelming impact when it appeared in the early 1590s is evident from the surviving record of performances both in the London theatres and in the household of Sir John Harington at Burley-on-the-Hill in Rutland on 1 January 1596. This popularity is also clear from the demand for 'the book of the play', which went into three quarto editions between 1594 and 1611 before its canonization in the definitive Folio of 1623; and also from miscellaneous printed evidence, such as a ballad, 'Titus Andronicus' Complaint', associated with the play's first success, and a passing reference by the 'bookkeeper' of Ben Jonson's *Bartholomew Fair*, produced in 1614, to an Andronicus fan club still alive and well 'some five and twenty, or thirty years' on. However, for a period of nearly three hundred years, stretching from the Restoration to the Second World War, *Titus Andronicus* was taken seriously only by a handful of textual and bibliographical scholars. Readers, when they could be found, mostly regarded it as a contemptible farrago of violence and bombast, while theatrical managers treated it either as a script in need of radical rewriting, or as a show-biz opportunity for a star actor, especially in the role of Aaron.

All this has changed. The reputation of *Titus Androni-cus* – among directors, actors, critics, editors, academics, audiences and students – has never been higher since the play's heyday at the end of the sixteenth century. Theatrically, the turning point was Peter Brook's 1955 Stratford-upon-Avon production, with Laurence Olivier and Anthony Quayle beyond competition as Titus and Aaron, and a cut text projecting effects of barbaric violence and ritualized cruelty. This success prompted a sequence of independent productions by serious companies, which was brought to an unforgettable climax in Deborah Warner's uncut version – the first such since, presumably, the 1590s – at the Stratford Swan Theatre in 1987, which, without mitigating the play's ferocity, did full justice to its intellectual brilliance and social sophistication, but also to a richness of humanity that had still not yet been fully understood.

II

The first known performance of *Titus Andronicus* was given by Sussex's Men at the Rose Theatre on 24 January 1594. Performances were however soon suspended following a fresh outbreak of plague at the end of January. The play was entered in the Stationers' Register on 6 February 1594 and published shortly afterwards.

Both internal and external evidence suggests a slightly earlier date of composition. The title-page of the First Quarto, which appeared in 1594, carries the play's theatrical history thus: 'As it was Plaide by the Right Honourable the Earle of Darbie, Earle of Pembrooke, and the Earle of Sussex their Servants.' We have independent evidence that Pembroke's Men went bankrupt and ceased production in August 1593, and no sign of their existence predates 1592. We also know from strong circumstantial evidence that

Shakespeare had close associations with the company pro-
tected by the Earls of Derby. It is therefore reasonable to
assume that the title-page list is chronological, a fact that
gains yet further confirmation from the title-page of the
Second Quarto (1600), which, though repeating the list in
a slightly different order at a time when memories had
faded, brings the stage history up to date by printing last
the name of Shakespeare's current company, the famous
'Lorde Chamberlaine [his] Servants'; and by that of the
Third Quarto (1611) which now dispenses wholly with
ancient history in favour of the current holders of the play,
'the Kings Majesties Servants' – the name assumed by the
Lord Chamberlain's Men under James I.

An allusion to *Titus Andronicus* in a play called *A Knack
to Know a Knave* –

> *As welcome shall you be . . .*
> *As Titus was unto the Roman senators,*
> *When he had made a conquest on the Goths,*
> *That in requital of his service done,*
> *Did offer him the imperial diadem*

– also suggests a slightly earlier date of composition. This
memorially reconstructed text was first published in 1594,
but Philip Henslowe's Diary records seven performances
of *A Knack* by the Lord Strange's [or Admiral's] Men at
the Rose, between 9 and 12 June 1592 and 24 January
1593. I find unconvincing the claim that this near-exact
reference to the play could have been the result of a 1594
memorial confusion of the two texts; it is possible that
these lines could have been an insertion in *A Knack* to
advertise a new play by Shakespeare; but to me what they
seem to be doing is making opportunistic use for expressive
purposes of already well-known material; indeed they
assume the celebrity of a play which, as we have seen, was

still remembered by the audience of *Bartholomew Fair*. In this perspective, it would seem that *Titus Andronicus* must already have entered the repertoire of Derby's Men by the end of 1591 or the start of 1592 at the latest.

The plague continued to grip London for the whole of 1593, forcing the large urban companies to act before provincial audiences. Strange's Men had to appeal to the Privy Council for special treatment, and, as Henslowe reported to Alleyn in a letter of 23 September, Pembroke's Men collapsed altogether in mid-August, and were driven to pawn their costumes and sell their play-texts (including the titles mentioned above), in order to satisfy their creditors. This disastrous year also saw the twenty-nine-year-old Christopher Marlowe's violent death on 30 May, and Thomas Kyd's arrest and torture for alleged atheism, which precipitated his death fifteen months later at the age of thirty-six.

The third company to perform *Titus Andronicus*, Sussex's Men, had run uninterrupted under three earls from 1569. In the early nineties they had made one appearance at court, in 1591–2 when Strange's Men had shown their six plays. They seem to have survived 1593 better than most, for between 27 December of that year and 6 February of the next, they had a successful run at the Rose, with very profitable performances of *Titus Andronicus*, explicitly recorded by Henslowe as theirs, on 24 January, 28 January and 6 February – the very day on which the printer John Danter registered 'a booke intituled a Noble Roman Historye of Tytus Andronicus'. How did Sussex's Men gain the rights over the production of *Titus*? The most plausible story is that they picked up some actors and their plays from Pembroke's broken company. In any event, by the start of 1594 the whole system of play-production was coming apart. Sussex's patron, the 4th

Earl, had died just before the beginning of their run at the Rose, leaving their future uncertain. As for Derby's Men, they had been left destitute by the sudden death of their new patron, Lord Strange's son, Ferdinando Stanley, after only seven months. And to cap these disasters, on 6 February a further recrudescence of the plague once again closed the theatres.

When the epidemic finally lifted in April, the two theatre supremos, the Queen's Chamberlain Henry Carey Lord Hunsdon, who was responsible for ensuring court entertainment during the long Christmas season, and his son-in-law Charles Howard, himself a former Chamberlain and now Lord Admiral, decided to consolidate the best available dramatic talent into two strong companies. Hunsdon himself took charge of the first, which became known as The Chamberlain's Men. Made up of top actors from Strange's/Derby's Men and from Pembroke's Men, it was led by Richard Burbage, with William Shakespeare as resident playwright, and with 'The Theatre' – soon to be rebuilt as 'The Globe' – as its playhouse. Hence Shakespeare's entire corpus, *Titus Andronicus* included, passed into the new company's control. The second company, under Howard, became the new Admiral's Men, with Edward Alleyn as their star actor, Marlowe's plays as their prestige repertoire and Henslowe's 'Rose' as their base.

Thus ended what could be called the heroic phase of Elizabethan drama, in which *Titus Andronicus* occupied a central place. The appearance of Marlowe's two *Tamburlaine* plays and Thomas Kyd's *Spanish Tragedie* in *c*. 1587–8 unlocked the theatrical energies that had been intermittently building up since Thomas More's play-writing circle under Henry VIII. As Marlowe's *Dr Faustus* and *The Jew of Malta* (*c*. 1589–91) show, traditional genres were stunningly revitalized or transformed. But what dominated this seven-year phase was a succession of increasingly powerful and ambitious historico-tragic dramas, with escalating casts and a growing ability to represent collective life on stage. These plays, which all have demonstrable connections with *Titus Andronicus*, included: Thomas Lodge's *The Wounds of Civil War* (*c.* 1589) staging the conflict between Marius and Sulla (the first surviving theatrical depiction of Roman history); George Peele's *The Battle of Alcazar* (*c.* 1589) and Marlowe's *Massacre at Paris* (*c.* 1592), the first dramatizations of near-contemporary real-life events (respectively the catastrophic destruction of the Portuguese by the Moroccan Moors in 1578, and the St Bartholomew's Eve massacre of French Huguenots in 1572); Robert Greene's *Selimus* (*c.* 1591) evoking the murderous dynastic rivalries of the Ottoman sultinate in the Turkey of 1512; and most of all the English history plays: Shakespeare's *Henry VI* trilogy (1591–2) and Marlowe's *Edward II* (*c.* 1591–2). These wonderfully productive six or seven years found perhaps their most characteristic expression in a dramatic form that could be called tragical history, and of which Shakespeare's *Titus Andronicus* (1591) and *Richard III* (1592–3) are the supreme instances.

III

In 1589 a twenty-year-old Thomas Nashe launched an attack on playwrights who 'could scarcely Latinise their neck verse if they should have need' – that is to say, who were barely able to convert into Latin the biblical verse proving they could claim 'benefit of clergy' and so escape the gallows; or who ransacked 'English Seneca ... by candlelight' for 'many good sentences' (quotations); or who at a moment's notice would supply 'handfuls of tragical speeches' ('To the Gentlemen Students of Both Universities', *Works*, ed. R. B. McKerrow and F. P. Wilson, Oxford University Press, 1958, vol. 3, pp. 315–16). Various puns and allusions make it clear that Nashe's particular target was Thomas Kyd, who, like Shakespeare, presumed to write plays without the advantage of a university degree, and who, incapable of distinguishing Rome from England or evil from good, 'thrust Elysium into hell' – a phrase maliciously culled from *The Spanish Tragedie*.

In such a context there can be little doubt that despite his phenomenal early success Shakespeare had something to prove. *Titus Andronicus* was the first of a group of Rome-inspired texts, which included *Venus and Adonis* (1592–3), *The Rape of Lucrece* (1593–4) and *The Comedy of Errors* (1594). These works, however, represent a challenge less to Shakespeare's contemporaries (the so-called 'university wits' championed by the precocious Nashe) than to antiquity itself. The two narrative poems comprehensively outdo their Latin sources, Ovid's *Metamorphoses* X and his *Fasti* II, in their elaboration of emotional conflict. *The Comedy of Errors* adds a second pair of identical twins to Plautus's *Menachmi* to complicate the source plot by a factor of four. *Titus Andronicus* not only introduces one of its main 'sources', the Philomela episode of *Metamorphoses* VI into the narrative – to the point of bringing Ovid's very book on stage – but, as we shall see, explicitly improves on it. In Ovid, Pandion, King of Athens, gives his daughter Procne to Tereus, King of Thrace, for saving Athens; Tereus takes her back to his country, and a son, Itys, is born of the marriage. After five years, Procne persuades Tereus to fetch her sister Philomela from Athens for a visit. Tereus falls insanely but secretly in love with her. Pandion entrusts his second daughter to him; but when they reach Thrace, Tereus takes her to a 'hut deep hidden in the ancient woods'. She pleads for mercy, then for death. Incensed, he rapes her repeatedly and cuts out her tongue. He then leaves her under guard, returns to Procne and pretends that Philomela is dead. In the ensuing year, Philomela stitches the story of her wrongs in a tapestry and sends it to Procne. Under cover of the wild festival of Bacchus celebrated by the uninhibited Thracian women, Procne finds Philomela in the woods and brings her back home disguised as a bacchante. Uncovering the 'shame-blanched face' of her sister, she becomes deranged with hate for Tereus. She notices that her small son Itys looks like his father, represses her maternal love, cuts his throat like 'a tigress', and cooks him, offering him to Tereus as part of a sacred feast. Having 'gorged himself with the flesh of his own flesh', he calls for Itys, only to receive the reply 'You have, within, him whom you want', while Philomela thrusts the boy's head into his face. Beside himself with rage and grief, Tereus pursues Pandion's daughters with drawn sword. As they flee, Philomela turns into a nightingale, Procne into a swallow and Tereus into a hoopoo. In *Titus Andronicus*, it is the self-conscious Aaron who proposes to out-do Ovid, both in ingenuity (doubling the mutilations) and in rhetoric (by turning art into life); but it is Titus who in his turn will eventually overtake him in both departments.

Shakespeare was, as it were, competing with Rome, not with Nashe, or Greene – who, three years after Nashe, was himself to attack Shakespeare as 'the only Shake-scene in the country' in his *Greene's Groat's-Worth of Witte 1592* (literally reprinted by G. B. Harrison in *Elizabethan and Jacobean Quartos*, Edinburgh University Press, 1967, pp. 45–6). It almost seems as if Shakespeare's response to humanist snobbery was to set up a premature quarrel of the ancients and the moderns, in order to demonstrate the superiority of the latter. If the depth and intensity of Shakespeare's interest in Rome as such is still under question after this first classical phase, it is put beyond doubt by his second, when his encounter with Plutarch produced three masterpieces, *Julius Caesar* (1599), *Antony and Cleopatra* (1606) and *Coriolanus* (1608), which have never been equalled in their capacity to resurrect, without the faintest taint of antiquarianism or pedantry, Rome and its Romans on the modern stage.

Titus Andronicus is not, of course, in any sense a Plutarchian play. Its principal model is probably a pseudo-historical prose narrative which resurfaced between 1736 and 1764 under the title 'The History of Titus Andronicus ... Newly Translated from the Italian Copy printed at Rome'. The nineteenth-century Shakespearean scholar J. O. Halliwell-Phillips reported that he owned a version of this history. The only surviving copy is now in the Folger Library, Washington. There is no compelling reason for ruling out the existence of an Italian source. Renaissance Italy was very interested in the history of the later Roman empire, and Italian translations of virtually all the major Greek sources were available. Nor is there any special reason to question the claim of the eighteenth-century pamphlet's publisher that it represented a new, or at least revised, translation. Of course, the existence of such a source in Elizabethan translation would not bring greater discredit to *Titus* than Arthur Brooke's 'Tragicall Historye of Romeus and Juliet', ultimately derived from the Italian, brought to Shakespeare's next tragedy, *Romeo and Juliet*. Moreover, the existence of such a source would in no way diminish our perception of Shakespeare's creative engagement with his predecessors, though it would not lend support to the magpie version of that engagement, which represents the playwright as collecting bits and pieces of narrative material from a whole variety of sources until they spontaneously cohered to form a new narrative. What it would do, however, is to explain why, unlike Lodge's *Wounds of Civil War* or Shakespeare's own later Roman plays, *Titus Andronicus* fails to recreate a specific period of Roman history – or rather why it creates an historical hybrid, combining the stern republican Rome of Cato the Elder with the third-century imperial Rome of, say, the emperors Decius and Severus, with its internal persecutions and its frontiers permeable to Gothic invaders who, even then, were starting to assimilate the civilization of their victims. Yet for all its apparent chronological irresponsibility, *Titus* provides astonishing evidence of the depth of Shakespeare's imaginative assimilation of Rome and its culture.

Explanations of Shakespeare's powers of assimilation must start with the recognition that his historical drama is much more 'sociological' or 'anthropological' than moral or political. Of course Shakespeare is not lacking in political or moral concepts; but if plays like *Titus Andronicus* or the stupendous *Coriolanus* are political, they are so more by virtue of their awareness of how political projects are formed and conducted than for their endorsement of this or that political programme. The evolution of the historical play over the seven years that followed the appearance of *Tamburlaine I* (1587) was essentially a movement from a conception of society as docile before individual will to one of society as resistant to it.

The simultaneous movement of late Elizabethan drama towards such a relativized conception of character is owed as much to dramaturgical developments as to new conceptions of the relationship of the self to the social. Much the most important of the former is the emergence of interactive dialogue as a theatrical norm. In a play like *Gorboduc* (1561), by no means a contemptible text, the dialogue for the most part takes the form of speeches describing off-stage events which could be addressed equally to other actors or the audience, in order to enforce a lesson: that unless the Queen begets an heir or appoints a successor, the realm of England will disintegrate. With the appearance of *Tamburlaine*, speeches given and received become expressions of a mighty personality whose existence evolves in its relation to the other members of the cast, but only in order to dominate them by seduction or authority or terror. With *Titus Andronicus* (*c*.1591–2), however, the entire dramatic script, soliloquies included, functions as a network of responses and reactions. Although the language of the play of course exhibits more formal registers – symbolic, ritualistic, intertextual – its primary and consistent function is interlocutory.

How far and deep this goes can be demonstrated from its most stylized scene, Act 2, scene 4, in which Titus's brother, Marcus, finds his niece Lavinia wandering in the forest chase outside Rome, having been raped and mutilated by the sons of the Gothic queen, Tamora. Confronted by the appalling spectacle, Marcus notoriously launches into a 47-line allegedly Ovidian speech which seems to defy every convention of interactive realism. What accord can there be between Lavinia's monstrous disfigurement and Marcus's display of verbal luxuriance? Each, it appears, makes the other unacceptable: her pain turns his fluency into an affront; his verbiage demeans her suffering; and the scene between them becomes humanly trivial and theatrically chilled. For many, as for Peter Brook who simply omitted Marcus's speech from his historic 1955 production, it is unrescuable. For others, salvaging it can only be accomplished indirectly. Here, the standard line of defence has been that the speech is not a dramatic failure because it was never designed to be a dramatic success. Thus, in *Shakespeare's Early Tragedies* (1968), Nicholas Brooke wrote: 'Lavinia is turned into a stone in the formalized language of the poetry . . . [She] is dumb and unmoving like the woodcuts in an emblem book, while Marcus provides the interpretative verses that were usually printed beneath.' Stage animation is petrified into a tableau, and the momentum of dialogue suspended into a commentary. Still more ingeniously, the play's distinguished (1984) Oxford editor, Eugene Waith, claimed that what Marcus is trying to bring about, through sheer force of incantation, is an Ovidian metamorphosis, transforming a brutalized scenario into a pastoral idyll, but that he is checked by the reality of the woman before him – the literal refusing conversion into the metaphorical. Finally, and most recently, in an ambitious book entitled *Shakespeare's Troy* (1997), Heather James reads the play as an Ovidian 'deformation' of conservative Virgilian eloquence, arguing that Shakespeare 'transforms Lavinia's body into a site for a skeptical analysis of metaphor'. In the *Aeneid*, Virgil's Dido, sexual victim of the imperializing Aeneas, is absorbed into the imperialist project by virtue of a noble style that refuses to call a seduction a seduction. In the *Metamorphoses*, Ovid applies the epic simile to Philomela's rape, but only to show up its inability to ennoble Tereus's contemptible act. In *Titus Andronicus*, Shakespeare associates Lavinia's and thus Philomela's rape with Dido's seduction, thereby showing up the latter as 'a scene of violation [sic] in which responsibility cannot be obscured' (p. 63). The moral responsibility in question is Aeneas's, for in *this* reading of Virgil, it is only Dido who has been seduced. The general argument is as such intelligible: the imperial idea travels west, from Troy to Rome and from

Rome to Britain. Shakespeare is an anti-imperialist, so he writes a play proving that Aeneas was no better than a rapist, and that the Elizabethan establishment is immoral. The question is, however, one of plausibility.

What these readings, culled from three decades of commentary, overlook is the fact that a play is primarily dialogic – for example, that Marcus is first and foremost addressing his niece. What Marcus's speech offers is in fact a highly original form of interactive dialogue in which one party cannot speak and the other, perforce, cannot hear. This means that the sub-text – the stage direction implied in the spoken text – becomes hyperactive. Marcus enters 'from hunting'. His first line (11) shows that Lavinia is trying to avoid being seen. His next line (12) tells us not only that she stops and turns, but why she does so: Marcus's enquiry as to the whereabouts of Bassianus touches a reflex need to report his murder. But in turning she has revealed her visible mutilations. Marcus's change of tone (from 12 to 13) shows that he has fully registered the shock of her condition. Appalled at the discovery that she is without hands (13–15), he asks her to reveal the name of the perpetrator (16–21). Her silence prompts him to ask again (21). Her effort to reply causes a fresh haemorrhage, which shows him the extent of her physical mutilation (22–5) and provokes him to guess the reason for it (26–7). She turns away in shame, which confirms his insight (28–32); so she allows him to come closer to her (33–7) and, as Donald Sumpter did in Deborah Warner's revelatory production, to hold her (38–43), and even cradle her in his arms (44–51). He ends by raising her to lead her to her father (52–5); she shrinks back at the prospect (56), but finally yields to his persuasion (57). That this is a scene consisting of two characters reacting and responding to each other must surely put pay to claims that Lavinia is turned into an emblem and her sufferings into a ritual.

If Lavinia, at least in the theatre, is neither a motionless image in need of commentary (Brooke), nor a broken body provoking a vain lyricism of healing (Waith), nor even an emblem of the true meaning of the poetic blazon (James), we are still left with Marcus's expressive volubility. That, dramatically speaking, it is seen to be as problematic as Lavinia's silence can be detected in the fear of commentators that any attempt to 'humanize' Marcus will reveal him to be little better than a talking machine, or an unperceiving sentimentalist, or an unfeeling Ovidian lyricist. But even a simple review of his speech in the context of an interactive relationship will, I think, show these anxieties to be misplaced. His first two lines (11–12) are cast in the language of normal life which takes for granted ordinary familial relations ('niece', 'cousin', 'husband'). This tone is required for the concussive change of register of the next three lines (13–15), which express his sense of cosmic dislocation ('dream', 'wake', 'planet'). In his next six lines (16–21), he asks for the identity of her assailant; but he does so with an overpowering sense of the irreparability and the incomprehensibility of what that assailant has done. This is effected through the conceit of disbranching, which conveys not only the brutality ('lopped', 'hewed') but the perversion of the deed: some 'stern ungentle hands' cutting off gentle, sensitive hands, and thus extinguishing the 'beauty' and 'happiness' of a life-restoring embrace ('circling shadows'). The following six lines (22–27), which enact the discovery of her further mutilation and rape begin by horribly heightening the sense of a perverted nature (a wind-stirred water-spring as a bubbling 'river of warm blood'), prompting him to summon the figure of Tereus, here less a 'literary allusion' to Ovid than an inspired guess which Marcus communicates to her in the literal plainness of

> *But sure some Tereus has deflowered thee,*
> *And, lest thou shouldst detect him, cut thy tongue.*

The next five lines (28–32) evoking Lavinia's gestures of shame, release in their sudden baroque extravagance (blood pouring out of the open taps of her wounds, her face suffused with redness like a sky) a recognition of the enormity of what has happened to her, and by implication to him.

Marcus's response to Lavinia's state exhibits two qualities seldom found together: an unevasive emotional recognition of the horror of her injuries, and the knowledge that, despite her transformation into a living grave of herself, she remains the person he knows and loves. He may not possess her story ('O that I knew thy heart', 34), but his protective identification with her, which the rest of his speech dramatizes, never wavers. In the five lines (33–7) that express the pain of blocked grief, the distinctions between his heart-burning (37) and hers, and between speaking on his own and on her behalf (33) become blurred. This sets the course for the rest of his speech, in which he offers her the consolation of a full knowledge of what she has lost, and thereby of her continuing worth. In his next six lines (38–43), he not only recognizes that her suffering is worse than 'fair' Philomela's, but also that her beauty ('lovely niece') and accomplishments outstripped her Ovidian predecessor's. Because Marcus does not minimize the significance of what has happened to her, he enables her to re-approach the familial household of which she feels herself to have become unworthy. Hence his next eight lines (44–51) are able to bring this process of reclamation to some sort of conclusion. The 'beast' (34) who cut off the 'pretty fingers' (42) of the embroiderer becomes the 'monster' (44) who tears off the hands and tongue of the singer-lutenist. In such a context, the comparison of Lavinia and her ravisher to Orpheus and Cerberus must and does remain a conceit. She is indeed a wondrous musician both literally (45) and symbolically (48); but in the world of this play, where there is no second chance, the 'silken strings' can offer no resistance to the chopper. With the six-line coda (52–7) of, as it were, Marcus's monologue of two – in this reading one of the memorable expressions of protective love in Shakespeare – he achieves the only victory available to him: coaxing his niece, despite her last recoil, to accept the community of woe (see III.1.148) that their family is becoming: 'Do not draw back, for we will mourn for thee' – even as he knows that such a comfort cannot repair the irreparable: 'O, could our mourning ease thy misery.'

IV

Interactive dialogue enacts one of the ways in which individuals can be imagined to exist in society. In so far as they are the centre of their own lives, individuals belong to themselves; but in so far as they are members of a community, with its history, its institutions and its social and cultural divisions, they belong to others. The kind of dramatic dialogue we have been examining expresses such a community, not discursively or analytically, but at the moment of its operation. It is therefore the least abstract representation of social life we possess. No play deserves the name that does not in some measure display this property. Ritualistic or religious drama tends to blend conflicting points of view into a single vision; naturalistic drama, on the other hand, tends to treat such differences deterministically, as the products of society, and history; yet both depend on actors capable of reacting to one another. Such homogenizing tendencies, however, are absent from the finest plays of the London stage of the early 1590s. They distinguish between the individual and the social, of course, but that distinction is perspectival: that is to say, it permits two equally valid descriptions of the same piece of dialogue – as the expression of individual agency, and as the reflection of social process. On *that* stage, every utterance is simultaneously a message and a symptom.

Even in the scene between Marcus and Lavinia, in which one party is mute, and during which both are drawn together into the solidarity of grief, we remain aware of discrepant consciousnesses. Just as our perception of Lavinia's state is variously intensified by Marcus's responses to her, as his predicament is by her reactions, so we cannot but become aware that together they reveal the marks of a recognizable social group. For example, whether we are conscious of it or not, we very early register the fact that they are patricians. The traumatized Lavinia is introduced into the play, as 'Rome's rich ornament' (Bassianus, I.1.55), and her subsequent conduct shows her as being confident and at ease in that role. It is in part because of this loss of status that initially she shrinks from her uncle. Marcus, civilized, self-possessed, sympathetic and rational, is appalled by the surgery that has been practised on her body. His instinct is to draw her into the protective resources of the Roman family; but even so, his consciousness of defeat is palpable, particularly as one begins to be aware that he laments the destruction of talent and beauty not only for her sake, but also for his own as an Andronicus and a Roman.

That the effects of interactive dialogue extend beyond the personal to the social becomes overwhelmingly apparent as soon as we locate Lavinia and Marcus's encounter within the whole of the scene. Marcus's speech is prefaced by an infernal duet between Demetrius and Chiron, the perpetrators of the outrage, who have been egged on by Aaron and Tamora to rape and maim the young woman Tamora has called 'this trull' (II.3.191). Having made Lavinia safe, the brothers can now gloat over their handiwork. They are provoked into crass inventiveness by their discovery that her mutilations have turned normal language into nonsense. For example, Chiron's 'Go home, call for sweet water, wash thy hands', prompts Demetrius's

> *She hath no tongue to call, nor hands to wash,*
> *And so let's leave her to her silent walks.* (II.4.7–8)

These loutish exchanges are obviously venomous with misogyny. What is less obvious, but quite as brutal, is their class hatred: 'Sweet water' is perfumed water, 'silent walks' are solitary walks, in the quiet part of a garden, for the purposes of meditation. These are plainly aristocratic practices, and they drive these Goths, at once spoilt and half-educated, into a frenzy of aggression. It seems scarcely extravagant to suggest that the author of this play may at such moments have remembered the sack of Rome, either of AD 410 (by the Visigoths) or of 1527 (by the Germans). Be that as it may, my point is that his capacity to see through the eyes of a particular character gives him, by virtue of the fact that there is always more than one character, his point of entry into the forms of life that this individual perspective implies. One of the effects of the opening ten lines on the rest of the scene is to establish a relativity of perspectives that allows the playwright to make the barbarian status of these 'Goths' as perceptible as the patrician status of those 'Romans'.

The notoriety of *Titus Andronicus* as the most violent of all Elizabethan plays has (if my dating is right) concealed its importance as the first sustained attempt to put a consistent foreign world on the stage. Despite occasional anachronisms mostly Christian, and almost entirely associated with Aaron, who attracts them because he raises the problem of 'irreligiousness', or what we would now call atheism – problems which cannot readily be dramatized, or even imagined, in relation to Jupiter or Diana – Shakespeare's re-creation of pagan antiquity takes dramatic art on to a new level of mimetic sophistication. In this respect it far outstrips Lodge's *Wounds of Civil War*, which competently translates Appian's *Civil Wars* into the staged rivalries of Marius and Sulla, or Greene's *Selimus*, which portrays Islamic Turkey as some sort of hell of competing dynastic ambitions within a geography of resonant place-names. The crucial point of difference is not how well Shakespeare's knowledge of Roman life compares with our own stock of accumulated hindsight, but the degree to which he has been able to imagine a different form of life *from the inside*.

What this achievement entails can be illustrated from his use of so-called classical allusions which he deploys more liberally in *Titus* than in any other of his plays. A comparison with Marlowe's use of such allusions is instructive. Try to strike me, Tamburlaine tells Theridamas, who has been charged by the King of Persia to put an end to the banditry of the Scythian shepherd, 'And Jove himself will stretch his hand from heaven | To ward the blow'. This is the brilliant new language of hyperbolic glamour. It does not disclose Tamburlaine's religious allegiances, but merely embodies his sense, and ours, of his effortless power. Shakespeare's Titus, who does not keep his victories for himself but brings them back to Rome, also invokes Jove:

> *Thou great defender of this Capitol,*
> *Stand gracious to the rites that we intend.*

(I.1.80–81)

Titus's Jove is Jupiter Capitolinus – not a verbal gesture, or even a symbol, but a god, the object of specific 'rites' of worship, the recipient of prayers of intercession, the owner of a great temple which is the historical and religious centre of the city, and which Titus sees before him as he speaks ('*this* Capitol'). The difference between the two playwrights is not, of course, that Shakespeare is a better Roman historian than Marlowe, the translator of Lucan's *Pharsalia* and Ovid's *Amores*; it is that Rome is inside Shakespeare's Titus as well as outside of him, or more explicitly, that Titus contains much more of his environment than Marlowe's Tamburlaine does of his. The fact not merely of an interdependence, but of an interaction, between the individual and the social – the fact that the individual lives in society to the extent to which society lives in him – distinguishes of course human from natural communities such as the bee-swarm or the sardine-school, where the life of the collectivity is identical to that of the collected.

The way in which the characters of *Titus Andronicus* invoke their classical and Roman past shows that they are its product. That past is astonishingly comprehensive, descending, as it does, from the pre-Olympian and Olympian gods (Ovid), to the Trojan founders of Rome (Virgil), to the creators of the Republic (Livy) and the degenerates of Empire (Suetonius). We can only glance at a couple of examples. As early as line 23 of the play, the incorruptibly humane tribune, Marcus, introduces his brother, the incorruptibly valorous general Titus, as 'Andronicus, surnamed Pius' – the honorary epithet bestowed by Virgil on Aeneas, and by Aeneas on his deserving successors. Titus himself, by virtue of his ten-year defence of Rome against the Goths, which has cost him the lives of twenty-one out of his twenty-five sons – 'Half of the number that King Priam had' (I.1.83) – proclaims his descent from that heroic ancestry. By the middle of the play, three more of Titus's sons having met summary executions (two by edict of the Senate, one at his own hand), his sole surviving son Lucius, having been unjustly banished, raises an army of disaffected Goths in the name of ancient virtue, and takes over Rome. At the end of the play, the continuity affirmed at its start is re-established. Marcus, once again, enrolls him in the same succession as his father, as 'the Roman Hector' (IV.1.87) and 'our ancestor [Aeneas]' (V.3.79). In general, Roman *integritas* is achieved by keeping alive the past in the present.

It cannot be an accident, therefore, that at the very climax of the play's denouement, Titus chooses to give the decadent Saturninus a lesson in the meaning of Roman history. Having, with the veiled Lavinia's help, served his guests, Titus turns to the head of state:

> *My lord the Emperor, resolve me this:*
> *Was it well done of rash Virginius*
> *To slay his daughter with his own right hand*
> *Because she was enforced, stained, and deflowered?*

SATURNINUS

> *It was, Andronicus.*

TITUS

> *Your reason, mighty lord?*

SATURNINUS
> *Because the girl should not survive her shame,*
> *And by her presence still renew his sorrows.*

TITUS
> *A reason mighty, strong, and effectual;*
> *A pattern, precedent, and lively warrant*
> *For me, most wretched, to perform the like.*   (35–44)

And he does. The parallel is not perfect. In Livy the centurion Virginius kills his daughter before, and not after the rape threatened by the ruthless *decemvir* Appius Claudius. (But see the explanatory note to V.3.36.) However, as Livy himself observes, Virginia's killing became as exemplary as Lucrece's suicide, both events testifying to the austere virtue on which Rome's greatness was thought to rest. Titus, as embodiment of this virtue, kills not one but two of his children: Mutius, in the name of absolute paternal authority (but also in unconscious terror that his elevation of Saturninus to the purple is undoing Rome) at the beginning of the play, and Lavinia, in the name of female chastity, at the end. Saturninus as a Roman knows the story of Virginia, but a story is all it is to him. A free-thinking epicure and sensualist in a position that enables him to satisfy his every impulse, he cannot take seriously a fable that would cast him in the role of a Tarquin or an Appius Claudius. Thus, at the play's defining moment, Titus confronts Saturninus as Rome confronting Rome; and just as the deaths of Lucrece and Virginia once led to the banishment of kings and executive magistrates, so the killing of Lavinia sets off a cascade of executions that sweeps the Gothicized court out of Italy.

This triumph of ancestral Roman virtue does not mean, however, that Shakespeare has given up the irony inherent in his dramaturgy. The presence of a division within Rome between two sorts of Roman, the traditional and the modern, already signals that *Titus* as a text will not easily be hospitable to simple affirmations. This is reinforced by the fact that the restoration of Roman virtue requires the assistance of a Gothic army, which in turn suggests that the idea of the 'Gothic' is not a unitary one either. *Romanitas* itself, however, is more subtly destabilized by the way in which foreigners like the Gothic queen Tamora and her Moorish agent-lover Aaron, both of whom have acquired a veneer of Latin culture, invoke Roman history. Aeneas may be the founding father of Rome, but he has attributes other than piety – sexual passion, for example. This is noticed by the enamoured Tamora, now Roman empress, who invites her lover Aaron to an erotic 'conflict' – her word – 'such as was supposed | The wand'ring prince [Aeneas] and Dido once enjoyed' (II.3.21–2). The sceptical precision of that 'was supposed' should not be overlooked: Tamora may be a naturalized Roman, but her Gothic roots are alive and well. Not only is she drawn to the transgressive aspects of Virgil's great epic, but she maintains an emotional distance from its imperial claims. She displays a similar scepticism towards classical myth. When, for instance, she threatens the doomed Bassianus with 'Had I the power that *some say* Dian had' (II.3.61), it is Diana's divinity as well as her chastity that she despises.

Aaron's use of classical names is different again. Plays set in Islamic locations, such as *Selimus* or *The Battle of Alcazar*, use classical allusions in a routine way, generally to give an overall and undiscriminating colouring of non-Christianity – for instance, 'Latona's son' (73) and 'Bellona' (729) for 'the sun' or 'war' in *Selimus*, or 'Phlegeton' (177) and 'Erebus' (1136) for 'hell' in *Alcazar*. Shakespeare eschews such one-dimensional usages in the speech he gives his Aaron. Aaron's classical deities, which he calls on at moments of aggressive self-definition, are primitive, violent and obscure: Tamora is sexually bound to him like the tortured 'Prometheus tied to Caucasus' (II.1.17); his 'desires' are dominated by the grisly Saturn (II.3.31); he swears to keep his black child against the assaults of Enceladus (IV.2.92), the largest of the giants, whose breath fired Etna. Like his self-image (the black panther), his pantheon antedates human society, reaching back to an era of 'big-boned men framed of the Cyclops' size' – to cite Titus's granite-like phrase (IV.3.47). In this play, even the language of the classical past, which had long been the mythological lingua franca of Europe, becomes incorrigibly perspectival.

V

Shakespeare's attempt to imagine Roman culture from the inside is of course that of a man whose orientation is Tudor–Christian. In culturally naïve writers, who take their own environment as the norm of reality, the imagining of another world retains no essential distinguishing marks, and achieves no genuine otherness. Such writers cannot solve the problem by seeking to become culturally neutral. On the contrary, it is precisely because of his grip on his own social perspective that Shakespeare is able to perceive Rome as something other. Shakespeare's England is part of the differential equation. But his Rome is also distinguished internally in various ways, notably by means of the inclusion of an alien presence – though scarcely a culture in its own right – in the form of the Gothic captives.

Nothing testifies more subtly to Shakespeare's instinctive grasp of the essentials of *romanitas* than his placement of the Andronici's mortuary monument within the entrance to his play. No victorious return to Rome is less triumphalist than Titus's. Following the coffins of his dead sons, he greets Rome as if his bereavement were inseparable from hers; he calls on the graciousness of Jupiter; he opens the tomb that contains his earliest ancestors and their descendants, including his score of sons killed in previous campaigns; he ritually sacrifices a prisoner; and he completes the ceremony with a petitionary prayer echoed by his daughter (I.1.73–171).

In just under a hundred powerful lines, Shakespeare has established ancestor worship as the defining principle of the patrilineal Roman family. The tomb of the Andronici unites the living and the dead in a single community. Both rely on each other for pacification and fulfilment: without the performance of prescribed rites (which, according to Fustel de Coulanges's classic study, *La Cité Antique*, first published in 1864, included in primitive times the slaughter of horses and slaves to serve the dead) the dead would continue to 'hover on the dreadful shore of Styx' (91) while the living would be 'disturbed with prodigies on earth' (104). The continuity of their history would be broken. Titus receives his authority as priest and father from this monument, which he tends as a sacred duty that he calls a 'cell of virtue and nobility' (96; where 'cell' evokes the Roman 'cella', the body of the temple as opposed to its portico), and which had stood for five hundred years before he 're-edified' it (353–4). It is by virtue of this office that he embodies the family honour and upholds the family name, that he serves Rome and the gods with unswerving fidelity, and that he retains the power of life and death over his dependants. Later in the scene his consent is required before even Mutius, the son who resisted him and paid the penalty, is allowed to enter into the immortality of the monument. The traditional Roman was bound by a

xlv

sacred tie to his 'house' and its 'sacred receptacle' (95), as to his City and its Capitol (80), both of which are addressed by name in Titus's salutation speech. This meant that sacredness was linked to a specific spot on the face of the earth. Thus to die in defence of one's 'altars and fires' (*pro aris et focis*) was the supreme mark of piety. In such a context, exile became the cruellest chastisement, for to be banished from 'home' was to be excluded from community not only in life but for ever. More than a trace of this can be found in Lucius's exile, to which he is sentenced in part fulfilment of the Tamora–Saturninus plot to 'raze' the Andronicus 'faction and . . . family' out of Rome (454). In their vindication speeches to the Roman people after the *coup d'état*, Marcus and Lucius allude to exile as the worst of fates, the one evoking 'a forlorn and desperate castaway' driven to doing 'shameless execution on himself' (V.3.74–5), the other describing himself as 'unkindly [unnaturally] banishèd, | The gates shut on me and turned weeping out' (V.3.103–4).

The Andronici in general, and Titus in particular, represent the persistence, within decadent imperial Rome, of traditions of ancient virtue receding into the penumbra of prehistory. But the play's mighty opening scene no sooner presents these traditions than it drives them to their limits by making the funeral rites which Titus performs include human sacrifice. As we have just seen, in ancestor worship the dead retain a form of existence responsive to the ministrations of the living. As his dead brothers are about to be consigned to the family sepulchre, Titus's eldest son, Lucius, demands the life of 'the proudest prisoner of the Goths' (I.1.99) as a sacrifice *ad manes fratrum* ('to the sacred shades of our brothers'). Overriding the pleas of the Gothic queen, Titus grants the brothers Tamora's eldest son Alarbus, who is summarily killed, cut into parts and burnt.

It has been argued that Shakespeare could not have written this scene (but Peele, we are told, could), or that he invented an anthropology that had no precedent in Rome. Both claims are surely mistaken. Shakespeare took this barbaric rite seriously enough to treat it as normal Roman, and even more normal British, practice at the end of one of his last plays, *Cymbeline* (V.5.70–80). Moreover, the literature of antiquity offered several cases, notably in the *Iliad* (the funeral of Patroclus, XXIII.158–60) and in the *Aeneid* (the funeral of Pallas, XI.81). Tamora's passionate maternal pleas, inviting the patristic Titus to share her perception of her child's fate, and concluding with the very argument which Portia would use to launch her appeal to Shylock's mercy (*The Merchant of Venice*, IV.1.184–97), makes any identification of Titus's perspective with Shakespeare's impossible to sustain. The sacrifice of Alarbus marks the limiting point of the lineage-family because to that family it is the fulfilment of its identity (the link between the dead and the living is preserved) while representing its contradiction (one family's piety is another's atrocity). Once again, the audience is placed simultaneously inside and outside a given perspective, the only difference being that now it is the perspective of a clan rather than of an individual. In Shakespeare's dramaturgy, all points of view, whether individual or collective, carry their cultural horizons with them.

Traditional Rome is in deep trouble in this play. Internally, it appears to be falling apart. There are three candidates for the 'diadem' (Saturninus, Bassianus and Titus) and three methods of choice (primogeniture, electoral college, plebiscite). The method favoured by traditionalists – primogeniture – produces Saturninus, an unstable hysteric. On the Roman frontier, despite Titus's repeated victories, the human cost of defence has become intolerable. Titus's grand entry (in Olivier's rendering of it) brings into view a 'battered veteran', whose every word seems to be 'dredged up from an ocean-bed of fatigue' (Kenneth Tynan, *Curtains*, 1961, pp. 103–5), and whose subsequent decisions in Act I, scene 1 – the summary rejection of Tamora's pleas (124–32), the wilful appointment of Saturninus to the purple (206–36), the reckless promise of Lavinia to him (237–60), the savage slaying of Mutius (280–95) – all reinforce the impression of disintegrating control. What are the reasons for this breakdown? Is it that traditional Rome has failed to respond to the pluralism of Empire? That it has clung too long to its absolute sense of identity, refusing to accept its place on the expanding map of the world it has created?

This extra-Roman world is represented in the play by the Goths, who appear in two guises. The Gothic army which the exiled Lucius joins, and which restores the Andronici to power in Rome is 'warlike' (II.1.61, IV.4.110, V.2.113, V.3.27) – an epithet which Lucius himself receives (IV.4.69). What we see of them shows that they are respectful of military prowess (V.1.9–11, 20), secure in the simple integrity and vigour of their northern fields and forests (V.1.14–15, 19, 20–21), and sturdily contemptuous of tyrants (V.1.12, 16). These Goths are Germans, descendants of those tribes depicted by Tacitus in his *Germania*; and in supporting the Andronici's political cause, they share the values of the common Romans, who, like the compassionate Messenger who returns Titus's severed hand to him, along with the heads of his two sons, grow increasingly restive under Saturninus's incompetent tyrannical rule (IV.4.73–80).

But there is, of course, another group of Goths – as different from the soldier Goths as Saturninus is from Titus – which is given a much higher profile in the play.

The defining adjective for them is provided, appropriately enough, by Marcus who, with his equally rational but tougher nephew, Lucius, will help keep the play from spilling into a carnival of butchery. Pleading for the burial of Mutius, he reminds Titus: 'Thou art a Roman, be not barbarous' (I.1.381). This says, in effect, 'Do not become your anti-self.' In a brilliant study, *Inventing the Barbarians* (1989), Edith Hall has shown how fifth-century Athenians, in a gesture which we have come to call 'orientalist', learnt to define themselves by stereotyping foreigners as their own opposites. Athenian dramatists and historians, prompted perhaps by their heroic resistance to Darius and Xerxes, represented to themselves the populations of the 'Asiatic vague immensities' to the North and East of them – especially the Thracians, the Scythians and the Persians – as 'defeated, luxurious, emotional, cruel, and always dangerous' (Hall, p. 99). Every one of these epithets is applicable to Tamora.

Tamora and her sons constitute, after all, the royal family of the Goths; yet their relationship with the pastoral warriors who march through the last two acts of the play is not dramatized. Tamora's name is certainly not Germanic. It is related to the Thracian names of 'Thamyris' or 'Thamyras' and to that of Tomyris, the warrior-queen of the Massagetae – an Asian nation from the unending steppes east of Scythia, whose vengeful ferocity and cunning destroyed the Persian monarch Cyrus. (See Herodotus, *The Histories*, Penguin Classics, translated by Aubrey de Selincourt, 1954, and revised by John Marincola, 1997, pp. 81–4.) As if to reinforce these associations, Tamora is called Semiramis twice: admiringly by her lover Aaron (II.1.22), who, elated by her sudden transformation into the ruler of Rome, confers on her the opulence, prowess and lustfulness of the legendary Queen of Babylon; and as a term of abuse by the chaste and classy Lavinia:

> *Ay, come, Semiramis, nay, barbarous Tamora,*
> *For no name fits thy nature but thy own.*

> (II.3.118–19)

Moreover, Tamora is indeed 'very dangerous', not only because of her implacable cruelty, but because that cruelty is linked with what Aaron calls her 'wit' (II.1.10), that is, her virtuosity as an histrionic manipulator. This combination of mimicry and sadism is exhibited by the speech in which she publicly urges Saturninus to 'pardon' the Andronici while privately assuring him that she will 'find a day to massacre them all' (I.1.453). Can this hypocritical eloquence be distinguished from the sincere eloquence of her plea for the life of Alarbus? Or must we conclude that she is a sham, even when she means what she says? But this would be to judge her by Roman standards, which make fidelity to one's word a sacred duty. Her 'wit' is accountable not to truth, but to emotion, in this case maternal passion. In a complete negation of the Roman world of the fathers, she turns motherhood into a form of promiscuity, which knows no scruple of restraint, and reduces her sons to vicious puppets. This maternal appetite even enters into her relations with the admittedly infantile Saturninus, as she demonstrates in her spontaneous nuptial 'contract' with him – her oath that

> *She will a handmaid be to his desires,*
> *A loving nurse, a mother to his youth.*

> (I.1.334–5)

It is tempting to conclude that because the Gothic queen and her sons are not anchored in the culture of the Germanic Goths, they are products of 'orientalism', and thus

1

merely melodramatic figures. That, however, would be partially mistaken, for they obviously possess a degree of individual power to which the term 'melodrama' does no justice. Tamora is a deviant Goth imagined out of barbarian elements which include sexual appetite, cunning and arrogance. To be sure, she enters the play as the head of a family, to find herself in collision with the Andronici, whose social reality is not in question. Moreover, her attack on them plainly has that status as its target. She contemptuously deconstructs Roman religious practices ('O cruel, irreligious piety', I.1.133); she is echoed by Chiron's 'Was never Scythia half so barbarous' (134), and by Demetrius's 'Oppose not Scythia to ambitious Rome' (135) – which implies that Roman 'barbarity' so outstrips Scythia's that comparisons are meaningless. That the charge of barbarism is aimed specifically at Titus, licenser of human sacrifices, is shown by Demetrius's derisive identification of Titus with the savage 'Thracian tyrant' Polymestor, killer of the son of the Trojan queen Hecuba, whose revenge Tamora is exhorted to repeat (138–44).

This cultural aggression comes to a climax in Act II with the confrontation of Tamora and Lavinia, who, for a variety of reasons including conflicting ideals of womanly conduct, cannot endure each other. During the hunt celebrating the nuptials of Saturninus and Tamora, Lavinia and Bassianus come upon Tamora as Aaron is taking his leave of her, and turn on her the full weight of Roman sexual contempt, mostly in the form of sarcastic references to the huntress-goddess Diana, salted with racist allusions to the Moor's blackness. They are interrupted by Tamora's sons, whom Tamora incites against Bassianus and, with Bassianus killed, on Lavinia, who is ready for death, but not for what amounts to a gang rape. In the truly harrowing scene that follows, Lavinia's attempts to plead for the values of chastity are systematically counterproductive, only exciting the queen's sadistic appetite, to the point when she has her forcibly silenced and dragged away.

The scene in question also brings out something in Tamora that is more radically disturbing than cultural aggression. It is introduced by two speeches which, as Aaron puts it, place Tamora under the sign of Venus, and himself under that of Saturn – the god of 'blood and revenge' that is 'hammering' (II.3.39) in his head. This mixture opens up a prospect that instantly heightens Tamora's sexual excitement: 'Ah, my sweet Moor, sweeter to me than life!' (51). This excitement continues to rise as the next episode unfolds before her, with her rampant sons, Bassianus's corpse ('his dead trunk pillow to our lust', 130) and the frantic Lavinia; and it reaches a climax with:

> Now will I hence to seek my lovely Moor,
> And let my spleenful sons this trull deflower.
>
> (190–91)

Saturn and Venus have indeed conjoined, but in her.

But this scene's sadism takes an even subtler form. It notoriously contains a pair of contradictory descriptions of a single woodland prospect, first by an amorous Tamora, who depicts for Aaron's benefit the forest glade with its singing birds, its sunlit shadows and the echoing calls of hounds and horns, as a *locus amoenus* (10–29); then, again by Tamora, but now in a murderous mood, who converts it into a Gothic forest of terror and death, into which she claims to have been enticed by Bassianus, and which so works up her sons that they instantly knife him (91–115). This inconsistency of descriptions of the same landscape has generated a number of inconclusive explanations. From the dramatic perspective I am attempting to develop, this second description, with its luxuriating accumulation of *rhetorical* imagery designed to provoke a murder, remembers its erotic predecessor as it transforms it, and acquires an *expressive* layering of sadistic fantasy which an audience, with what is being twice described before them on stage, would be responsive to. A somewhat similar contrapuntal effect is achieved in the next episode, which depicts the entrapment of Martius and Quintus in the hunting pit that already contains Bassianus's freshly killed corpse. Titus's sons are overcome by an 'uncouth' (uncanny, 211) lassitude that may seem no more than a convenience to get them into the pit. In the real time of performance, however, we cannot forget that this strange affliction settles on them at the very moment their sister is being raped and dismembered off stage. The sinister double effect once again focuses on a description. Quintus asks Martius who has just fallen into the pit:

> *What subtle hole is this,*
> *Whose mouth is covered with rude-growing briers,*
> *Upon whose leaves are drops of new-shed blood*
> *As fresh as morning dew distilled on flowers?*

> (198–201)

This obviously evokes the fate of the freshly slaughtered Bassianus. But, as others have noticed before me, it cannot at the same time fail to remind us of what is simultaneously happening out there in the wings. It is scarcely surprising if Quintus and Martius have the feeling that they have strayed into some sort of magnetic field of malevolence.

Act II of *Titus Andronicus* enacts scenes of torture and carnage muffled in woods as deep as the Katyn forests of eastern Poland. It therefore invites readings in terms of metaphysical or xenophobic evil. But Shakespeare also seems to be asking for something less. In creating his 'barbaric' Goths, he makes a virtue of necessity by exploiting the fact that the concept of barbarism is devoid of social content. What these Goths have revealed about themselves is not that they are possessed by satanic powers, but that they are as it were socially moronic. I have argued that the Romans are Romans by virtue of the fact that they have internalized Rome; at an elementary level, the Germanic Goths, too, are shown to have assimilated the qualities of a real if unsophisticated culture. In contrast, these 'barbaric' Goths do not seem to have properly internalized anything, not even Thrace or Scythia. They possess the trappings of a culture, which include the unabsorbed basics of a grammar-school education (IV.2.22–5); they have ferocious maternal–filial affections; but essentially they remain morally incomplete. It is for this reason that they regard the massively integrated Andronici as their pre-ordained foes, and that they pursue them with a visceral as well as an avenging fury.

VI

The one figure of the play who seems entirely to have evaded emotional dependence on others is Aaron. To be sure, he is a Moor (his name is a variant of 'Haroun'), but one that has no more than a nominal connection with the Muslim world. His literary forebears are less the fiendish villain of Peele's *Alcazar*, Muly Mahomet, or the truly monstrous eponymous hero of Greene's *Selimus*, than Marlowe's atheistical Jew, Barabas, but without even a religion to deride, or a daughter to kill, or an audience to cajole and conspire with. Indeed, in creating Aaron, Shakespeare exploits the strongest theatrical techniques to project an impression of complete autonomy. Because of his colour and stance, Aaron remains extremely visible throughout Act I, but he also remains completely silent. Once the play's great expository scene is over, however, he steps forward and virtually explodes into his soliloquy. This speech, incandescent with the possibilities of Tamora's elevation, is less a tribute to her than to himself. In a mere twenty-four lines, Aaron imprints himself on our perceptions as a resourceful, virile, ruthless and self-exhilarating nihilist. Yet the more we see of him and his exuberant self-delight, the more baffling he becomes. Every moment of his life represents a nullification of those collaborations that build up and preserve human communities. Aaron keeps up a continuous fusillade of self-assertive acts that appear to be wholly self-referential. What matters to him is the perception of his victims' humiliation or pain, rather than the knowledge that he is the cause of it. This holds of his most trivial as of his most destructive performances. At one extreme, his encounters with Tamora's sons are peppered with taunts and sarcasms which they are too dense to register (II.1 and IV.2). At the other extreme, the most cynical of the few actions he performs without intermediaries – the chopping off of Titus's hand at Titus's own request to save the lives of his already executed sons, whom Aaron himself has framed for the murder of Bassianus – may well be the most monstrous practical joke in the history of theatre. But here too my point is that the perpetrator of the 'joke' does not require its victim to know the identity of his tormentor in order to relish its effects (III.1.201–4, V.1.111–20). The Messenger that returns Titus's hand to him blames Saturninus and his entourage; nor does Titus ever learn the contents of Aaron's eventual 'confession' to Lucius (V.1). Aaron's reticence may seem perverse, but it is not incoherent. To seek to be known for the virtuosity of one's criminal invention is to acknowledge the need for applause, that is to say, to accept dependency. At the same time, such autonomy is a perversion that needs constant reassurance that dependent beings are self-deceived. Aaron's preference is for acting through agents like Tamora (who is never more than a mirror for his exploits), and Demetrius and Chiron (who are merely his butts) in the destruction of Bassianus and of Lavinia, and even at second hand through Saturninus in the inculpation and execution of Martius and Quintus. His relish of the role of invisible power behind far-reaching interlocking plots seems to satisfy his deepest needs. He may be a virtuoso performer of villainies, but it is the pain of others that is the oxygen of his life.

In his contemptuous self-sufficiency Aaron claims to be the author of himself. But within the context of this play, his nullification of social reciprocity cannot be taken as a mere given. There is clearly something obsessive about his general aggressiveness – and in particular about his persecution of the Andronici – which, I repeat, cannot be explained in terms of a commitment to Tamora founded on her appetite for *him*, and which excludes taking her into his confidence. He comes close to acknowledging this himself when he tells her, in response to a blatant sexual invitation: 'Blood and revenge are hammering in my head' (II.3.39). Like Tamora, what he cannot bear about the Andronici is their tradition of rectitude and cultural distinction. Although he, and perhaps Shakespeare, are not yet capable of Iago's awesome justification for killing Cassio ('He has a daily beauty in his life | That makes me ugly', *Othello*, V.1.19–20), his need to humiliate as well as torment them suggests that the claim to self-authorship entails what we have learnt to call *repression* – what is repressed being the social self whose inevitable 'return' must be accompanied by the usual symptoms of psychic damage.

Only by invoking what might be called 'the social unconscious' can we begin to account not merely for Aaron's persecution of the Andronici, but also for the famous *volte face* of Act IV, scene 2. I refer, of course, to Aaron's unconditional acknowledgement of the 'coal-black' son (98) that his imperial mistress has just begotten and sent to him for instant extermination. The moment he sees the colour that identifies the child as his own, his acknowledgement of it overrides all other obligations: 'My mistress is my mistress, this myself' (106). He discards at once the political programme, such as it is, that he has based on Tamora. In its place, with equal abruptness, arises a new but no less ruthless agenda: the survival of his son. For what the child has done is to convert his father's black skin from a badge of defiant self-sufficiency into a social bond. Indeed, it has turned him inside out, for the social self, until then buried within him, is now in front of him, smiling back at him (119), forcing him into the role of a father who puts down the Gothic brothers' racial threats – Demetrius's 'I'll broach the tadpole on my rapier's point' (84) – with the truly ferocious: 'Sooner this sword shall plough thy bowels up!' (86). Aaron has been struck by a bolt of 'parentage' (to use the term repudiated by Marlowe's Tamburlaine); but if this bolt deprives him of his survivor's flair, it also alerts him to the danger of seeking refuge with a Gothic army now under Lucius's command. After the double murder of the Nurse (144) and the Midwife (166), and the cradle-switching required for the infant's survival (152–60), Aaron is left alone with him:

> *I'll make you feed on berries and on roots,*
> *And feed on curds and whey, and suck the goat,*

> *And cabin in a cave, and bring you up*
> *To be a warrior and command a camp.*   (176–9)

The protective paternal voice marks Aaron's release into family feeling, but also into the culture, if not the comradeship, of those military pastoralists we have identified as the German Goths. The irony, of course, is that it is this 'humanization' of Aaron that drives him headlong into the hands of the one man who has the power, as well as the cause, to destroy him. Aaron may have acquired a future, but as he shall shortly discover, he has not thereby lost his past.

When Lucius captures him, Aaron is no longer the self-created plotter who might, like his successor Iago, have sworn:

> *Demand me nothing; what you know you know;*
> *From this time forth I never will speak word.*
> *(Othello, V.2.304–5)*

On the contrary, Aaron now spills the beans, and continues to do so as long as he has breath in his body. Has he taken leave of his 'character' of radical independence? It seems to me that his acknowledgement of his child has brought to the surface what before had remained quite unperceived: the contradictions inherent in his stance of autonomy. As soon as he sees who commands the Goths, he knows the game is up; but since, as he has told us, his son is an extension of himself into futurity, that will not matter so long as the child survives. What he has to offer Lucius in exchange for his child's life is the revelation of his part in the destruction of the Andronici. The reason why Lucius is not only ready but eager to accept this deal is that, were the story of the death of his two brothers and his brother-in-law and of the martyrdom of his father and sister to remain suppressed, he would not be able to ensure, as the patrilineal survivor, their rightful place in the ancestral annals. Aaron achieves the survival of his son, but to do so he has to pay the price of consistency. As a 'misbeliever' (see V.3.142) or atheist, he is obliged to rely on the piety that guarantees Lucius's word. Lucius questions the logic of Aaron's request: how can he put his trust in what he despises? But Aaron sees at once that what counts is not *his* word, but Lucius's (V.1.70–85). However, all this does is to relocate the contradiction. Aaron is a metaphysical utilitarian: the value of anything is its usefulness for himself; but Lucius's oath can only be of use to him if Lucius holds it absolutely, that is to say, on grounds that rule out usefulness.

Thus the contract Aaron forces on Lucius ensures his own defeat, and in two ways. On the one hand, it condemns him to a *confession of impenitence* that, once Lucius has been told what he needs to know (87–120), can only repeat itself with increasing vacuousness, as Aaron's replaying of the gramophone record of Barabas's catalogue of transgressions ('Set fire to barns and haystacks in the night' etc., V.1.124–44) from the *Jew of Malta* indicates. On the other hand, the survival of Aaron's infant son, depending on the integrity of Lucius's oath, guarantees the survival of those values which Aaron is now condemned mechanically to repudiate. And indeed, this effect is subtly enhanced by Marcus's presentation of the boy to the Roman population, as the play concludes, with the biblical 'Behold the child' (V.3.118, cf. Luke 2:34) perceptible only to Shakespeare's audience, not Marcus's, of course, but not the less symbolically redemptive for that.

VII

The intelligibility of a culture presupposes normal states of mind and body. Any radical abnormality, such as dismemberment, puts human beings out of synchronization with their common life. As we have noted, language is defamiliarized by the loss of hands. Marcus, for example, chiding Titus for his extravagant laments over his daughter, warns him not to drive her to lay 'violent hands upon her tender life'; Titus retorts that this is crazy talk:

> *Why, Marcus, no man should be mad but I.*
> *What violent hands can she lay on her life?*
>
> (III.2.24–5)

Ready-made phrases, unnoticed in daily life, suddenly rear up against their users when that life ceases to be daily. In *Titus Andronicus* such disruptions can take subtle forms. Lavinia's fate is the result of a decision by Aaron, 'Chief architect and plotter of these woes' (V.3.121), to convert a sensational tale by Ovid into a real-life scenario – in other words, to produce a strictly crazy confusion of categories.

Most readers and playgoers recognize that Act III, scene 1, in which Titus as a Roman father is exposed to a succession of Aaron-devised hammer-blows – the sentencing to death of two of his sons, the perpetual banishment of a third, the wrecking of his daughter, the vain act of self-mutilation to reprieve his two sons – represents a high point in the early Shakespeare's representation of suffering. Scholars such as Wolfgang Clemen, who studied the conventions of the pre-Shakespearean set-speech lament (see *English Tragedy before Shakespeare*, 1955) have provided us with a yardstick for measuring Shakespeare's achievement in transforming what might have been three hundred lines of formal complaint into perhaps the most intense *enactment* of grief in Elizabethan drama. Every new development ratchets up yet further Titus's psychological anguish, until his moral resistance finally breaks. Although this great scene has to my knowledge not been analysed in detail, its merits challenge the art of the greatest of actors. What is relevant to my argument, however, is its role in the play's structure of meanings.

What the scene offers is a murderous attack on the central pillar of the Roman patrilineal family. This assault on the father is not principally aimed at severing familial attachments, although it certainly tries to do so. Its essential target is what connects that family to the city. Its campaign against the Andronici is an attempt, as it were, to take *romanitas* out of Rome. To what extent this is consciously calculated is unnecessary to determine: Act II has shown Aaron to be a master-plotter; yet Act IV has also revealed him to possess the defining characteristic of the Shakespearean villain: intellect in the service of unexamined feeling. It may not therefore be possible to disentangle the mix of reason and obsession in him. As far as Titus, his principal victim, is concerned, however, there can be little doubt that what the scene of his agony delivers is a man in whom the need for vengeance takes the form of mental derangement.

An intense experience of grief constitutes a social abnormality. Marcus, who is always in full possession of the norms of rationality, finds Titus's outbursts of anguish difficult to take. In the brief respite provided by Aaron's cynical deal (the father's hand for the sons' lives) Titus, who now shares Lavinia's mutilation, threatens to 'breathe the welkin dim | And stain the sun with fog' – the fog of their sighs – if heaven does not respond to their prayers (III.1.210–11). Marcus reproves him:

> *O brother, speak with possibility . . .*
> *But yet let reason govern thy lament*   (213–17)

– to which Titus retorts:

> *If there were reason for these miseries,*
> *Then into limits could I bind my woes.*   (218–19)

But since there are none, the use of outrageous hyperboles is appropriate, even natural: he and Lavinia must respond to each other as the earth to a deluge or the sea to a tempest (218–30).

Titus's extremity of sorrow also possesses a political dimension. The scene under examination opens with his pleas for a reprieve of his 'condemnèd sons'. This is represented by a scenario or tableau – Titus face-down imploring the earth for pity while the Roman judges pass over the stage with the two prisoners 'to the place of execution' – which enacts the gap that has opened up between Titus and Rome. Soon afterwards, he tells the banished Lucius that the city is 'a wilderness of tigers' (54), that is to say, the very essence of banishment itself. Thereupon Marcus enters with Lavinia. The horror of her condition draws out of Titus a response in which the paternal and the political fuse:

> *Give me a sword, I'll chop off my hands too:*
> *For they have fought for Rome, and all in vain.*
>
>   (72–3)

The image of the exile's feral 'wilderness' is now no longer adequate to Titus's sense of disorientation; it modulates into the image of a 'castaway' clinging to a rock surrounded by a rising 'wilderness of sea' (94). Aaron's illusory reprieve momentarily revives Titus's collapsing sense of Roman identity:

> *Good Aaron, give his majesty my hand.*
> *Tell him it was a hand that warded him*
> *From thousand dangers. Bid him bury it;* (192–4)

But as we know, the Emperor sends it back, and Titus, even though he cannot help being a Roman, ceases to be one.

The ominously prolonged silence with which Titus receives this final reversal, when even Marcus is forced to invoke 'Etna' and 'hell' (240–41), is something new. He finally breaks it with a yet more ominous burst of laughter, followed by a brief explanation for it that lapses into the predatory 'Then which way shall I find Revenge's cave?' (269). The old hyperboles of grief marking the rising tension between fatherhood and 'romanhood' have gone. Revenge, the supreme barbarian trait, is now in control. Titus can scarcely be said to have chosen his new role; it rises within him in a surge of madness. The scene is almost over, but it reserves a final surprise. It opened with a poignant tableau, and ends with another: the Andronici make a group exit, with Titus carrying the one head, Marcus the other, and Lavinia her father's hand 'between [her] teeth' (281), while Lucius, bound for exile, swears restitution. This is one of the moments which have given this play a bad name. But it is surely possible to perform it, as I think it should be, as a visual representation of a family, though quite literally cut into pieces, refusing to let go, and drifting out of sight still literally holding itself together. The theatrical effect of such visual puns, which are characteristic of the play, may be incongruous, but need not be trivial.

VIII

Aaron's improvement of Ovid's already fearsome tale is etched on Lavinia's living flesh by Tamora and her sons, who have been given a motive by the ritual sacrifice of Alarbus. Aaron, as we have seen, lacks a specific cause. It does not follow, however, that his is a case of motiveless malignancy. As I have argued, he is in a state of generalized aggression produced by a stance of autonomy requiring the repression of the social dimension of the self. Why then does he feel the need to convert his assault on Lavinia into a rewriting of Ovid? It serves no practical purpose: it adds nothing to her physical pain or her moral shame. It may prevent her from communicating her sufferings, but certainly not from putting an end to them herself. If Ovid does nothing for Lavinia, however, he does something for Aaron. By seeking to out-rival the poet in the medium of life rather than art, Aaron adopts before a living woman the posture of the artist before his own handiwork – the product and display of his 'wit'. In short, he aestheticizes Lavinia's suffering in ways undreamt of by Mallarmé or Wilde, in order to express a contempt for human suffering that can only be called satanic.

The imprinting of a fictional character on a living person is certainly pathological. Although Aaron is technically in control of what he is doing – he has a precise intention which is exactly carried out – morally he does not know what he is doing. Plainly, his notion of the human is deficient; less obviously, so is his notion of art. Ovid's fiction is more than a report of imagined events: it is also a *meaningful* report, for even if Ovid is no friend of *romanitas*, his tale shows that Pandion's Athenian family is destroyed by a resurgence in Tereus of Thracian savagery that proves horribly contagious, infecting its two civilized victims, Philomela and Procne, with an even more rabid barbarism. That Shakespeare – who could not have written *King Lear* unless he had written *Titus Andronicus* first – was fully aware of this is shown by Lear's assertion, in the play's opening scene, that he is more likely to welcome the 'barbarous Scythian, | Or he that makes his generation messes | To gorge his appetite' (I.1.126–8), than his disinherited daughter. Stories by writers like Ovid are not merely virtuoso narratives: they are cultural messages which may explore the limits of civil virtue. In this perspective, Aaron improves not on Ovid but on Tereus, and in so doing puts himself at risk, for by neglecting the status of the *Metamorphoses* as a significant cultural document, he overlooks the fact that as such it will have found its way into Titus's library, waiting to let the cat out of the bag.

If, as I am implying, the super-self-possessed Aaron is a covert paranoiac, how mad is his arch opponent Titus? (For Titus is indeed Aaron's contrary, since if in Shakespeare's patterning of the action it is Lucius who destroys Aaron (V.1) and Titus Tamora (V.2), in the patterning of the *design* Aaron is to Tamora what Titus is to Lucius.) This question is smudged by the interpolated scene (III.2) which gives us a seriously disturbed Titus. In the (original) scene that follows Act III, scene 1, namely Act IV, scene 1, which finds Titus and the remnants of his family in his house, his general conduct – his handling of his grandson's fear of his aunt, of Lavinia's impeded attempts to explain what she is trying to do with her copy of Ovid, and of Marcus's inspired solution of her difficulties – seems perfectly rational. But once the terrible truth is disclosed, Titus suddenly becomes a mysterious figure both to Marcus and to us. He utters an appeal, in momentous

Latin, '*Magni dominator poli*' (to 'the master of the great heavens', IV.1.80–81), which persuades Marcus that he needs calming. Marcus therefore invites Titus to participate in a formal oath of vengeance. Although Titus does so, he privately suspends collaboration, warning Marcus that he is out of his depth (100), that Tamora remains in power (96–9), and that a long delay must be expected (101–3). Titus decides to send some provocative gifts to the now 'detected' Chiron and Demetrius through his grandson, whose combativeness he seems to reprove (118). Marcus interprets this correction as a sign that Titus is too 'just' for revenge (127), and thenceforth seeks to manage Titus's illness. Marcus has lost touch with Titus's thoughts; but although we can see this, we do not know what Titus is thinking either. Is the threat conveyed by the gifts to Tamora's sons sinister or merely deranged? (Aaron, who spots at once what the sons do not, that they have been identified, regards the gift as a 'conceit' worthy of Tamora's applause (IV.2.30): Shakespeare thus underlines the fact that the arrival of the black infant stops him from warning her against Titus.) Is Titus's archery display (IV.3.50–76) – ostensibly a postal service to the gods above, which, like digging the earth or dragging the seas, is a search for vanished Justice – craziness or camouflage? Marcus and his household, opting for the former, continue to humour Titus's whims; Marcus even redirects, privately, the discharge of the arrows into the Emperor's court (62–3), enraging Saturninus and inadvertently provoking the Clown's execution (IV.4.45). But what is Titus up to? He highjacks the Clown's petitionary appeal in order to get an extremely threatening message to Saturninus, but in total disregard for the life of his appealing messenger. Is this advertised craziness a cover for an attempt to destabilize the Roman populace, as Saturninus thinks

(IV.4.20)? Or is the very pretence of madness – as it is with another of Titus's inheritors, Hamlet – itself a mark of mental disturbance? Caught between the verdicts of the socialized Marcus, who thinks him mad, and the narcissistic Saturninus, who thinks him sane, we are forced to conclude that he is both. But what this means is not revealed until the long-prepared and overwhelmingly shocking *coup de théâtre* of Act V, scene 2, hot on the heels of scene 1 with its equally unexpected exhibitionistic confession by Aaron.

Until Act IV, scene 2, Aaron and Tamora have been complementary allies. However, the birth of the black child – to Tamora a disgusting as well as a dangerous object, to Aaron the revelation of fatherhood – splits their confederacy, although she does not know it. Even so, their respective fates continue to be structurally related. As we have seen, the autonomous Aaron is turned inside-out by the upsurge of the instinct of paternity; Tamora's power over others, owed to her command of the histrionic and rhetorical arts, converts her into a self-destructive victim. Mistress of virtual reality, she ends by losing her capacity to deal with the real thing.

The consequences of this are shown in the exceptionally sophisticated dramatization of her visit to Titus. That visit is prompted by a political project, which is to use Titus to separate Lucius from the army of advancing Goths. To her, Titus's madness is, as it were, fictional, in that it takes the form of impotent fantasies of revenge. She therefore presents herself to him in the guise of a personified 'Revenge', accompanied by her sons as Revenge's agents, 'Murder' and 'Rapine', who are, of course, what they pretend to be, but who are offered to Titus because 'they take vengeance on such kind of men' (V.2.63). She therefore invites Titus to play his part in the make-believe of her masque. However, in a striking reversal of expectations, failure to distinguish between fact and fiction is shown to be hers, not his. The degree to which, despite or perhaps because of her track-record in *realpolitik*, she is under the spell of wish-fulfilment is probed in the high-wire tension of Shakespeare's dramaturgy, which has Titus again and again tell her to her face that he is 'not mad', and that he knows her 'well enough' (21), that Rape and Murder are extraordinarily 'like the Empress' sons' (64, 84), that she should 'stab them' (47), and – when he is 'assured' that they are personifications – that they should kill themselves (99–103), and indeed that as Revenge she should give the 'queen, attended by a Moor . . . some violent death' because, as he says with a moving simplicity, they 'have been violent to me and mine' (109). Tamora's failure to see what is staring at her in the face, not once but continuously, suggests that it is she, not Titus, who has lost control of her wits.

But this first reversal, dramatic as it is, exists in order to prepare us for a second and this time conclusive one. It takes place in the course of the forty lines during which Titus, with patient explicitness, tells the gagged and bound Demetrius and Chiron – whom he has tricked Tamora into leaving with him – exactly what is going to happen to them, and why. Nothing could be less allegorical than the literalism of this speech, nor starker than the enormity of what it is saying. Titus is preparing to turn his house and its household gods, the source and anchor of Roman piety, into a human abattoir to prepare for a cannibal feast. More generally, he is proposing to convert the social institution of the banquet, traditionally the *convivium* of communal festivity (which Tamora had herself planned to pervert into an entrapment) into an obscene rite of retro-maternity in which 'Like to the earth'

Tamora will be made to 'swallow her own increase' (V.2.190).

Titus's justification of this grotesque design is explicit and assured:

> *For worse than Philomel you used my daughter,*
> *And worse than Procne I will be revenged.* (193–4)

He takes up Ovid's master-narrative exactly at the point at which Aaron left it. In one sense, this is a well-merited implied lesson to Aaron, the incompetent critic, who has taken the part for the whole. But in another, it is an amplification, and not a correction, of Aaron's original aestheticism. Like Aaron, Titus conflates the fictional and the real; but he does so for a very different reason. Aaron's was an expression of solipsistic power, Titus's is a symptom of demented suffering. His aggression, unlike Aaron's, is the reflex of a radical injury to personal identity, which this play regards as relational. Thus it is an injury which legal justice, even when it can intervene – as it emphatically cannot in the Rome of Saturninus and Tamora – is unable to heal. It recalls that self-assertion which Gordon Braden, in his revelatory reading of Seneca's tragedies (*Renaissance Tragedy and the Senecan Tradition: Anger's Privilege*, New Haven, Yale University Press, 1985), finds at the centre of the revenger's madness. Shakespeare, however, makes greater demands than Seneca.

Titus's decision to assume the mantle of Procne is not, as with Aaron's adoption of the role of Tereus, to disregard the meaning of Ovid's tale, but to construct a defiant performance of it. Procne commits what is probably the most barbaric crime in *The Metamorphoses*, an anthology that does not skimp on outrages; but what she does she has been taught to do by Tereus. Titus learns exactly the same lesson from Aaron and Tamora. But unlike Procne, who abandons herself to the luxury of undiluted vengeance, Titus's revenge purposes to be, as I have implied, an affirmation of ancient virtue. At once chef and host to his guests, he presides over his feast as high priest of *romanitas*, beginning with a demonstration for the benefit of the Emperor of Roman tradition at its most intransigent (a re-enactment of Virginius's execution of his daughter), and concluding with the performance of a spectacularly barbaric rite (the killing of a mother filled with the cooked flesh of her own sons). Thus Rome and Scythia co-inhabit Titus as implacably as patience and policy do the mad Lear, who starts his sermon to Gloucester with one exhortation: 'Thou must be patient', in order to cap it, eight lines later, with another: 'Kill, kill, kill, kill, kill kill' (*op. cit.* IV.6.180, 188). With such contradictions, which are defined by morality but which morality cannot unravel, we are brought into the presence of a tragic impasse.

IX

The final movement of the play sees the surviving Andronici persuade the Roman people to elect Marcus to the supreme office on a platform of reconciliation and reconstruction. It then brings the play to a close by segregating the Andronici and the Goths, which it accomplishes by repeating the ritual that opened the play: the burial of the dead. Titus and Lavinia are laid in the family mortuary monument by their grieving survivors, who, though few, represent three generations: Marcus, Lucius and Young Lucius. As for Tamora and the still-living Aaron, they are denied all ceremony and left uninterred under the sky, prey to scavenging birds. This narrative coda is as theatrically skilful as anything preceding it. However, despite the masterly eloquence of the orations, which persuade their audiences because they deserve to, and the structural relevance and clarity with which the corpses delivered by Titus's banquet are distributed, many productions omit, and commentaries neglect or even disregard, these 130 concluding lines.

Among the several reasons for this indifference, which would include the fear of a theatrical anticlimax, one in particular has prevailed over the last two decades: that the reassurance of this moral tidying-up and closing of ranks is a betrayal of the transgressive imagination that has created the play.

For what the play has revealed is not a conflict between outsiders and insiders, but a radical disconnection within Rome itself, a city which indifferently nurtures a Saturninus and a Marcus, and which generates an ideology, embodied in the military Andronici, in which duty and violence are two names for a single thing. The claim is that in *Titus Andronicus* Shakespeare's imagination has opened up and stared into a terrifying reality, but that, as the play winds down, and imagination cools down with it, the normal Shakespearean conservatism takes over, battens down the hatches and looks forward to ever-improving box-office takings.

The assumption behind such a critique is that society, in the sense of civility, collaboration and continuity, is at best a necessary illusion which protects its members from knowledge of the repressions and cruelties which these values entail. Such a view, which may well be as religious or moral as it is political, is not one which I wish to contest. My only point is that it is not relevant to an understanding of plays like *Titus Andronicus*. Such plays are not directly concerned with social diagnosis and reform. Their task is to restore reality to human experience; and this can only be accomplished by the ability to see two things at once. William Blake once noted that no man can understand true art who has not explored and rejected bad art. The reverse is also true: no one will understand the true meaning of violence who does not care for its opposite. To grasp the reality of such phrases as 'barbaric destructiveness' or 'intellectual nihilism', it is necessary to be able to take delight in the playing of a lute (II.4.44–7) or to feel the past alive in the future (V.3.160–65). It is Shakespeare's unconditional commitment to human society that gives his depictions of its disruptions and disintegrations such power.

Jacques Berthoud

THE PLAY IN PERFORMANCE

I Survival

As we have noted in our Introduction, *Titus Andronicus* first appeared on stage late in 1593, at the climax of seven years' production of large-scale tragedies inspired by contemporary European history. The play was a hit from the start, and it went on to survive the plague closures and the death of Elizabeth, and to maintain its prestige under James I until at least 1612. After the Commonwealth interregnum, which closed the theatres for nearly three decades, it experienced a brief revival. In 1708, John Downes, a professional prompter, remembered it in his *Roscius Anglicanus* (a theatrical survey named after Classical Rome's greatest actor) as one of the old plays 'acted now and then' by Charles II's 'Company of Comedians', which 'being well performed, were very satisfactory to the town' (p. 9). But this did not last. In 1687 a new version entitled *Titus Andronicus or the Rape of Lavinia* was produced. Its adaptor, Edward Ravenscroft, dismissed the Folio version as being 'rather a heap of Rubbish than a Structure', and reshaped it by suppressing much of the stage violence and by tilting the action towards Aaron and Tamora. In a major production of 1717 the actor James Quin turned Aaron into the dominating figure of the play, setting a 150-year fashion that culminated in the performance of a black American actor, Ira Aldridge, who in the 1850s over-whelmed audiences on both sides of the Atlantic in a heavily rewritten version by playing him as a nobly impassioned figure. Indeed, such was the grip of this reading that when, at long last, Robert Atkins put on *Titus Andronicus,* Folio version, at the Old Vic in 1923 as part of his complete Shakespeare cycle, the scene-stealing Aaron, George Hayes, once again derailed the tragedy into farce so that, as one witness remarked, 'at the end some of us fairly broke down and laughed' (Gordon Gosse, *Fifty Years of Shakespearean Playgoing*, London, 1969, p. 79). No one could have predicted then that the next major production, thirty-two years and a second world war later, would restore Shakespeare's script to its proper place as the first of his tragedies.

This outline suggests that *Titus Andronicus* is a very tricky play. Obviously a product of the so-called 'theatre of blood' of 1585–92, it had from the start no affinities whatever with Shakespeare's later Roman dramas quarried out of Plutarch's *Lives*. Its closest links were with the Roman history and mythology that Shakespeare had learned at school, and with Holinshed's British *Chronicles* of 1579, which had inspired the terrifying baronial wars of Shakespeare's first tetralogy. *Titus* was therefore completely out of synchrony with the taste of a Restoration whose neoclassical culture, consolidated in France during the Commonwealth, required a neoclassical theatre. Thus these new audiences, now composed of professional classes for whom Rome meant Cicero and Virgil rather than Gothic hordes on the frontiers, ceased to be able to take the play seriously except by promoting the visibly non-Roman Aaron into the star of the show.

The long-term consequence was that, of all the Folio's play-scripts, *Titus* alone failed to acquire a viable tradition of performance between the closure of the theatres in 1642 and the derisory failure of its attempted recovery in 1923. Thus an examination of the challenges and opportunities it offers directors and actors can be undertaken only for the period between Peter Brook's sensational production of 1955 and Deborah Warner's first complete representation in 1987.

II Peter Brook

When Brook, rising prodigy of post-war British theatre, was invited to direct a play for the 1955 Stratford season, he accepted on condition that it be *Titus* and not, as originally proposed, *Macbeth*. This represented, of course, a statement of confidence in that play; but it also implied a commitment to a new kind of theatre. With hindsight it has been suggested that Brook was already acquainted with the 'theatre of cruelty' promoted in the 1930s by Antonin Artaud. However, although no direct influence existed (Brook's first acquaintance with Artaud dates from 1959 when he picked up *The Theatre and Its Double* in a New York bookshop), Brook discovered an instant affinity with a man who, like himself, despised the 'theatre of entertainment' – the play as a 'conversation of actors' rather than as a ritual designed to invade and transport the feelings of an audience. Only retrospectively can we see that Brook's *Titus* already contained the essentials of the Theatre of Cruelty which he would present to London audiences nearly nine years later.

Although Brook retained three assistants for *Titus*, he took charge of its overall style, including set, lighting, music and costumes, in order to turn the play into a sustained assault on the Stratford audience's conventional expectations. His set, consisting of three massively square, fluted, grey-bronze pillars able to open so as to reveal upper stages, proclaimed the inhuman weight of Roman power. The lighting, from the brutal opening triumph over which it spread a greenish darkness to the concluding carnage which it bathed in a blood-red glow, distilled an aura of menace over the entire production. The taped music blended instrumental sounds with magnified noises to achieve unprecedented aural terror: for example, to accompany the cutting off of Titus's hand Brook produced a throbbing effect (two piano chords recorded inside the piano and slowed down) which one of the reviewers described as 'a mixture of an immense organ and a gigantic double-bass in a primitive blood-lust rhythm'. The costumes, which could be described as 'Renaissance Roman' (except for Aaron's, which converted him into a Rubens-like figure in blue, jet and gold), played variations on the colours of lighting and set: bile green, red, black, and what one reviewer called 'the liverish colour of dried blood' (Alan C. Dessen, in his majestic 1989 digest of the reviews of the play *Titus Andronicus*, published by Manchester University Press).

How this worked in practice can be shown by Lavinia's stage-entrance after her rape and mutilation by Tamora's psychopathic sons. Her ravishers brought her in through the opened arch of the central pillar now leafy with forest branches. A catatonic ruin of herself, she held one of her handless arms away from her side, and raised the stump of the other to her mouth, her head tilted to one side. Three scarlet ribbons streamed from her mouth and amputated wrists. The horror was ratcheted up still further by the frail beauty of the white-gowned actress (Vivien Leigh), whom the psychopathic youths mocked with sadistic gentleness as she drifted with helpless anguished movements downstage. Brook orchestrated this unforgivable moment with a slow plucking of harp-strings emitting notes like (in Richard David's phrase) 'drops of blood falling into a pool' (as quoted by Harold Metz, in *Shakespeare Quarterly* 28, 1977). The intensity of the sadism was preserved by the banishment of the 'garrulous' Marcus from the scene.

Exactly the same kind of visual intensification returned at the play's horrific climax. Brook eliminated the opening episode of the final scene, in which Lucius imprisons Aaron, so as to launch the audience straight into Titus's apocalyptic revenge. The cascade of killings occurred almost instantly. Under the glare of the torchlight, the victims collapsed one after the other across the dinner table to form an opulent row, the corpses of the two women (Lavinia and Tamora) flanked by those of the two men (Titus and Saturninus), while the surviving witnesses lined up in calm amazement behind them, and above them, marking a third level, Lucius and Marcus were held by a visionary spotlight within the frame of the upper stage. Plainly, Brook could not allow this stunning climactic tableau to bleed into the play's concluding 134 lines of political reconstruction. As in the scene of Lavinia's rape, therefore, he once again silenced Marcus, cutting his compassionate pleas to the Roman people for legality and peace, allowing only Lucius's final twenty-five lines ordering the disposal of the four corpses.

These spectacles, by arresting the action and dialogue, concentrated the cruelty into climactic moments strong enough to ensure that, every night, at least three spectators (a figure rising on one occasion to twenty) passed out, and memorable enough to obliterate three centuries of derision for the play. Brook has claimed that *Titus* worked for him because he was able to find in it a ritualistic dimension. He reminded us, for example, that Lavinia's crimson ribbons, which conveyed the horror of her mutilations far more shockingly than the phoney realism of stage blood, were derived from Korean masked-dance drama. This is plausible in so far as theatre, like ritual, is a collaborative activity. But even Brook who, as we have seen, despises anecdote, would have acknowledged that he could not have achieved his triumph without Olivier, Quayle and Vivien Leigh. Laurence Olivier's Titus was indeed one of the summits of a great career. From his entrance as 'a battered veteran, stubborn and shambling' yet capable of 'great cries . . . dredged up from an ocean-bed of fatigue', to the seemingly endless challenges of Act III where 'he so grew and proliferated in the astounding variety of his reactions to disaster . . . that with "I am the sea"' he seemed to become 'madness itself' (Richard David, *Shakespeare Survey*, 10, 1957, p. 126), and finally to the demented slyness that planned and produced the concluding holocaust, he confounded history to reveal Shakespeare's first tragic hero. Anthony Quayle's 'superbly corrupt flamboyance', his 'muffled organ-throb voice', his savagery and 'sudden tenderness' (David, p. 126) for his black infant son, not only must have matched the best his post-Restoration predecessors had had to offer, but for the first time revealed Aaron as a major presence in a dramatic whole. As for Vivien Leigh's Lavinia, she remained the still centre of an action convulsed by two parties, one crazed by insider inflexibility and arrogance, the other by outsider resentment and incontinence.

Thus the intensity of Brook's production was owed less to his interpretation of the dialogue – a task which he evidently left to his actors – than to his command of stage effects. Every scene became an opportunity for theatrical panache. For example, marginal or transitory episodes such as those featuring the clown or the arrow-shooting in Act IV were turned into show-stoppers. In scene 3, set outside the palace, the clown did not enter like a yokel on foot with his pigeons; he descended spectacularly from the flies, explaining to Titus (courtesy of a limping pentameter supplied by Brook) that he was 'fetching down his pigeons from the wall'. Even more spectacularly, Brook turned Titus's impotent arrow-shooting in scene 4 into a stunning episode by shifting it back to the end of scene 3 when Titus shot his arrows into the wings, then by instantly opening scene 4 with the flight of those arrows streaking in from the opposite wings to clatter against the wall of Saturninus's throne room.

Brook's production of *Titus Andronicus* owes its place in the history of British theatre to his ability to bring together ritualistic intensity and great individual acting. However, in his determination to turn the script into an overpowering theatrical event, he was driven to cut well over a quarter of the dialogue, including almost the whole of Marcus's role. This meant that he had to sacrifice contextualized interaction between the characters to the creation of mind-blowing theatrical moments. He thus left his successors a double legacy: that the play was supremely worth doing, and that there remained much to be done.

III Trevor Nunn

After 1955 it was no longer possible to regard *Titus Andronicus* as Shakespeare's major aberration. Between 1955 and 1989 there appeared ten professional productions in the USA and at least four in the UK – if one counts John Barton's drastically abbreviated version for Stratford in 1981. It does not seem, however, that the American productions, several of which are reported to have been unusually powerful, markedly altered perception of the play's possibilities on stage. This is not the case, however, with two full-scale Royal Shakespeare Company productions, one which sought explicitly to unlock the play's political applications, the other which achieved an enhancement of the play's classic status as momentous, in its own way, as Brook's had been.

It is not surprising that connections between Brook's recovery of *Titus*'s fortunes and the two world wars that preceded his production have been ignored. The energies of war and art are almost certainly in contradiction, despite the existence of combatant poets. When, however, some seventeen years after Brook, Trevor Nunn decided as part of his season of Roman plays at Stratford to revisit the script, he was drawn to what Brook had disregarded – the history and politics of the play. To Shakespeare's contemporaries Rome had been civilization's supreme model, and its decay their worst scenario: what the play would have offered them, therefore, was a brutalized version of *romanitas* in the dehumanizing effect on Titus of ten years' military service, and a degenerate version of it in the viciously self-indulgent civilian ambitions that had developed during his absence. Nunn was less concerned, however, with the condition of ancient Rome than with the morality of contemporary life. In 1972 the United States was locked in an ideological 'frontier war' in Vietnam, where they had resorted to the saturation bombing of the north at the rate of 200 sorties a day. Meanwhile modern Rome, the very centre of Christendom, had apparently collapsed into the decadent hedonism so vividly evoked by Fellini's great movies, *La Dolce Vita* (1960) and *Satyricon* (1969). Nunn concluded that the sybaritic condition of the Eternal City was intimately related to the savagery of the Vietnam War. Thus, in the words of his programme note, 'Shakespeare's Elizabethan nightmare had become ours.'

To support this reading of the play Nunn recruited some very talented actors: the great Colin Blakely as Titus, with his squat, powerful figure and gravelly voice lending a tragic virility to Titus's transformation from autocratic general to demented avenger; John Wood as a viciously unstable and narcissistic Saturninus bent on upstaging his historical predecessors, Nero and Caligula; and – in unforgettable contrast – Janet Suzman, a magnificently vital Lavinia reduced by her double rape and triple amputation into a crouching, jerking, deformed creature who yet retained a gleam of defiance in her eyes. This refusal to submit was perhaps the production's subtlest endorsement of its director's political agenda, which, in complete contradiction of Brook's aesthetic sensationalism, was committed to a moral-religious reading of the play.

With such a cast and principles Nunn could only opt for the realism eschewed by Brook, if he wished to awaken complacent British audiences to what violence and degeneracy were really like. Titus was hit 'as if with hammer blows' (*The Times*, 13 October 1972) by a peace much worse than war, which gradually transformed him from a craggy, grizzled soldier into a bull at bay, then into a state of melancholy madness. Saturninus's palace became the site of orgies in which its mercurial Emperor would fling himself to the ground and bite the legs of his courtiers. As for the set, it evoked gaunt, wind-blown trees in an empty landscape to which Nunn transferred many scenes usually played indoors.

This realism, however, consorted uneasily with the play's fundamental convictions. To be sure, Shakespeare had concluded *Titus* with the restoration of Rome's political institutions and the election of a new emperor – an outcome which had been made possible only by Lucius's perception that Rome's sole salvation lay in a Gothic victory under his command. Thus Nunn, who provided a less curtailed script than Brook, was committed, whether he liked it or not, to preserving at least the essentials of the final 154 lines laying the foundations of reconstruction – political in the election of Lucius as successor to Saturninus, and domestic in the Andronici's leave-taking of their dead sire. What should be noted, however, is Nunn's unease at a return of that 'calm of mind, all passion spent' which brings Milton's *Samson Agonistes* to its memorable close.

The twenty-five lines of private grief that Shakespeare allocates to Marcus Lucius and young Lucius reaffirm a profoundly Roman value which the action of the play has done its utmost to destroy: family piety. Nunn, however, being committed to the idea of the decline of the West on the pattern of the decline of Rome, had no alternative to modifying some of these lines. More exactly, he could not allow an essentially Roman Lucius to have the last word. This his production made perfectly clear. After the appalling horror of Act III, scene 1, Lucius, in true Roman fashion, announces to the audience his decision to join the Goths against Rome in order to 'make proud Saturnine and his empress | Beg at the gates like Tarquin and his queen' (296–7). This did not fit Nunn's moral allegory. He therefore converted some of these thirteen lines into a kind of doggerel that not only offered to 'bring back justice to the lives of men', but also proclaimed his faith in a 'power that sees all things on earth', and concluded with a carefully qualified resolve: 'Then here before my god I make this vow: | If Lucius live, he will requite these wrongs.' Thus when Lucius joins the surviving Andronici in a tender but non-Christian little ceremony of parting from their dead sire, Nunn retains only three of the thirteen lines Shakespeare had allocated to it, and has an essentially pacifist Lucius preside over it. Nunn's Lucius did *not* kill Saturninus at the end of the Thyestean banquet: Saturninus killed himself. Nor did Nunn's Lucius leave Aaron's infant child to his father: he carried him 'aloft' to accept his election to the purple, and he brought him down in his arms to bid farewell to his sire. The play thus concluded in a Christian image of redemptive peace. The only thing wrong with this is that it is not Shakespeare.

For all its inventiveness, Nunn's engagement as director of *Titus Andronicus* was driven by his condemnation of modern political and cultural life rather than a desire to discover the meaning and merit of Shakespeare's first and fiercest tragedy. Thus despite the sincerity of his ideals and the support of his cast, he was unable to create a legacy of interpretative possibilities for his successors.

IV Deborah Warner

When, fifteen years after Nunn's production, Warner was invited by the RSC to direct *Titus* for the 1987 Stratford season, she already possessed an enviable reputation as director of the minimalist London fringe company known as the Kick Start. She was therefore allocated not the cavernous main theatre at Stratford but the much more intimate *Swan*, which, with its long projecting stage, its Elizabethan-type balcony and its auditorium rising high on three sides of the playing space, represented conditions as near to the original Elizabethan playhouse as any modern theatre until the erection of the 1997 Bankside replica. Even more important, she brought to the play the conviction that it did not represent journeyman work – which prompted her to opt, almost certainly for the first time

lxxxiii

since the Restoration, for an uncut script. This enabled her to demonstrate once and for all that the play's treatment of madness was not unreal, its use of classical myth not dated, its conception of Rome not anachronistic and its verse completely adapted to the demands of performance.

Under a director determined not only to present the script complete but to involve the whole cast in its realization, the actors discovered that *Titus Andronicus* should and could be trusted to overcome the scepticism of audiences. The outstanding Titus, Brian Cox, has left an eloquent account of how the script was made to reveal itself. Praising Warner for creating 'a responsibility within the ensemble towards the play as a totality and not just to the individual characters', he was able to provide a reading of Titus as a man 'forced to pay the price for the self-brutalization of his own nature' by being made to experience all the consequences of his self-damage. Similarly, as Titus's brother, Donald Sumpter (the first recorded Marcus to be allocated his full quota of lines) was able radically to alter the balance of the play's action by revealing the seriousness of its commitment to rational conduct. Indeed, in collaboration with Titus's ultimately surviving son, Lucius, played 'straight' by Derek Hutchinson, he brought out all the seriousness of Shakespeare's representation of *romanitas* – the civic virtue of Rome which in this production put the play's all-too-evident military ethos under much more pressure than had previously been thought possible. Thus Warner's *Titus*, though lacking the furnace-like intensity of Brook's production, was able to examine a dysfunctional social world without ever implying that it represented a norm. In sum, of the entire cast, the only performance not quite able to rise to the demands of the script was that of Peter Polycarpou's Aaron. A lightweight Moor, he failed to incarnate the demonic glamour of the role, so that when the great reversal came – his instant identification with his black infant son – the implications of this reversal went unnoticed.

For Warner, the duty to keep communications open between stage and auditorium was paramount, not least because of the play's history of audience incredulity, which Brook had dealt with by giving playgoers the fix of a lifetime, and Nunn by offering them a sermon for the seventies. Everything about her production, therefore, was aimed at persuading playgoers that the dramatis personae were not alien beings. She treated costumes as signals rather than disguises: togas and armour were suggested, not replicated; women wore full-length dresses, but hairstyles and shoes remained unobtrusively modern. Her use of make-up was highly original: as the action unfolded, she got her actors to apply clay to themselves to suggest that the brutalities of Roman war and peace were slowly reducing them to elementary existences. The garments of the exhausted veterans were daubed with it; and as the Roman patricians began to discover what owning bodies really meant, they too lost their glitter and sank back into unprotected humanity. In a similar way blood (which in previous productions had been splashed about) was used sparingly, and usually on white cloth: streaks on the heads of the brothers after their sacrifice of Alarbus, but stains on a white bag containing Titus's hand, or a sudden profuse spillage on Titus's white apron as he slaughtered Tamora's sons. The same potent minimalism determined the choice of props, which mainly consisted of everyday objects. To cite two instances, Titus's triumphant entry had him seated like a primitive chief on a horizontal ladder borne on the shoulders of his subjugated war-prisoners; and a naked light bulb, reminiscent of post-war East European interrogation rooms, lit the scene of the mad Titus's entrapment of Tamora's sons.

Equally subtle was the management of audience laughter, which had often in previous productions been disastrously inapposite. Sensing the danger, Warner went out of her way to provoke it in order to heighten the shock of the pay-off when it came. Her handling of Titus's cannibal banquet provided a sustained example of her technique of audience engagement. Servants entered with table and benches, whistling as cheerfully as the seven dwarfs; then, turning themselves into ordinary guests, they sat at the table, their backs to the audience, and watched the entrance of the guests of honour – Saturninus, Tamora, Lucius, Marcus and the catatonic Lavinia. Titus, who, in a chef's hat, had busily set the plates, then fetched the meal (the cannibal pie) and, returning with it held up, walked right over the table, a mad clown provoking laughs in the house. With such a preamble, which cunningly interlinked the responses of stage-guests and audience, the denouement exploded with concussive force. The killings cascaded one after the other, the servants rose in horror, and the audience froze. Warner's management of violence, however, was more than a technique of audience control: by locating cruelty in the very ordinariness of human existence she revealed to them something they had not brought with them into the theatre.

More generally, by performing the script complete, Warner was able to reveal the defining quality of a Shakespearean play, and indeed of classical drama in general: that the dialogue is always and everywhere completely interactive – even when one actor has literally lost her tongue and the other can only speak (see Introduction, pp. xxxi–xxxvi). Moreover, textual completeness provided further pay-offs: it revealed that interaction between individuals was conditioned (rather than determined) by relation between cultures. For example, Warner's uncut *Titus* offered the script's fully integrated mythology, mostly derived from Ovid's *Metamorphoses*. By exhibiting it Warner empowered her players to embody a Rome in part defined, like all other human societies, by a legendary inheritance active in the thoughts of its members. Thus Demetrius's and Chiron's treatment of Lavinia emerged as being more than sexual sadism: it became a savage cultural manifesto. As Marcus was (at last) allowed to make clear, Lavinia's torture was cast as a literal re-enactment of an episode from Rome's stock of myths – the Thracian (or Gothic) rape and mutilation of Philomela. Tamora's sons are thugs, but their actions speak: 'You represent us as barbarians,' they seem to be saying, 'we'll show you what that means'.

Warner's complete text allowed her players to show that the sadistic cultural challenge that concludes Act II provokes the demented countercultural challenge that generates the Act V holocaust. Before slaughtering Chiron and Demetrius, Titus tells them exactly why he is doing it: 'For worse than Philomel you have used my daughter, | And worse than Procne I will be revenged' (V.2.193–4). Twenty-four hours later, in a re-enactment of Roman history (Virginius's slaying of his daughter Virginia), he kills his daughter Lavinia: then in a further invocation of Greek-Gothic myth, he re-enacts the legendary 'Thyestean banquet' in which Thyestes, who had seduced the wife of his brother Atreus as a prelude to seizing his throne, has (as it were) the tables turned on him when Atreus invites him to a feast of 'reconciliation' and serves him the cooked flesh of his sons. Shakespeare's version of this horror story is usually taken to be an expression of Titus's dementia – which it surely is. But only in a complete performance of the play, which we finally received on 28 April 1987, were we able to see how far its individual conflicts, usually construed in terms of personal vengeance, are generated by what asks to be recognized as a cultural unconscious.

V Conclusion

What these three Stratford productions have achieved is the rediscovery of a Shakespearean theatrical script which three centuries of textual perversion had suppressed from the stage. Brook's production provided an overpowering audio-visual context to support major performances by three great mid-century British actors; but it cannot be said to have explored a script which it reduced to its highlights. Nunn's production, driven by pacifist anger and cultural despair, relied on a team of loyal actors to generate a sermon for the times. Only Deborah Warner – though, to be sure, with the work of her two predecessors behind her – opted to take on board the complete authorial text preserved by the Quartos and the Folio. She was thus able to show, for the first time since the turn of the sixteenth century, that the text of *Titus Andronicus* was indubitably a performance script as Shakespearean as *Julius Caesar* or *Coriolanus*.

However, the establishment of a play on the stage does not yet constitute a performance tradition of the kind long enjoyed by nearly all the other Folio plays. Hence this essay has had to confine itself to describing the re-creation of such a tradition. This in part accounts for its neglect of the American performances of *Titus* so well served by Alan Dessen's exemplary study. Scattered as they are over an entire continent, stagings of the obscurer Shakespeare plays in the United States and Canada tend to be discrete events, understandably more concerned perhaps to draw and retain audiences than to construct a continuity of representation.

Jacques Berthoud

FURTHER READING

Single-text editions of *Titus Andronicus* currently available include Eugene Waith's Oxford edition (1984) and Alan Hughes's New Cambridge edition (1994). These provide substantial introductions to the stage history and critical reception of the play. Jonathan Bate's edition (1995) in the Third Series of Arden replaces J. C. Maxwell's authoritative but out-dated Arden edition of 1953. Bate distances himself from Maxwell's view that the first act was written by George Peele and that the play is 'much less interesting in itself than as foreshadowing several of Shakespeare's mature tragedies'. Bate persuasively shows that 'not only the play's staging but also its aesthetics and politics are in fact complicated and sophisticated'. Bate is inclined to regard the play not as 'a piece of juvenilia but a new work performed for the first time as a showpiece in January 1594', thus proposing a slightly later date of composition.

Prior to Peter Brook's 1955 Stratford production, which generated new critical and theatrical interest in the play, the reception of *Titus Andronicus* was dominated by the controversial issue of authorship. The most significant contributions to the authorship debate this century range from *Did Shakespeare Write 'Titus Andronicus'?* (London: Watts, 1905), in which J. M. Robertson argues against the hypothesis of Shakespeare's sole authorship, to H. T. Price's *Construction in Shakespeare* (Ann Arbor, Mich.: University of Michigan Press, 1951), which provides internal evidence to support the opposite view.

Critics and editors are now more inclined to focus on

the play's intrinsic merits than on the vexed issue of its origins. Shakespeare's imaginative reworking of his sources, which are reprinted in Geoffrey Bullough's *Narrative and Dramatic Sources of Shakespeare*, vol. VI (London: Routledge, 1966), is explored in Heather James's article 'Cultural Disintegration in *Titus Andronicus*: Mutilating Titus, Virgil, and Rome', in *Themes in Drama* 13 (1991) and her book *Shakespeare's Troy* (Cambridge: Cambridge University Press, 1997), and in Jonathan Bate's, *Shakespeare and Ovid* (Oxford: Clarendon Press, 1993). In her article, James argues that 'Shakespeare first invokes the *Aeneid* as the epic of empire-building, order, and *pietas*, and then allows Ovid's *Metamorphoses* to invade it . . . In [his] treat[ment of] the classical texts of imperial Rome', James continues, 'Shakespeare replicates the tragedy's patterns of competition, mutilation and digestion.' Bate similarly emphasizes Shakespeare's experimental and self-conscious use of his Ovidian source, and argues that *Titus Andronicus* is 'an archetypal Renaissance humanist text in that it is patterned on the classics', and not on an early modern source, as was widely believed. Bate and James, along with Eugene Waith, in his seminal article 'The Metamorphosis of Violence in *Titus Andronicus*', in *Shakespeare Survey* 10 (1957), pp. 39–49, and Ann Thompson, in 'Philomel in *Titus Andronicus* and *Cymbeline*', in *Shakespeare Survey* 31 (1978), pp. 23–32, have amply demonstrated that the influence of Ovid is stronger than any other model and have thus departed from a conventional assumption that *Titus Andronicus* can be best interpreted as belonging to the Senecan tradition of Elizabethan revenge tragedies. See, for example, F. Bowers, *Elizabethan Revenge Tragedy* (Princeton, 1940); Irving Ribner, 'Senecan Beginnings: *Titus Andronicus*, *Richard III*, *Romeo and Juliet*', in *Shakespearian Tragedy* (London, 1960), A. C.

Hamilton, *The Early Shakespeare* (San Marino, Calif., 1967); Nicholas Brooke, *Shakespeare's Early Tragedies* (London, 1968); and G. K. Hunter, *Dramatic Identities and Cultural Tradition* (Liverpool, 1978).

The advent of critical theory has produced a varied range of new readings of the play. In 'Rape and Revenge in *Titus Andronicus*', *English Literary Renaissance* 8 (1978), pp. 159–82, David Willbern applies a psychoanalytic approach in order to demonstrate that the play exemplifies a 'structural reciprocity' between rape and revenge. Alan Sommers's structural analysis in ' "Wilderness of Tigers": Structure and Symbolism in *Titus Andronicus*', in *Essays in Criticism* 10 (1960), pp. 275–89, focuses on Shakespeare's subtle exploration of the binary opposition between the Romans and the Goths. Feminist criticism has also produced interesting essays on the relationship between rape as a literal threat against the female body, and as a metaphorical threat against the body politic. See, for example, R. S. White, *Innocent Victims: Poetic Injustice in Shakespearean Tragedy* (London, 1986) and Catherine R. Stimpson, 'Shakespeare and the Soil of Rape', in *The Woman's Part: Feminist Criticism of Shakespeare*, edited by C. R. S. Lenz, G. Green and C. T. Neely (Urbana, Ill., 1980). The anthropological approach inspired by C. L. Barber and N. Frye, and subsequently qualified by M. Bakhtin and C. Geertz, has also identified the roots of Titus's tragedy with perversions of 'relationships of proximity and conviviality', see Richard Marienstras, *New Perspectives on the Shakespearean World* (Cambridge: Cambridge University Press, 1985) and conflicting ritual observations, see Naomi Conn Liebler, *Shakespeare's Festive Tragedy* (London: Routledge, 1995).

Eugene Waith's article on 'The Metamorphosis of Violence in *Titus Andronicus*' (see p. xci) and his investigation of the relationship between the excess of violence and the highly stylized quality of the play's language has proved to be the most influential contribution to its critical reception. Waith believes that Shakespeare was more interested by Ovid's exploration of the transforming powers of intense passions than by the medieval tradition of *Ovide Moralisé*, but that 'in taking over certain Ovidian forms, [he] takes over part of an Ovidian conception which cannot be fully realised by the techniques of drama'. Although inspired by Waith, A. H. Tricomi rejects the view that 'the play fails to transpose a narrative tale into a convincing dramatic story', and explains instead how its figurative language imitates the literal events of the plot in order to 'keep the excruciating images of mutilation before us even when the visual spectacle is no longer before us' ('The Aesthetics of Mutilation in *Titus Andronicus*', in *Shakespeare Survey* 27 (1974), pp. 11–19). In a slightly earlier and less incisive article, 'The Unspeakable in Pursuit of the Uneatable; Language and Action in *Titus Andronicus*', in *Critical Quarterly* 14 (1972), pp. 320–39, D. J. Palmer develops a similar line of argument to Waith and Tricomi.

The stage history of the play over the last thirty years is covered by A. C. Dessen's *Titus Andronicus*, Shakespeare in Performance Series (Manchester and New York: Manchester University Press, 1989), whereas Gustav Ungerer, 'An Unrecorded Elizabethan Performance of *TA*', in *Shakespeare Survey* 14 (1961), pp.102–9, reveals documentary evidence on a private performance of the play, which took place in the household of Sir John Harington in Rutland on New Year's Day, 1596. Antony Sher and Greg Doran's *Woza Shakespeare: Titus Andronicus in South Africa* (London: Methuen, 1996) provides an entertaining and enlightening account of a production of *Titus Andronicus* staged in South Africa in 1995.

Renewed critical and theatrical interest in the play has prompted collections of essays and casebooks, such as Philip C. Kolin, *Titus Andronicus: Critical Essays* (New York and London: Garland, 1995), Harold Metz, *Shakespeare's Earliest Tragedy: Studies in Titus Andronicus* (Madison, NJ: Fairleigh Dickinson University Press, 1996) and Maurice Charney, *Titus Andronicus*, Harvester New Critical Introductions to Shakespeare (New York and London: Harvester, 1990). Useful introductions to the play can also be found in Dieter Mehl, *Shakespeare's Tragedies: An Introduction* (Cambridge: Cambridge University Press, 1986) and Neil Taylor and Bryan Loughrey, *Shakespeare's Early Tragedies: 'Richard III', 'Titus Andronicus' and 'Romeo and Juliet': A Casebook* (Basingstoke: Macmillan, 1990).

Sonia Massai

Note to the Play in Performance

General

Alan C. Dessen's *Titus Andronicus* (Manchester and New York: Manchester University Press, 1989), mentioned above, is the indispensable study, covering every major production of the play in the United Kingdom and North America. After a survey stretching from the last years of the sixteenth to the second decade of the twentieth centuries, it draws on a wealth of reviews and other sources (including many instances of direct experience) to produce in-depth analyses of eight major twentieth-century productions. These include in England: Peter Brook's (Stratford, 1955), Trevor Nunn's (Stratford, 1972), Jane

Howell's (BBC television, 1985) and Deborah Warner's (Stratford, 1987); and in North America: Gerald Freedman's (New York, 1967), Laird Williamson's (Oregon, 1974), Brian Bedford's (Stratford, Ontario, 1978) and Pat Patton's (Oregon, 1986).

G. Harold Metz, 'The Early Staging of *Titus Andronicus*', *Shakespeare Quarterly* 28 (1977), pp. 154–9.

Peter Brook

Peter Brook, *The Shifting Point, 1946–87* (London: Methuen, 1988).

Richard Helfer and Glen Loney (eds.), *Peter Brook: Oxford to Orghast* (Amsterdam: Harwood Academic Publishers, 1998), pp. 66–73.

J. C. Trewin, *Peter Brook: A Biography* (London: Macdonald, 1971), pp. 80–81.

Kenneth Tynan, *'Curtains': Selections from the Drama Criticism and Related Writings* (New York: Atheneum, 1961), pp.103–5.

Evelyn Waugh, *The Spectator*, 2 September 1955, in *Shakespeare in the Theatre: An Anthology of Criticism*, edited by Stanley Wells (Oxford: Oxford University Press, 1999).

Trevor Nunn

Judith Cook, *Shakespeare's Players* (London: Harrap, 1983), pp. 88–9.

Deborah Warner

Brian Cox, 'Titus Andronicus' in *Players of Shakespeare* 3, edited by Russell Jackson and Robert Smallwood (Cambridge: Cambridge University Press, 1993).

Stanley Wells, 'Shakespeare's Performances in Stratford and London, 1986–7' in *Shakespeare Survey* 41 (1989), pp. 178–81.

Jacques Berthoud

THE MOST
LAMENTABLE
ROMAN TRAGEDY OF

TITUS ANDRONICUS

THE CHARACTERS IN THE PLAY

SATURNINUS, newly elected Emperor of Rome
BASSIANUS, brother of Saturninus

TITUS ANDRONICUS, Roman general
MARCUS ANDRONICUS, Roman Tribune, brother of
   Titus
LUCIUS ⎫
QUINTUS ⎪
MARTIUS ⎬ sons of Titus Andronicus
MUTIUS ⎭
LAVINIA daughter of Titus Andronicus
YOUNG LUCIUS a boy, son of Lucius and grandson to
   Titus Andronicus
SEMPRONIUS ⎫
CAIUS ⎬ kinsmen of Titus Andronicus
VALENTINE ⎭
AEMILIUS a noble Roman

TAMORA Queen of the Goths, afterwards Empress of
   Rome
ALARBUS ⎫
DEMETRIUS ⎬ Tamora's sons
CHIRON ⎭
AARON, a Moor, and Tamora's lover

NURSE
CLOWN
MESSENGER

Senators, Tribunes, Roman Soldiers, Attendants, Goths

3

Flourish. Enter the tribunes and senators aloft; and
then enter below Saturninus and his followers at one
door, and Bassianus and his followers at the other,
with drums and colours

SATURNINUS

Noble patricians, patrons of my right,
Defend the justice of my cause with arms.
And, countrymen, my loving followers,
Plead my successive title with your swords.
I am his first-born son that was the last
That wore the imperial diadem of Rome;
Then let my father's honours live in me,
Nor wrong mine age with this indignity.

BASSIANUS

Romans, friends, followers, favourers of my right,
If ever Bassianus, Caesar's son,   10
Were gracious in the eyes of royal Rome,
Keep then this passage to the Capitol,
And suffer not dishonour to approach
The Imperial seat, to virtue consecrate,
To justice, continence, and nobility;
But let desert in pure election shine,
And, Romans, fight for freedom in your choice.
        Enter Marcus Andronicus aloft with the crown

MARCUS

Princes that strive by factions and by friends
Ambitiously for rule and empery,
Know that the people of Rome, for whom we stand   20

5

A special party, have by common voice
In election for the Roman empery
Chosen Andronicus, surnamèd Pius
For many good and great deserts to Rome.
A nobler man, a braver warrior,
Lives not this day within the city walls.
He by the senate is accited home
From weary wars against the barbarous Goths,
That with his sons, a terror to our foes,
30   Hath yoked a nation strong, trained up in arms.
Ten years are spent since first he undertook
This cause of Rome, and chastisèd with arms
Our enemies' pride. Five times he hath returned
Bleeding to Rome, bearing his valiant sons
In coffins from the field, and at this day
To the monument of the Andronici
Done sacrifice of expiation,
And slain the noblest prisoner of the Goths.
And now at last, laden with honour's spoils,
40   Returns the good Andronicus to Rome,
Renownèd Titus, flourishing in arms.
Let us entreat, by honour of his name
Whom worthily you would have now succeed,
And in the Capitol and senate's right
Whom you pretend to honour and adore,
That you withdraw you and abate your strength,
Dismiss your followers, and, as suitors should,
Plead your deserts in peace and humbleness.

SATURNINUS
How fair the tribune speaks to calm my thoughts.

BASSIANUS
50   Marcus Andronicus, so I do affy
In thy uprightness and integrity,
And so I love and honour thee and thine,

Thy noble brother Titus and his sons,
And her to whom my thoughts are humbled all,
Gracious Lavinia, Rome's rich ornament,
That I will here dismiss my loving friends
And to my fortune's and the people's favour
Commit my cause in balance to be weighed.

Exeunt his soldiers; his other followers remain

SATURNINUS
Friends that have been thus forward in my right,
I thank you all and here dismiss you all,   60
And to the love and favour of my country
Commit myself, my person, and the cause.

Exeunt his soldiers; his other followers remain
(*To the tribunes and senators above*)
Rome, be as just and gracious unto me
As I am confident and kind to thee.
Open the gates and let me in.

BASSIANUS
Tribunes, and me, a poor competitor.

Flourish. They go up into the senate house.
Enter a Captain

CAPTAIN
Romans, make way. The good Andronicus,
Patron of virtue, Rome's best champion,
Successful in the battles that he fights,
With honour and with fortune is returned   70
From where he circumscribèd with his sword
And brought to yoke the enemies of Rome.

Sound drums and trumpets. Then enter two of Titus's
sons, Martius and Mutius, then two men bearing a
Coffin covered with black, then two other sons, Lucius
and Quintus, then Titus Andronicus, and then
Tamora, the Queen of Goths, and her three sons,
Alarbus, Chiron and Demetrius, with Aaron the Moor,

7

and others as many as can be. Then set down the coffin,
and Titus speaks

TITUS

Hail, Rome, victorious in thy mourning weeds!
Lo, as the bark that hath discharged his freight
Returns with precious lading to the bay
From whence at first she weighed her anchorage,
Cometh Andronicus, bound with laurel boughs,
To re-salute his country with his tears,
Tears of true joy for his return to Rome.
80   Thou great defender of this Capitol,
Stand gracious to the rites that we intend.
Romans, of five-and-twenty valiant sons,
Half of the number that King Priam had,
Behold the poor remains alive and dead.
These that survive, let Rome reward with love;
These that I bring unto their latest home,
With burial amongst their ancestors.
Here Goths have given me leave to sheathe my sword.
Titus, unkind and careless of thine own,
90   Why suffer'st thou thy sons unburied yet
To hover on the dreadful shore of Styx?
Make way to lay them by their brethren.

They open the tomb

There greet in silence as the dead are wont,
And sleep in peace, slain in your country's wars.
O sacred receptacle of my joys,
Sweet cell of virtue and nobility,
How many sons hast thou of mine in store
That thou wilt never render to me more!

LUCIUS

Give us the proudest prisoner of the Goths,
100   That we may hew his limbs and on a pile
Ad manes fratrum sacrifice his flesh

8

Before this earthy prison of their bones,
That so the shadows be not unappeased,
Nor we disturbed with prodigies on earth.

TITUS

I give him you, the noblest that survives,
The eldest son of this distressèd queen.

TAMORA (*kneeling*)

Stay, Roman brethren! Gracious conqueror,
Victorious Titus, rue the tears I shed,
A mother's tears in passion for her son;
And if thy sons were ever dear to thee,   110
O, think my son to be as dear to me.
Sufficeth not that we are brought to Rome
To beautify thy triumphs, and return
Captive to thee and to thy Roman yoke,
But must my sons be slaughtered in the streets
For valiant doings in their country's cause?
O, if to fight for king and commonweal
Were piety in thine, it is in these.
Andronicus, stain not thy tomb with blood.
Wilt thou draw near the nature of the gods?   120
Draw near them then in being merciful;
Sweet mercy is nobility's true badge.
Thrice-noble Titus, spare my first-born son.

TITUS

Patient yourself, madam, and pardon me.
These are their brethren whom your Goths beheld
Alive and dead, and for their brethren slain
Religiously they ask a sacrifice.
To this your son is marked, and die he must
T'appease their groaning shadows that are gone.

LUCIUS

Away with him, and make a fire straight,   130
And with our swords upon a pile of wood

9

Let's hew his limbs till they be clean consumed.

Exeunt Titus's sons with Alarbus

TAMORA (*rising*)

O cruel, irreligious piety.

CHIRON

Was never Scythia half so barbarous.

DEMETRIUS

Oppose not Scythia to ambitious Rome.
Alarbus goes to rest and we survive
To tremble under Titus' threat'ning look.
Then, madam, stand resolved; but hope withal
The selfsame gods that armed the Queen of Troy
140 With opportunity of sharp revenge
Upon the Thracian tyrant in his tent
May favour Tamora, the Queen of Goths –
When Goths were Goths, and Tamora was queen –
To quit these bloody wrongs upon her foes.

Enter the sons of Andronicus, with their swords bloody

LUCIUS

See, lord and father, how we have performed
Our Roman rites. Alarbus' limbs are lopped,
And entrails feed the sacrificing fire,
Whose smoke like incense doth perfume the sky.
Remaineth naught but to inter our brethren,
150 And with loud 'larums welcome them to Rome.

TITUS

Let it be so, and let Andronicus
Make this his latest farewell to their souls.

Sound trumpets, and lay the coffin in the tomb

In peace and honour rest you here, my sons;
Rome's readiest champions, repose you here in rest,
Secure from worldly chances and mishaps.
Here lurks no treason, here no envy swells,
Here grow no damnèd drugs, here are no storms,

No noise, but silence and eternal sleep.
        Enter Lavinia
In peace and honour rest you here, my sons.

LAVINIA

In peace and honour live Lord Titus long;   160
My noble lord and father, live in fame.
Lo, at this tomb my tributary tears
I render for my brethren's obsequies,
(*Kneeling*) And at thy feet I kneel with tears of joy
Shed on this earth for thy return to Rome.
O bless me here with thy victorious hand,
Whose fortunes Rome's best citizens applaud.

TITUS

Kind Rome, that hast thus lovingly reserved
The cordial of mine age to glad my heart.
Lavinia live, outlive thy father's days   170
And fame's eternal date for virtue's praise.
        Lavinia rises

MARCUS (*above*)

Long live Lord Titus, my belovèd brother,
Gracious triumpher in the eyes of Rome!

TITUS

Thanks, gentle tribune, noble brother Marcus.

MARCUS

And welcome, nephews, from successful wars,
You that survive, and you that sleep in fame.
Fair lords, your fortunes are alike in all
That in your country's service drew your swords;
But safer triumph is this funeral pomp,
That hath aspired to Solon's happiness   180
And triumphs over chance in honour's bed.
Titus Andronicus, the people of Rome,
Whose friend in justice thou hast ever been,
Send thee by me, their tribune and their trust,

I.1

>This palliament of white and spotless hue,
>And name thee in election for the empire
>With these our late-deceasèd emperor's sons.
>Be *candidatus* then and put it on,
>And help to set a head on headless Rome.

TITUS

190 >A better head her glorious body fits
>Than his that shakes for age and feebleness.
>What should I don this robe and trouble you?
>Be chosen with proclamations today,
>Tomorrow yield up rule, resign my life,
>And set abroad new business for you all?
>Rome, I have been thy soldier forty years,
>And led my country's strength successfully,
>And buried one-and-twenty valiant sons
>Knighted in field, slain manfully in arms,
200 >In right and service of their noble country.
>Give me a staff of honour for mine age,
>But not a sceptre to control the world.
>Upright he held it, lords, that held it last.

MARCUS

>Titus, thou shalt obtain and ask the empery.

SATURNINUS (*above*)

>Proud and ambitious tribune, canst thou tell?

TITUS

>Patience, Prince Saturninus.

SATURNINUS   Romans, do me right!
>Patricians, draw your swords and sheathe them not
>Till Saturninus be Rome's emperor.
>Andronicus, would thou were shipped to hell
210 >Rather than rob me of the people's hearts.

LUCIUS

>Proud Saturnine, interrupter of the good
>That noble-minded Titus means to thee.

TITUS

    Content thee, prince; I will restore to thee
    The people's hearts, and wean them from
        themselves.

BASSIANUS (*above*)

    Andronicus, I do not flatter thee,
    But honour thee, and will do till I die.
    My faction if thou strengthen with thy friends,
    I will most thankful be, and thanks to men
    Of noble minds is honourable meed.

TITUS

    People of Rome and people's tribunes here,   220
    I ask your voices and your suffrages.
    Will ye bestow them friendly on Andronicus?

TRIBUNES (*above*)

    To gratify the good Andronicus
    And gratulate his safe return to Rome,
    The people will accept whom he admits.

TITUS

    Tribunes, I thank you, and this suit I make,
    That you create our emperor's eldest son,
    Lord Saturnine, whose virtues will, I hope,
    Reflect on Rome as Titan's rays on earth,
    And ripen justice in this commonweal.   230
    Then if you will elect by my advice,
    Crown him and say, 'Long live our emperor!'

MARCUS

    With voices and applause of every sort,
    Patricians and plebeians, we create
    Lord Saturninus Rome's great emperor,
    And say, 'Long live our Emperor Saturnine!'
        A long flourish till Marcus, Saturninus, Bassianus,
        tribunes and senators come down.
        Marcus crowns Saturninus

I.1

SATURNINUS
    Titus Andronicus, for thy favours done
    To us in our election this day
    I give thee thanks in part of thy deserts,
240   And will with deeds requite thy gentleness.
    And for an onset, Titus, to advance
    Thy name and honourable family,
    Lavinia will I make my empress,
    Rome's royal mistress, mistress of my heart,
    And in the sacred Pantheon her espouse.
    Tell me, Andronicus, doth this motion please thee?
TITUS
    It doth, my worthy lord, and in this match
    I hold me highly honoured of your grace,
    And here in sight of Rome to Saturnine,
250   King and commander of our commonweal,
    The wide world's emperor, do I consecrate
    My sword, my chariot, and my prisoners,
    Presents well worthy Rome's imperious lord.
    Receive them then, the tribute that I owe,
    Mine honour's ensigns humbled at thy feet.
SATURNINUS
    Thanks, noble Titus, father of my life.
    How proud I am of thee and of thy gifts
    Rome shall record, and when I do forget
    The least of these unspeakable deserts,
260   Romans, forget your fealty to me.
TITUS (*to Tamora*)
    Now, madam, are you prisoner to an emperor,
    To him that for your honour and your state
    Will use you nobly and your followers.
SATURNINUS (*aside*)
    A goodly lady, trust me, of the hue
    That I would choose were I to choose anew.

(*To Tamora*)

Clear up, fair queen, that cloudy countenance;
Though chance of war hath wrought this change of
    cheer,
Thou com'st not to be made a scorn in Rome.
Princely shall be thy usage every way.
Rest on my word, and let not discontent   270
Daunt all your hopes. Madam, he comforts you
Can make you greater than the Queen of Goths.
Lavinia, you are not displeased with this?

LAVINIA

Not I, my lord, sith true nobility
Warrants these words in princely courtesy.

SATURNINUS

Thanks, sweet Lavinia. Romans, let us go.
Ransomless here we set our prisoners free;
Proclaim our honours, lords, with trump and drum.
    Flourish

BASSIANUS (*seizing Lavinia*)

Lord Titus, by your leave, this maid is mine.

TITUS

How, sir? Are you in earnest then, my lord?   280

BASSIANUS

Ay, noble Titus, and resolved withal
To do myself this reason and this right.

MARCUS

Suum cuique is our Roman justice;
This prince in justice seizeth but his own.

LUCIUS

And that he will and shall, if Lucius live.
    Exeunt Tamora, Demetrius, Chiron and attendants

TITUS

Traitors, avaunt! Where is the Emperor's guard?
Treason, my lord! Lavinia is surprised.

SATURNINUS
Surprised? By whom?
BASSIANUS   By him that justly may
Bear his betrothed from all the world away.
                    Exeunt Bassianus and Marcus with Lavinia

MUTIUS
290   Brothers, help to convey her hence away,
And with my sword I'll keep this door safe.
                    Exeunt Quintus and Martius at one door
TITUS (*to Saturninus*)
Follow, my lord, and I'll soon bring her back.
                    Exit Saturninus at the other door

MUTIUS
My lord, you pass not here.
TITUS   What, villain boy,
Barr'st me my way in Rome?
        He attacks Mutius
MUTIUS   Help, Lucius, help.
        Titus kills him

LUCIUS
My lord, you are unjust, and more than so,
In wrongful quarrel you have slain your son.
TITUS
Nor thou, nor he, are any sons of mine;
My sons would never so dishonour me.
Traitor, restore Lavinia to the Emperor.

LUCIUS
300   Dead, if you will, but not to be his wife
That is another's lawful promised love.   *Exit*
                    *Enter aloft the Emperor with Tamora and her two
                    sons, and Aaron the Moor*

SATURNINUS
No, Titus, no, the Emperor needs her not,
Nor her, nor thee, nor any of thy stock.

16

I'll trust by leisure him that mocks me once,
Thee never, nor thy traitorous haughty sons,
Confederates all thus to dishonour me.
Was none in Rome to make a stale
But Saturnine? Full well, Andronicus,
Agree these deeds with that proud brag of thine,
That saidst I begged the empire at thy hands.   310

TITUS

O monstrous! What reproachful words are these?

SATURNINUS

But go thy ways, go give that changing piece
To him that flourished for her with his sword.
A valiant son-in-law thou shalt enjoy,
One fit to bandy with thy lawless sons,
To ruffle in the commonwealth of Rome.

TITUS

These words are razors to my wounded heart.

SATURNINUS

And therefore, lovely Tamora, Queen of Goths,
That like the stately Phoebe 'mongst her nymphs
Dost overshine the gallant'st dames of Rome,   320
If thou be pleased with this my sudden choice,
Behold, I choose thee, Tamora, for my bride,
And will create thee Empress of Rome.
Speak, Queen of Goths, dost thou applaud my choice?
And here I swear by all the Roman gods,
Sith priest and holy water are so near,
And tapers burn so bright, and everything
In readiness for Hymenaeus stand,
I will not re-salute the streets of Rome
Or climb my palace, till from forth this place   330
I lead espoused my bride along with me.

TAMORA

And here in sight of heaven to Rome I swear,

If Saturnine advance the Queen of Goths,
She will a handmaid be to his desires,
A loving nurse, a mother to his youth.

SATURNINUS

Ascend, fair queen, Pantheon. Lords, accompany
Your noble Emperor and his lovely bride,
Sent by the heavens for Prince Saturnine,
Whose wisdom hath her fortune conquerèd.
340   There shall we consummate our spousal rites.

Exeunt all but Titus

TITUS

I am not bid to wait upon this bride.
Titus, when wert thou wont to walk alone,
Dishonoured thus and challengèd of wrongs?

Enter Marcus and Titus's sons, Lucius, Quintus, and
Martius

MARCUS

O Titus, see! O see what thou hast done:
In a bad quarrel slain a virtuous son.

TITUS

No, foolish tribune, no. No son of mine,
Nor thou, nor these, confederates in the deed
That hath dishonoured all our family,
Unworthy brother, and unworthy sons.

LUCIUS

350   But let us give him burial as becomes;
Give Mutius burial with our brethren.

TITUS

Traitors, away! He rests not in this tomb.
This monument five hundred years hath stood,
Which I have sumptuously re-edified.
Here none but soldiers and Rome's servitors
Repose in fame; none basely slain in brawls.
Bury him where you can, he comes not here.

MARCUS

My lord, this is impiety in you.
My nephew Mutius' deeds do plead for him;
He must be buried with his brethren.   360

MARTIUS *and* QUINTUS

And shall, or him we will accompany.

TITUS

'And shall'? What villain was it spake that word?

MARTIUS

He that would vouch it in any place but here.

TITUS

What, would you bury him in my despite?

MARCUS

No, noble Titus, but entreat of thee
To pardon Mutius and to bury him.

TITUS

Marcus, even thou hast struck upon my crest,
And with these boys mine honour thou hast
    wounded.
My foes I do repute you every one,
So trouble me no more, but get you gone.   370

QUINTUS

He is not with himself; let us withdraw.

MARTIUS

Not I, till Mutius' bones be burièd.
        The brother and the sons kneel

MARCUS

Brother, for in that name doth nature plead –

MARTIUS

Father, and in that name doth nature speak –

TITUS

Speak thou no more, if all the rest will speed.

MARCUS

Renownèd Titus, more than half my soul –

LUCIUS

Dear father, soul and substance of us all –

MARCUS

Suffer thy brother Marcus to inter
His noble nephew here in virtue's nest,
380 That died in honour and Lavinia's cause.
Thou art a Roman, be not barbarous.
The Greeks upon advice did bury Ajax
That slew himself, and wise Laertes' son
Did graciously plead for his funerals.
Let not young Mutius then, that was thy joy,
Be barred his entrance here.

TITUS   Rise, Marcus, rise.
      They rise
The dismall'st day is this that e'er I saw,
To be dishonoured by my sons in Rome.
Well, bury him, and bury me the next.
      They put Mutius in the tomb

LUCIUS

390 There lie thy bones, sweet Mutius, with thy friends,
Till we with trophies do adorn thy tomb.

ALL (*kneeling*)

No man shed tears for noble Mutius;
He lives in fame, that died in virtue's cause.
      They rise

                              Exeunt all but Marcus and Titus

MARCUS

My lord, to step out of these dreary dumps,
How comes it that the subtle Queen of Goths
Is of a sudden thus advanced in Rome?

TITUS

I know not, Marcus, but I know it is.
Whether by device or no, the heavens can tell.
Is she not then beholden to the man

That brought her for this high good turn so far? 400
MARCUS

Yes, and will nobly him remunerate.

> *Flourish.*
>
> *Enter the Emperor, Tamora and her two sons, with the Moor, at one door. Enter at the other door Bassianus and Lavinia, with Lucius, Quintus and Martius*

SATURNINUS

So, Bassianus, you have played your prize.

God give you joy, sir, of your gallant bride.
BASSIANUS

And you of yours, my lord. I say no more,

Nor wish no less, and so I take my leave.
SATURNINUS

Traitor, if Rome have law or we have power,

Thou and thy faction shall repent this rape.
BASSIANUS

'Rape' call you it, my lord, to seize my own,

My true betrothèd love, and now my wife?

But let the laws of Rome determine all; 410

Meanwhile am I possessed of that is mine.
SATURNINUS

'Tis good, sir. You are very short with us,

But if we live, we'll be as sharp with you.
BASSIANUS

My lord, what I have done, as best I may

Answer I must, and shall do with my life.

Only thus much I give your grace to know:

By all the duties that I owe to Rome,

This noble gentleman, Lord Titus here,

Is in opinion and in honour wronged,

That in the rescue of Lavinia 420

With his own hand did slay his youngest son

In zeal to you, and highly moved to wrath

To be controlled in that he frankly gave.
Receive him then to favour, Saturnine,
That hath expressed himself in all his deeds
A father and a friend to thee and Rome.

TITUS

Prince Bassianus, leave to plead my deeds.
'Tis thou and those that have dishonoured me.
(*Kneeling*) Rome and the righteous heavens be my
    judge,

430   How I have loved and honoured Saturnine.

TAMORA

My worthy lord, if ever Tamora
Were gracious in those princely eyes of thine,
Then hear me speak indifferently for all,
And at my suit, sweet, pardon what is past.

SATURNINUS

What, madam, be dishonoured openly,
And basely put it up without revenge?

TAMORA

Not so, my lord. The gods of Rome forfend
I should be author to dishonour you.
But on mine honour dare I undertake

440   For good Lord Titus' innocence in all,
Whose fury not dissembled speaks his griefs.
Then at my suit look graciously on him;
Lose not so noble a friend on vain suppose,
Nor with sour looks afflict his gentle heart.
(*Aside to Saturninus*)
My lord, be ruled by me, be won at last,
Dissemble all your griefs and discontents.
You are but newly planted in your throne.
Lest then the people, and patricians too,
Upon a just survey take Titus' part

450   And so supplant you for ingratitude,

22

Which Rome reputes to be a heinous sin,
Yield at entreats, and then let me alone:
I'll find a day to massacre them all,
And raze their faction and their family,
The cruel father and his traitorous sons
To whom I suèd for my dear son's life,
And make them know what 'tis to let a queen
Kneel in the streets and beg for grace in vain.
(*To all*) Come, come, sweet Emperor; come,
    Andronicus.
Take up this good old man, and cheer the heart   460
That dies in tempest of thy angry frown.

SATURNINUS

Rise, Titus, rise; my Empress hath prevailed.

TITUS (*rising*)

I thank your majesty and her, my lord.
These words, these looks, infuse new life in me.

TAMORA

Titus, I am incorporate in Rome,
A Roman now adopted happily,
And must advise the Emperor for his good.
This day all quarrels die, Andronicus;
(*To Saturnine*) And let it be mine honour, good my
    lord,
That I have reconciled your friends and you.   470
For you, Prince Bassianus, I have passed
My word and promise to the Emperor
That you will be more mild and tractable.
And fear not, lords, and you, Lavinia:
By my advice, all humbled on your knees,
You shall ask pardon of his majesty.

> *Bassianus, Lavinia, Lucius, Quintus, and Martius*
> *kneel*

LUCIUS

We do, and vow to heaven and to his highness
That what we did was mildly as we might,
Tend'ring our sister's honour and our own.

MARCUS (*kneeling*)

480 That on mine honour here do I protest.

SATURNINUS

Away, and talk not, trouble us no more.

TAMORA

Nay, nay, sweet Emperor, we must all be friends.
The tribune and his nephews kneel for grace;
I will not be denied; sweetheart, look back.

SATURNINUS

Marcus, for thy sake, and thy brother's here,
And at my lovely Tamora's entreats,
I do remit these young men's heinous faults.
Stand up. (*They rise*)
Lavinia, though you left me like a churl,
490 I found a friend, and sure as death I swore
I would not part a bachelor from the priest.
Come, if the Emperor's court can feast two brides,
You are my guest, Lavinia, and your friends.
This day shall be a love-day, Tamora.

TITUS

Tomorrow, an it please your majesty
To hunt the panther and the hart with me,
With horn and hound we'll give your grace *bonjour*.

SATURNINUS

Be it so, Titus, and gramercy too.
    Sound trumpets

                    Exeunt all but Aaron

✳

Aaron is alone on stage

AARON

Now climbeth Tamora Olympus' top,
Safe out of fortune's shot, and sits aloft,
Secure of thunder's crack or lightning flash,
Advanced above pale envy's threat'ning reach.
As when the golden sun salutes the morn
And, having gilt the ocean with his beams,
Gallops the zodiac in his glistering coach
And overlooks the highest-peering hills,
So Tamora.
Upon her wit doth earthly honour wait,   10
And virtue stoops and trembles at her frown.
Then, Aaron, arm thy heart and fit thy thoughts
To mount aloft with thy imperial mistress,
And mount her pitch, whom thou in triumph long
Hast prisoner held, fettered in amorous chains,
And faster bound to Aaron's charming eyes
Than is Prometheus tied to Caucasus.
Away with slavish weeds and servile thoughts!
I will be bright and shine in pearl and gold
To wait upon this new-made Empress.   20
'To wait' said I? – to wanton with this queen,
This goddess, this Semiramis, this nymph,
This siren that will charm Rome's Saturnine,
And see his shipwreck and his commonweal's.
Hollo, what storm is this?

Enter Chiron and Demetrius braving

DEMETRIUS

Chiron, thy years want wit, thy wits wants edge

And manners to intrude where I am graced,
And may, for aught thou knowest, affected be.

CHIRON

Demetrius, thou dost overween in all,
30 And so in this, to bear me down with braves.
'Tis not the difference of a year or two
Makes me less gracious, or thee more fortunate:
I am as able and as fit as thou
To serve and to deserve my mistress' grace,
And that my sword upon thee shall approve,
And plead my passions for Lavinia's love.

AARON (*aside*)

Clubs, clubs! These lovers will not keep the peace.

DEMETRIUS

Why, boy, although our mother, unadvised,
Gave you a dancing-rapier by your side,
40 Are you so desperate grown to threat your friends?
Go to, have your lath glued within your sheath
Till you know better how to handle it.

CHIRON

Meanwhile, sir, with the little skill I have,
Full well shalt thou perceive how much I dare.

DEMETRIUS

Ay, boy, grow ye so brave?
                    They draw

AARON   Why, how now, lords?
So near the Emperor's palace dare ye draw,
And maintain such a quarrel openly?
Full well I wot the ground of all this grudge.
I would not for a million of gold
50 The cause were known to them it most concerns,
Nor would your noble mother for much more
Be so dishonoured in the court of Rome.
For shame, put up!

DEMETRIUS   Not I, till I have sheathed
   My rapier in his bosom, and withal
   Thrust those reproachful speeches down his throat,
   That he hath breathed in my dishonour here.
CHIRON
   For that I am prepared and full resolved,
   Foul-spoken coward, that thund'rest with thy
      tongue
   And with thy weapon nothing dar'st perform.
AARON
   Away, I say!   60
   Now, by the gods that warlike Goths adore,
   This petty brabble will undo us all.
   Why, lords, and think you not how dangerous
   It is to jet upon a prince's right?
   What, is Lavinia then become so loose,
   Or Bassianus so degenerate,
   That for her love such quarrels may be broached
   Without controlment, justice, or revenge?
   Young lords, beware; and should the Empress know
   This discord's ground, the music would not please.   70
CHIRON
   I care not, I, knew she and all the world:
   I love Lavinia more than all the world.
DEMETRIUS
   Youngling, learn thou to make some meaner choice:
   Lavinia is thine elder brother's hope.
AARON
   Why, are ye mad? Or know ye not in Rome
   How furious and impatient they be,
   And cannot brook competitors in love?
   I tell you, lords, you do but plot your deaths
   By this device.
CHIRON   Aaron, a thousand deaths

80   Would I propose to achieve her whom I love.

AARON
     To achieve her how?

DEMETRIUS   Why makes thou it so strange?
     She is a woman, therefore may be wooed;
     She is a woman, therefore may be won;
     She is Lavinia, therefore must be loved.
     What, man, more water glideth by the mill
     Than wots the miller of, and easy it is
     Of a cut loaf to steal a shive, we know.
     Though Bassianus be the Emperor's brother,
     Better than he have worn Vulcan's badge.

AARON (*aside*)
90   Ay, and as good as Saturninus may.

DEMETRIUS
     Then why should he despair that knows to court it
     With words, fair looks, and liberality?
     What, hast not thou full often struck a doe
     And borne her cleanly by the keeper's nose?

AARON
     Why then, it seems some certain snatch or so
     Would serve your turns.

CHIRON   Ay, so the turn were served.

DEMETRIUS
     Aaron, thou hast hit it.

AARON   Would you had hit it too,
     Then should not we be tired with this ado.
     Why, hark ye, hark ye, and are you such fools
100 To square for this? Would it offend you then
     That both should speed?

CHIRON
     Faith, not me.

DEMETRIUS   Nor me, so I were one.

AARON

For shame, be friends, and join for that you jar.
'Tis policy and stratagem must do
That you affect, and so must you resolve
That what you cannot as you would achieve,
You must perforce accomplish as you may.
Take this of me: Lucrece was not more chaste
Than this Lavinia, Bassianus' love.
A speedier course than ling'ring languishment   110
Must we pursue, and I have found the path.
My lords, a solemn hunting is in hand;
There will the lovely Roman ladies troop.
The forest walks are wide and spacious,
And many unfrequented plots there are,
Fitted by kind for rape and villainy.
Single you thither then this dainty doe,
And strike her home by force, if not by words.
This way, or not at all, stand you in hope.
Come, come; our Empress with her sacred wit   120
To villainy and vengeance consecrate,
Will we acquaint with all what we intend,
And she shall file our engines with advice
That will not suffer you to square yourselves,
But to your wishes' height advance you both.
The Emperor's court is like the house of fame,
The palace full of tongues, of eyes, and ears;
The woods are ruthless, dreadful, deaf, and dull.
There speak and strike, brave boys, and take your
        turns;
There serve your lust, shadowed from heaven's eye,   130
And revel in Lavinia's treasury.

CHIRON

Thy counsel, lad, smells of no cowardice.

29

DEMETRIUS

Sit fas aut nefas, till I find the stream
To cool this heat, a charm to calm these fits,
Per Stygia, per manes vehor.   *Exeunt*

II.2   *Enter Marcus, Titus Andronicus and his three sons,*
                       Lucius, Quintus, and Martius, making a noise with
                       hounds and horns

TITUS

The hunt is up, the morn is bright and grey,
The fields are fragrant, and the woods are green.
Uncouple here, and let us make a bay
And wake the Emperor and his lovely bride,
And rouse the Prince, and ring a hunter's peal,
That all the court may echo with the noise.
Sons, let it be your charge, as it is ours,
To attend the Emperor's person carefully.
I have been troubled in my sleep this night,

10   But dawning day new comfort hath inspired.
                       Here a cry of hounds and wind horns in a peal;
                       then enter Saturninus, Tamora, Bassianus, Lavinia,
                       Chiron, Demetrius, and their attendants
Many good morrows to your majesty;
Madam, to you as many and as good.
I promisèd your grace a hunter's peal.

SATURNINUS

And you have rung it lustily, my lords,
Somewhat too early for new-married ladies.

BASSIANUS

Lavinia, how say you?

LAVINIA   I say no:
I have been broad awake two hours and more.

SATURNINUS

    Come on then, horse and chariots let us have,

    And to our sport. (*To Tamora*) Madam, now shall ye

       see

    Our Roman hunting.

MARCUS   I have dogs, my lord,   20

    Will rouse the proudest panther in the chase

    And climb the highest promontory top.

TITUS

    And I have horse will follow where the game

    Makes way and run like swallows o'er the plain.

DEMETRIUS (*to Chiron*)

    Chiron, we hunt not, we, with horse nor hound,

    But hope to pluck a dainty doe to ground.   *Exeunt*

       Enter Aaron alone with gold   II.3

AARON

    He that had wit would think that I had none,

    To bury so much gold under a tree

    And never after to inherit it.

    Let him that thinks of me so abjectly

    Know that this gold must coin a stratagem

    Which, cunningly effected, will beget

    A very excellent piece of villainy.

       He hides the gold

    And so repose, sweet gold, for their unrest

    That have their alms out of the Empress' chest.

       Enter Tamora alone to the Moor

TAMORA

    My lovely Aaron, wherefore look'st thou sad,   10

    When everything doth make a gleeful boast?

    The birds chant melody on every bush,

    The snakes lies rollèd in the cheerful sun,

The green leaves quiver with the cooling wind
And make a chequered shadow on the ground.
Under their sweet shade, Aaron, let us sit,
And whilst the babbling echo mocks the hounds,
Replying shrilly to the well-tuned horns,
As if a double hunt were heard at once,
20   Let us sit down and mark their yellowing noise.
And after conflict such as was supposed
The wand'ring prince and Dido once enjoyed,
When with a happy storm they were surprised
And curtained with a counsel-keeping cave,
We may, each wreathèd in the other's arms,
Our pastimes done, possess a golden slumber,
Whilst hounds and horns and sweet melodious
    birds
Be unto us as is a nurse's song
Of lullaby to bring her babe asleep.

AARON

30   Madam, though Venus govern your desires,
Saturn is dominator over mine.
What signifies my deadly-standing eye,
My silence, and my cloudy melancholy,
My fleece of woolly hair that now uncurls
Even as an adder when she doth unroll
To do some fatal execution?
No, madam, these are no venereal signs.
Vengeance is in my heart, death in my hand,
Blood and revenge are hammering in my head.
40   Hark, Tamora, the empress of my soul,
Which never hopes more heaven than rests in thee,
This is the day of doom for Bassianus.
His Philomel must lose her tongue today;
Thy sons make pillage of her chastity
And wash their hands in Bassianus' blood.

He holds up a letter
Seest thou this letter? Take it up, I pray thee,
And give the King this fatal-plotted scroll.
Now question me no more, we are espied.
Here comes a parcel of our hopeful booty,
Which dreads not yet their lives' destruction.   50
Enter Bassianus and Lavinia
TAMORA
Ah, my sweet Moor, sweeter to me than life!
AARON
No more, great Empress; Bassianus comes.
Be cross with him, and I'll go fetch thy sons
To back thy quarrels, whatsoe'er they be.   *Exit*
BASSIANUS
Who have we here? Rome's royal Empress,
Unfurnished of her well-beseeming troop?
Or is it Dian, habited like her,
Who hath abandonèd her holy groves
To see the general hunting in this forest?
TAMORA
Saucy controller of my private steps,   60
Had I the power that some say Dian had,
Thy temples should be planted presently
With horns, as was Actaeon's, and the hounds
Should drive upon thy new-transformèd limbs,
Unmannerly intruder as thou art.
LAVINIA
Under your patience, gentle Empress,
'Tis thought you have a goodly gift in horning,
And to be doubted that your Moor and you
Are singled forth to try experiments.
Jove shield your husband from his hounds today: 70
'Tis pity they should take him for a stag.

33

BASSIANUS

Believe me, Queen, your swart Cimmerian
Doth make your honour of his body's hue,
Spotted, detested, and abominable.
Why are you sequestered from all your train,
Dismounted from your snow-white goodly steed,
And wandered hither to an obscure plot,
Accompanied but with a barbarous Moor,
If foul desire had not conducted you?

LAVINIA

80 And being intercepted in your sport,
Great reason that my noble lord be rated
For sauciness. (*To Bassianus*) I pray you, let us hence,
And let her joy her raven-coloured love.
This valley fits the purpose passing well.

BASSIANUS

The King my brother shall have note of this.

LAVINIA

Ay, for these slips have made him noted long.
Good king, to be so mightily abused!

TAMORA

Why, I have patience to endure all this.
                    Enter Chiron and Demetrius

DEMETRIUS

How now, dear sovereign and our gracious mother,
90 Why doth your highness look so pale and wan?

TAMORA

Have I not reason, think you, to look pale?
These two have 'ticed me hither to this place.
A barren detested vale, you see it is:
The trees, though summer, yet forlorn and lean,
O'ercome with moss and baleful mistletoe;
Here never shines the sun, here nothing breeds,
Unless the nightly owl or fatal raven.

34

And when they showed me this abhorrèd pit,
They told me here at dead time of the night
A thousand fiends, a thousand hissing snakes,   100
Ten thousand swelling toads, as many urchins,
Would make such fearful and confusèd cries
As any mortal body hearing it
Should straight fall mad, or else die suddenly.
No sooner had they told this hellish tale,
But straight they told me they would bind me here
Unto the body of a dismal yew
And leave me to this miserable death.
And then they called me foul adulteress,
Lascivious Goth, and all the bitterest terms   110
That ever ear did hear to such effect.
And had you not by wondrous fortune come,
This vengeance on me had they executed.
Revenge it as you love your mother's life,
Or be ye not henceforth called my children.

DEMETRIUS

This is a witness that I am thy son.
    He stabs Bassianus

CHIRON

And this for me, struck home to show my strength.
    He also stabs Bassianus, who dies.
    Tamora threatens Lavinia

LAVINIA

Ay, come, Semiramis, nay, barbarous Tamora,
For no name fits thy nature but thy own.

TAMORA

Give me the poniard. You shall know, my boys,   120
Your mother's hand shall right your mother's wrong.

DEMETRIUS

Stay, madam, here is more belongs to her:
First thrash the corn, then after burn the straw.

This minion stood upon her chastity,
Upon her nuptial vow, her loyalty,
And with that quaint hope braves your mightiness.
And shall she carry this unto her grave?

CHIRON

And if she do, I would I were an eunuch.
Drag hence her husband to some secret hole,
130 And make his dead trunk pillow to our lust.

TAMORA

But when ye have the honey ye desire,
Let not this wasp outlive, us both to sting.

CHIRON

I warrant you, madam, we will make that sure.
Come, mistress, now perforce we will enjoy
That nice-preservèd honesty of yours.

LAVINIA

O Tamora, thou bearest a woman's face –

TAMORA

I will not hear her speak. Away with her!

LAVINIA

Sweet lords, entreat her hear me but a word.

DEMETRIUS (*to Tamora*)

Listen, fair madam, let it be your glory
140 To see her tears, but be your heart to them
As unrelenting flint to drops of rain.

LAVINIA (*to Demetrius*)

When did the tiger's young ones teach the dam?
O, do not learn her wrath. She taught it thee:
The milk thou sucked'st from her did turn to marble,
Even at thy teat thou hadst thy tyranny.
(*To Chiron*) Yet every mother breeds not sons alike:
Do thou entreat her show a woman's pity.

CHIRON

What, wouldst thou have me prove myself a bastard?

LAVINIA

'Tis true, the raven doth not hatch a lark.
Yet have I heard – O, could I find it now! –   150
The lion, moved with pity, did endure
To have his princely paws pared all away.
Some say that ravens foster forlorn children
The whilst their own birds famish in their nests.
O be to me, though thy hard heart say no,
Nothing so kind, but something pitiful.

TAMORA

I know not what it means; away with her!

LAVINIA

O, let me teach thee for my father's sake,
That gave thee life when well he might have slain
      thee.
Be not obdurate, open thy deaf ears.   160

TAMORA

Hadst thou in person ne'er offended me,
Even for his sake am I pitiless.
Remember, boys, I poured forth tears in vain
To save your brother from the sacrifice,
But fierce Andronicus would not relent.
Therefore away with her, and use her as you will:
The worse to her, the better loved of me.

LAVINIA (clasping Tamora)

O Tamora, be called a gentle queen,
And with thine own hands kill me in this place,
For 'tis not life that I have begged so long.   170
Poor I was slain when Bassianus died.

TAMORA

What begg'st thou then, fond woman? Let me go!

LAVINIA

'Tis present death I beg, and one thing more
That womanhood denies my tongue to tell.

37

O, keep me from their worse-than-killing lust,
And tumble me into some loathsome pit
Where never man's eye may behold my body.
Do this, and be a charitable murderer.

TAMORA
So should I rob my sweet sons of their fee.
180 No, let them satisfy their lust on thee.

DEMETRIUS (*to Lavinia*)
Away, for thou hast stayed us here too long.

LAVINIA
No grace? No womanhood? Ah, beastly creature,
The blot and enemy to our general name,
Confusion fall –

CHIRON   Nay then, I'll stop your mouth.
        He seizes Lavinia
(*To Demetrius*) Bring thou her husband.
This is the hole where Aaron bid us hide him.
        Demetrius drags the body of Bassianus into the pit and
        covers the opening

TAMORA
Farewell, my sons. See that you make her sure.
                Exeunt Chiron and Demetrius with Lavinia
Ne'er let my heart know merry cheer indeed
Till all the Andronici be made away.
190 Now will I hence to seek my lovely Moor,
And let my spleenful sons this trull deflower.   *Exit*
        Enter Aaron with two of Titus's sons, Quintus and
        Martius

AARON
Come on, my lords, the better foot before.
Straight will I bring you to the loathsome pit
Where I espied the panther fast asleep.

QUINTUS
My sight is very dull, whate'er it bodes.

MARTIUS

    And mine, I promise you. Were it not for shame,
    Well could I leave our sport to sleep a while.
       He falls into the pit

QUINTUS

    What, art thou fallen? What subtle hole is this,
    Whose mouth is covered with rude-growing briers,
    Upon whose leaves are drops of new-shed blood   200
    As fresh as morning dew distilled on flowers?
    A very fatal place it seems to me.
    Speak, brother, hast thou hurt thee with the fall?

MARTIUS

    O brother, with the dismall'st object hurt
    That ever eye with sight made heart lament.

AARON (*aside*)

    Now will I fetch the King to find them here,
    That he thereby may have a likely guess
    How these were they that made away his brother. *Exit*

MARTIUS

    Why dost not comfort me and help me out
    From this unhallowed and blood-stainèd hole?   210

QUINTUS

    I am surprisèd with an uncouth fear:
    A chilling sweat o'erruns my trembling joints;
    My heart suspects more than mine eye can see.

MARTIUS

    To prove thou hast a true-divining heart,
    Aaron and thou look down into this den
    And see a fearful sight of blood and death.

QUINTUS

    Aaron is gone, and my compassionate heart
    Will not permit mine eyes once to behold
    The thing whereat it trembles by surmise.
    O tell me who it is, for ne'er till now   220

Was I a child to fear I know not what.
MARTIUS

Lord Bassianus lies berayed in blood
All on a heap, like to a slaughtered lamb,
In this detested, dark, blood-drinking pit.
QUINTUS

If it be dark, how dost thou know 'tis he?
MARTIUS

Upon his bloody finger he doth wear
A precious ring that lightens all this hole,
Which like a taper in some monument
Doth shine upon the dead man's earthy cheeks,
230 And shows the ragged entrails of this pit.
So pale did shine the moon on Pyramus
When he by night lay bathed in maiden blood.
O brother, help me with thy fainting hand –
If fear hath made thee faint, as me it hath –
Out of this fell devouring receptacle,
As hateful as Cocytus' misty mouth.
QUINTUS

Reach me thy hand, that I may help thee out,
Or, wanting strength to do thee so much good,
I may be plucked into the swallowing womb
240 Of this deep pit, poor Bassianus' grave.
I have no strength to pluck thee to the brink –
MARTIUS

Nor I no strength to climb without thy help.
QUINTUS

Thy hand once more; I will not loose again
Till thou art here aloft or I below.
Thou canst not come to me – I come to thee.
        He falls in.
        Enter the Emperor with attendants and Aaron, the
        Moor

SATURNINUS

    Along with me. I'll see what hole is here,
    And what he is that now is leapt into it.
    Say, who art thou that lately didst descend
    Into this gaping hollow of the earth?

MARTIUS

    The unhappy sons of old Andronicus,   250
    Brought hither in a most unlucky hour
    To find thy brother Bassianus dead.

SATURNINUS

    My brother dead? I know thou dost but jest.
    He and his lady both are at the lodge
    Upon the north side of this pleasant chase.
    'Tis not an hour since I left them there.

MARTIUS

    We know not where you left them all alive,
    But, out alas, here have we found him dead.
       Enter Tamora, Titus Andronicus, and Lucius

TAMORA

    Where is my lord the King?

SATURNINUS

    Here, Tamora, though grieved with killing grief.   260

TAMORA

    Where is thy brother Bassianus?

SATURNINUS

    Now to the bottom dost thou search my wound:
    Poor Bassianus here lies murderèd.

TAMORA

    Then all too late I bring this fatal writ,
    The complot of this timeless tragedy,
    And wonder greatly that man's face can fold
    In pleasing smiles such murderous tyranny.
       She gives Saturninus a letter

SATURNINUS (*reads*)
> *And if we miss to meet him handsomely,*
> *Sweet huntsman – Bassianus 'tis we mean –*
270   *Do thou so much as dig the grave for him.*
> *Thou know'st our meaning. Look for thy reward*
> *Among the nettles at the elder tree*
> *Which overshades the mouth of that same pit*
> *Where we decreed to bury Bassianus.*
> *Do this and purchase us thy lasting friends.*
> O Tamora, was ever heard the like?
> This is the pit, and this the elder tree.
> Look, sirs, if you can find the huntsman out
> That should have murdered Bassianus here.

AARON
280   My gracious lord, here is the bag of gold.

SATURNINUS (*to Titus*)
> Two of thy whelps, fell curs of bloody kind,
> Have here bereft my brother of his life.
> Sirs, drag them from the pit unto the prison.
> There let them bide until we have devised
> Some never-heard-of torturing pain for them.

> *Attendants pull Quintus, Martius, and Bassianus's*
> *body from the pit*

TAMORA
> What are they in this pit? O wondrous thing!
> How easily murder is discoverèd.

TITUS (*kneeling*)
> High Emperor, upon my feeble knee
> I beg this boon, with tears not lightly shed,
290   That this fell fault of my accursèd sons –
> Accursèd if the faults be proved in them –

SATURNINUS
> If it be proved? You see it is apparent.
> Who found this letter? Tamora, was it you?

TAMORA

Andronicus himself did take it up.

TITUS

I did, my lord; yet let me be their bail,
For by my fathers' reverend tomb I vow
They shall be ready at your highness' will
To answer their suspicion with their lives.

SATURNINUS

Thou shalt not bail them. See thou follow me.
    Titus rises
Some bring the murdered body, some the murderers.   300
Let them not speak a word, the guilt is plain;
For, by my soul, were there worse end than death,
That end upon them should be executed.   *Exit*

TAMORA

Andronicus, I will entreat the King;
Fear not thy sons, they shall do well enough.

TITUS

Come, Lucius, come; stay not to talk with them.
            Exeunt with Martius and Quintus under guard,
            and attendants with the body of Bassianus

            Enter the Empress' sons, Chiron and Demetrius, with II.4
            Lavinia, her hands cut off, and her tongue cut out,
            and ravished

DEMETRIUS

So now go tell, and if thy tongue can speak,
Who 'twas that cut thy tongue and ravished thee.

CHIRON

Write down thy mind, bewray thy meaning so,
And if thy stumps will let thee play the scribe.

DEMETRIUS

See how with signs and tokens she can scrawl.

II.4

CHIRON (*to Lavinia*)
Go home, call for sweet water, wash thy hands.
DEMETRIUS
She hath no tongue to call, nor hands to wash,
And so let's leave her to her silent walks.
CHIRON
An 'twere my cause, I should go hang myself.
DEMETRIUS
If thou hadst hands to help thee knit the cord.

Exeunt Chiron and Demetrius
Wind horns. Enter Marcus from hunting to Lavinia

MARCUS
Who is this? My niece, that flies away so fast?
Cousin, a word. Where is your husband?
If I do dream, would all my wealth would wake me;
If I do wake, some planet strike me down
That I may slumber an eternal sleep.
Speak, gentle niece, what stern ungentle hands
Hath lopped and hewed and made thy body bare
Of her two branches, those sweet ornaments,
Whose circling shadows kings have sought to sleep
       in,
And might not gain so great a happiness
As half thy love? Why dost not speak to me?
Alas, a crimson river of warm blood,
Like to a babbling fountain stirred with wind,
Doth rise and fall between thy rosèd lips,
Coming and going with thy honey breath.
But sure some Tereus hath deflowered thee,
And, lest thou shouldst detect him, cut thy tongue.
Ah, now thou turn'st away thy face for shame,
And notwithstanding all this loss of blood,
As from a conduit with three issuing spouts,
Yet do thy cheeks look red as Titan's face

Blushing to be encountered with a cloud.
Shall I speak for thee? Shall I say 'tis so?
O that I knew thy heart, and knew the beast,
That I might rail at him to ease my mind!
Sorrow concealèd, like an oven stopped,
Doth burn the heart to cinders where it is.
Fair Philomela, why she but lost her tongue
And in a tedious sampler sewed her mind;
But, lovely niece, that mean is cut from thee.   40
A craftier Tereus, cousin, hast thou met,
And he hath cut those pretty fingers off
That could have better sewed than Philomel.
O, had the monster seen those lily hands
Tremble like aspen leaves upon a lute
And make the silken strings delight to kiss them,
He would not then have touched them for his life.
Or had he heard the heavenly harmony
Which that sweet tongue hath made,
He would have dropped his knife and fell asleep,   50
As Cerberus at the Thracian poet's feet.
Come, let us go and make thy father blind,
For such a sight will blind a father's eye.
One hour's storm will drown the fragrant meads;
What will whole months of tears thy father's eyes?
Do not draw back, for we will mourn with thee.
O, could our mourning ease thy misery.   *Exeunt*

Enter the tribunes as judges and senators with Titus's   III.1
*two sons, Martius and Quintus, bound, passing over
the stage to the place of execution, and Titus going
before, pleading*

III.1

TITUS

Hear me, grave fathers; noble tribunes, stay!
For pity of mine age, whose youth was spent
In dangerous wars whilst you securely slept,
For all my blood in Rome's great quarrel shed,
For all the frosty nights that I have watched,
And for these bitter tears which now you see
Filling the agèd wrinkles in my cheeks,
Be pitiful to my condemnèd sons,
Whose souls are not corrupted as 'tis thought.
For two-and-twenty sons I never wept
Because they died in honour's lofty bed;

> *Andronicus lieth down, and the judges and others pass*
> *by him*

For these two, tribunes, in the dust I write
My heart's deep languor and my soul's sad tears.
Let my tears stanch the earth's dry appetite;
My sons' sweet blood will make it shame and blush.
O earth, I will befriend thee more with rain

> *Exeunt the judges and others with the prisoners*

That shall distil from these two ancient ruins
Than youthful April shall with all his showers.
In summer's drought I'll drop upon thee still,
In winter with warm tears I'll melt the snow
And keep eternal springtime on thy face,
So thou refuse to drink my dear sons' blood.

> *Enter Lucius with his weapon drawn*

O reverend tribunes, O gentle agèd men,
Unbind my sons, reverse the doom of death,
And let me say, that never wept before,
My tears are now prevailing orators.

LUCIUS

O noble father, you lament in vain:
The tribunes hear you not, no man is by,

46

And you recount your sorrows to a stone.

TITUS

Ah Lucius, for thy brothers let me plead.   30

Grave tribunes, once more I entreat of you –

LUCIUS

My gracious lord, no tribune hears you speak.

TITUS

Why, 'tis no matter, man. If they did hear,
They would not mark me; if they did mark,
They would not pity me; yet plead I must,
And bootless unto them.
Therefore I tell my sorrows to the stones,
Who, though they cannot answer my distress,
Yet in some sort they are better than the tribunes,
For that they will not intercept my tale.   40
When I do weep, they humbly at my feet
Receive my tears and seem to weep with me;
And were they but attirèd in grave weeds,
Rome could afford no tribunes like to these.
A stone is soft as wax, tribunes, more hard than stones.
A stone is silent and offendeth not,
And tribunes with their tongues doom men to death.
But wherefore stand'st thou with thy weapon drawn?

LUCIUS

To rescue my two brothers from their death,
For which attempt the judges have pronounced   50
My everlasting doom of banishment.

TITUS (rising)

O happy man, they have befriended thee!
Why, foolish Lucius, dost thou not perceive
That Rome is but a wilderness of tigers?
Tigers must prey, and Rome affords no prey
But me and mine; how happy art thou then
From these devourers to be banishèd.

But who comes with our brother Marcus here?
Enter Marcus with Lavinia

MARCUS
Titus, prepare thy agèd eyes to weep,
60   Or if not so, thy noble heart to break:
I bring consuming sorrow to thine age.

TITUS
Will it consume me? Let me see it then.

MARCUS
This was thy daughter.

TITUS   Why, Marcus, so she is.

LUCIUS (*falling to his knees*) Ay me, this object kills me.

TITUS
Faint-hearted boy, arise and look upon her.
        Lucius arises
Speak, Lavinia, what accursèd hand
Hath made thee handless in thy father's sight?
What fool hath added water to the sea,
Or brought a faggot to bright-burning Troy?
70   My grief was at the height before thou cam'st,
And now like Nilus it disdaineth bounds.
Give me a sword, I'll chop off my hands too:
For they have fought for Rome, and all in vain,
And they have nursed this woe in feeding life;
In bootless prayer have they been held up,
And they have served me to effectless use.
Now all the service I require of them
Is that the one will help to cut the other.
'Tis well, Lavinia, that thou hast no hands,
80   For hands to do Rome service is but vain.

LUCIUS
Speak, gentle sister: who hath martyred thee?

MARCUS
O, that delightful engine of her thoughts,

48

That blabbed them with such pleasing eloquence,
Is torn from forth that pretty hollow cage,
Where, like a sweet melodious bird, it sung
Sweet varied notes, enchanting every ear.

LUCIUS

O, say thou for her: who hath done this deed?

MARCUS

O, thus I found her, straying in the park,
Seeking to hide herself, as doth the deer
That hath received some unrecuring wound.   90

TITUS

It was my dear, and he that wounded her
Hath hurt me more than had he killed me dead.
For now I stand as one upon a rock
Environed with a wilderness of sea,
Who marks the waxing tide grow wave by wave,
Expecting ever when some envious surge
Will in his brinish bowels swallow him.
This way to death my wretched sons are gone,
Here stands my other son, a banished man,
And here my brother, weeping at my woes;   100
But that which gives my soul the greatest spurn
Is dear Lavinia, dearer than my soul.
Had I but seen thy picture in this plight
It would have madded me: what shall I do,
Now I behold thy lively body so?
Thou hast no hands to wipe away thy tears,
Nor tongue to tell me who hath martyred thee.
Thy husband he is dead, and for his death
Thy brothers are condemned, and dead by this.
Look, Marcus! Ah, son Lucius, look on her!   110
When I did name her brothers, then fresh tears
Stood on her cheeks, as doth the honey-dew
Upon a gathered lily almost witherèd.

III.1

MARCUS

    Perchance she weeps because they killed her husband,
    Perchance because she knows them innocent.

TITUS (*to Lavinia*)

    If they did kill thy husband, then be joyful,
    Because the law hath ta'en revenge on them.
    No, no, they would not do so foul a deed:
    Witness the sorrow that their sister makes.

120   Gentle Lavinia, let me kiss thy lips,
    Or make some sign how I may do thee ease.
    Shall thy good uncle and thy brother Lucius
    And thou and I sit round about some fountain,
    Looking all downwards to behold our cheeks,
    How they are stained like meadows yet not dry
    With miry slime left on them by a flood?
    And in the fountain shall we gaze so long
    Till the fresh taste be taken from that clearness
    And made a brine pit with our bitter tears?

130   Or shall we cut away our hands like thine?
    Or shall we bite our tongues, and in dumb shows
    Pass the remainder of our hateful days?
    What shall we do? Let us that have our tongues
    Plot some device of further misery
    To make us wondered at in time to come.

LUCIUS

    Sweet father, cease your tears, for at your grief
    See how my wretched sister sobs and weeps.

MARCUS

    Patience, dear niece;
    (*handing Titus his handkerchief*)
                       good Titus, dry thine eyes.

TITUS

    Ah Marcus, Marcus, brother, well I wot
140   Thy napkin cannot drink a tear of mine,

For thou, poor man, hast drowned it with thine own.

LUCIUS

Ah, my Lavinia, I will wipe thy cheeks.

TITUS

Mark, Marcus, mark! I understand her signs:
Had she a tongue to speak, now would she say
That to her brother which I said to thee.
His napkin with his true tears all bewet
Can do no service on her sorrowful cheeks.
O, what a sympathy of woe is this,
As far from help as limbo is from bliss.

Enter Aaron the Moor alone

AARON

Titus Andronicus, my lord the Emperor   150
Sends thee this word: that if thou love thy sons,
Let Marcus, Lucius, or thyself, old Titus,
Or any one of you, chop off your hand
And send it to the King. He for the same
Will send thee hither both thy sons alive,
And that shall be the ransom for their fault.

TITUS

O gracious Emperor, O gentle Aaron!
Did ever raven sing so like a lark
That gives sweet tidings of the sun's uprise?
With all my heart I'll send the Emperor my hand.   160
Good Aaron, wilt thou help to chop it off?

LUCIUS

Stay, father, for that noble hand of thine,
That hath thrown down so many enemies,
Shall not be sent. My hand will serve the turn:
My youth can better spare my blood than you
And therefore mine shall save my brothers' lives.

MARCUS

Which of your hands hath not defended Rome

And reared aloft the bloody battle-axe,
Writing destruction on the enemy's castle?
170 O, none of both but are of high desert.
My hand hath been but idle; let it serve
To ransom my two nephews from their death,
Then have I kept it to a worthy end.

AARON
Nay, come, agree whose hand shall go along,
For fear they die before their pardon come.

MARCUS
My hand shall go.

LUCIUS   By heaven, it shall not go.

TITUS
Sirs, strive no more. Such withered herbs as these
Are meet for plucking up, and therefore mine.

LUCIUS
Sweet father, if I shall be thought thy son,
180 Let me redeem my brothers both from death.

MARCUS
And for our father's sake and mother's care,
Now let me show a brother's love to thee.

TITUS
Agree between you: I will spare my hand.

LUCIUS
Then I'll go fetch an axe.

MARCUS   But I will use the axe.
                              Exeunt Lucius and Marcus

TITUS
Come hither, Aaron, I'll deceive them both:
Lend me thy hand, and I will give thee mine.

AARON (*aside*)
If that be called deceit, I will be honest,
And never whilst I live deceive men so;
But I'll deceive you in another sort,

52

And that you'll say ere half an hour pass.   190
    He cuts off Titus's left hand.
    Enter Lucius and Marcus again

TITUS

Now stay your strife; what shall be is dispatched.
Good Aaron, give his majesty my hand.
Tell him it was a hand that warded him
From thousand dangers. Bid him bury it;
More hath it merited, that let it have.
As for my sons, say I account of them
As jewels purchased at an easy price,
And yet dear too, because I bought mine own.

AARON

I go, Andronicus, and for thy hand
Look by and by to have thy sons with thee.   200
(*Aside*) Their heads, I mean. O, how this villainy
Doth fat me with the very thoughts of it.
Let fools do good, and fair men call for grace;
Aaron will have his soul black like his face.   *Exit*

TITUS (*kneeling*)

O, here I lift this one hand up to heaven,
And bow this feeble ruin to the earth.
If any power pities wretched tears,
To that I call. (*Lavinia kneels*)
             What, wouldst thou kneel with me?
Do then, dear heart, for heaven shall hear our prayers,
Or with our sighs we'll breathe the welkin dim   210
And stain the sun with fog, as sometime clouds
When they do hug him in their melting bosoms.

MARCUS

O brother, speak with possibility,
And do not break into these deep extremes.

TITUS

Is not my sorrows deep, having no bottom?

53

Then be my passions bottomless with them.

MARCUS

But yet let reason govern thy lament.

TITUS

If there were reason for these miseries,
Then into limits could I bind my woes.
220 When heaven doth weep, doth not the earth o'erflow?
If the winds rage, doth not the sea wax mad,
Threat'ning the welkin with his big-swoll'n face?
And wilt thou have a reason for this coil?
I am the sea. Hark how her sighs doth blow.
She is the weeping welkin, I the earth;
Then must my sea be movèd with her sighs,
Then must my earth with her continual tears
Become a deluge, overflowed and drowned.
For why my bowels cannot hide her woes,
230 But like a drunkard must I vomit them.
Then give me leave, for losers will have leave
To ease their stomachs with their bitter tongues.

Enter a messenger with two heads and a hand.
Titus and Lavinia rise

MESSENGER

Worthy Andronicus, ill art thou repaid
For that good hand thou sent'st the Emperor.
Here are the heads of thy two noble sons,
And here's thy hand in scorn to thee sent back.
Thy grief their sports, thy resolution mocked,
That woe is me to think upon thy woes
More than remembrance of my father's death.

Exit, after setting down the heads and hand

MARCUS

240 Now let hot Etna cool in Sicily,
And be my heart an ever-burning hell!
These miseries are more than may be borne.

To weep with them that weep doth ease some deal,
But sorrow flouted at is double death.

LUCIUS

Ah, that this sight should make so deep a wound
And yet detested life not shrink thereat!
That ever death should let life bear his name,
Where life hath no more interest but to breathe.

Lavinia kisses Titus

MARCUS

Alas, poor heart, that kiss is comfortless
As frozen water to a starvèd snake.   250

TITUS

When will this fearful slumber have an end?

MARCUS

Now farewell flatt'ry; die Andronicus.
Thou dost not slumber. See thy two sons' heads,
Thy warlike hand, thy mangled daughter here,
Thy other banished son with this dear sight
Struck pale and bloodless, and thy brother, I,
Even like a stony image, cold and numb.
Ah, now no more will I control thy griefs:
Rend off thy silver hair, thy other hand
Gnawing with thy teeth, and be this dismal sight   260
The closing up of our most wretched eyes.
Now is a time to storm. Why art thou still?

TITUS

Ha, ha, ha!

MARCUS

Why dost thou laugh? It fits not with this hour.

TITUS

Why? I have not another tear to shed.
Besides, this sorrow is an enemy
And would usurp upon my wat'ry eyes
And make them blind with tributary tears.

55

Then which way shall I find Revenge's cave?
For these two heads do seem to speak to me,
And threat me I shall never come to bliss
Till all these mischiefs be returned again
Even in their throats that hath committed them.
Come, let me see what task I have to do.
You, heavy people, circle me about,
That I may turn me to each one of you
And swear unto my soul to right your wrongs.

Marcus, Lucius, and Lavinia surround Titus.
He pledges them

The vow is made. Come, brother, take a head,
And in this hand the other will I bear;
And, Lavinia, thou shalt be employèd:
Bear thou my hand, sweet wench, between thy teeth.
(*To Lucius*) As for thee, boy, go get thee from my
     sight:
Thou art an exile, and thou must not stay.
Hie to the Goths and raise an army there,
And if ye love me, as I think you do,
Let's kiss and part, for we have much to do.

    They kiss.   *Exeunt all but Lucius*

LUCIUS

Farewell, Andronicus, my noble father,
The woefull'st man that ever lived in Rome.
Farewell, proud Rome, till Lucius come again:
He loves his pledges dearer than his life.
Farewell, Lavinia, my noble sister:
O, would thou wert as thou tofore hast been!
But now nor Lucius nor Lavinia lives
But in oblivion and hateful griefs.
If Lucius live, he will requite your wrongs,
And make proud Saturnine and his empress
Beg at the gates like Tarquin and his queen.

Now will I to the Goths and raise a power
To be revenged on Rome and Saturnine.   *Exit Lucius*

A banquet. Enter Titus Andronicus, Marcus, Lavinia, III.2
and the boy, Young Lucius

TITUS

So, so, now sit, and look you eat no more
Than will preserve just so much strength in us
As will revenge these bitter woes of ours.
     They sit
Marcus, unknit that sorrow-wreathen knot.
Thy niece and I, poor creatures, want our hands
And cannot passionate our tenfold grief
With folded arms. This poor right hand of mine
Is left to tyrannize upon my breast,
Who, when my heart, all mad with misery,
Beats in this hollow prison of my flesh,   10
Then thus (*striking his breast*) I thump it down.
(*To Lavinia*) Thou map of woe, that thus dost talk in
     signs,
When thy poor heart beats with outrageous beating,
Thou canst not strike it thus to make it still.
Wound it with sighing, girl, kill it with groans,
Or get some little knife between thy teeth
And just against thy heart make thou a hole,
That all the tears that thy poor eyes let fall
May run into that sink, and soaking in,
Drown the lamenting fool in sea-salt tears.   20

MARCUS

Fie, brother, fie! Teach her not thus to lay
Such violent hands upon her tender life.

TITUS

How now! Has sorrow made thee dote already?

57

Why, Marcus, no man should be mad but I.
What violent hands can she lay on her life?
Ah, wherefore dost thou urge the name of hands,
To bid Aeneas tell the tale twice o'er
How Troy was burnt and he made miserable?
O, handle not the theme, to talk of hands,
30 Lest we remember still that we have none.
Fie, fie, how franticly I square my talk,
As if we should forget we had no hands
If Marcus did not name the word of hands.
Come, let's fall to, and, gentle girl, eat this.
Here is no drink? Hark, Marcus, what she says;
I can interpret all her martyred signs:
She says she drinks no other drink but tears,
Brewed with her sorrow, mashed upon her cheeks.
Speechless complainer, I will learn thy thought.
40 In thy dumb action will I be as perfect
As begging hermits in their holy prayers.
Thou shalt not sigh, nor hold thy stumps to
	heaven,
Nor wink, nor nod, nor kneel, nor make a sign,
But I of these will wrest an alphabet,
And by still practice learn to know thy meaning.

YOUNG LUCIUS

Good grandsire, leave these bitter deep laments;
Make my aunt merry with some pleasing tale.

MARCUS

Alas, the tender boy in passion moved
Doth weep to see his grandsire's heaviness.

TITUS

50 Peace, tender sapling, thou art made of tears,
And tears will quickly melt thy life away.

Marcus strikes the dish with a knife

What dost thou strike at, Marcus, with thy knife?

MARCUS
    At that that I have killed, my lord – a fly.
TITUS
    Out on thee, murderer! Thou kill'st my heart.
    Mine eyes are cloyed with view of tyranny.
    A deed of death done on the innocent
    Becomes not Titus' brother. Get thee gone,
    I see thou art not for my company.
MARCUS
    Alas, my lord, I have but killed a fly.
TITUS
    'But'? How if that fly had a father and mother?   60
    How would he hang his slender gilded wings
    And buzz lamenting doings in the air.
    Poor harmless fly,
    That with his pretty buzzing melody
    Came here to make us merry, and thou hast killed him.
MARCUS
    Pardon me, sir, it was a black ill-favoured fly,
    Like to the Empress' Moor. Therefore I killed him.
TITUS
    O, O, O!
    Then pardon me for reprehending thee,
    For thou hast done a charitable deed.   70
    Give me thy knife. I will insult on him,
    Flattering myself, as if it were the Moor
    Come hither purposely to poison me.
    There's for thyself, and that's for Tamora.
    (Striking the fly) Ah, sirrah!
    Yet I think we are not brought so low
    But that between us we can kill a fly
    That comes in likeness of a coal-black Moor.
MARCUS
    Alas, poor man, grief has so wrought on him

59

80   He takes false shadows for true substances.

TITUS

    Come, take away. Lavinia, go with me;
    I'll to thy closet, and go read with thee
    Sad stories chancèd in the times of old.
    Come, boy, and go with me; thy sight is young
    And thou shalt read when mine begin to dazzle. *Exeunt*

IV.1   *Enter Young Lucius and Lavinia running after him,*
    and the boy flies from her with his books under his
    arm.
    Enter Titus and Marcus

YOUNG LUCIUS

    Help, grandsire, help! My aunt Lavinia
    Follows me everywhere, I know not why.
    Good uncle Marcus, see how swift she comes.
    Alas, sweet aunt, I know not what you mean.
    He drops his books

MARCUS

    Stand by me, Lucius; do not fear thine aunt.

TITUS

    She loves thee, boy, too well to do thee harm.

YOUNG LUCIUS

    Ay, when my father was in Rome she did.

MARCUS

    What means my niece Lavinia by these signs?

TITUS

    Fear her not, Lucius; somewhat doth she mean.

MARCUS

10   See, Lucius, see how much she makes of thee:
    Somewhither would she have thee go with her.

Ah, boy, Cornelia never with more care
Read to her sons than she hath read to thee
Sweet poetry and Tully's *Orator*.
Canst thou not guess wherefore she plies thee thus?

YOUNG LUCIUS

My lord, I know not, I, nor can I guess,
Unless some fit or frenzy do possess her;
For I have heard my grandsire say full oft
Extremity of griefs would make men mad,
And I have read that Hecuba of Troy   20
Ran mad for sorrow. That made me to fear,
Although, my lord, I know my noble aunt
Loves me as dear as e'er my mother did,
And would not but in fury fright my youth,
Which made me down to throw my books and fly,
Causeless perhaps. But pardon me, sweet aunt,
And, madam, if my uncle Marcus go,
I will most willingly attend your ladyship.

MARCUS

Lucius, I will.

Lavinia turns over the books dropped by Lucius

TITUS

How now, Lavinia? Marcus, what means this?   30
Some book there is that she desires to see.
Which is it, girl, of these? Open them, boy.
(*To Lavinia*) But thou art deeper read and better
    skilled.
Come and take choice of all my library,
And so beguile thy sorrow, till the heavens
Reveal the damned contriver of this deed.
Why lifts she up her arms in sequence thus?

MARCUS

I think she means that there were more than one
Confederate in the fact. Ay, more there was,

61

40 Or else to heaven she heaves them for revenge.

TITUS

    Lucius, what book is that she tosseth so?

YOUNG LUCIUS

    Grandsire, 'tis Ovid's *Metamorphoses*;
    My mother gave it me.

MARCUS   For love of her that's gone,
    Perhaps she culled it from among the rest.

TITUS

    Soft, so busily she turns the leaves.
    Help her! What would she find? Lavinia, shall I read?
    This is the tragic tale of Philomel,
    And treats of Tereus' treason and his rape;
    And rape, I fear, was root of thy annoy.

MARCUS

50 See, brother, see: note how she quotes the leaves.

TITUS

    Lavinia, wert thou thus surprised, sweet girl?
    Ravished and wronged, as Philomela was,
    Forced in the ruthless, vast, and gloomy woods?
    See, see. Ay, such a place there is where we did hunt –
    O, had we never, never hunted there –
    Patterned by that the poet here describes,
    By nature made for murders and for rapes.

MARCUS

    O, why should nature build so foul a den,
    Unless the gods delight in tragedies?

TITUS

60 Give signs, sweet girl, for here are none but friends,
    What Roman lord it was durst do the deed?
    Or slunk not Saturnine, as Tarquin erst,
    That left the camp to sin in Lucrece' bed?

MARCUS

    Sit down, sweet niece. Brother, sit down by me.

They sit
Apollo, Pallas, Jove or Mercury
Inspire me, that I may this treason find.
My lord, look here; look here, Lavinia.
This sandy plot is plain; guide, if thou canst,
This after me.
> *He writes his name with his staff, and guides it with*
> *feet and mouth*
                 I have writ my name
Without the help of any hand at all.   70
Cursed be that heart that forced us to this shift!
Write thou, good niece, and here display at last
What God will have discovered for revenge.
Heaven guide thy pen to print thy sorrows plain,
That we may know the traitors and the truth.
> *She takes the staff in her mouth, and guides it with*
> *her stumps, and writes*
O, do ye read, my lord, what she hath writ?
TITUS
'*Stuprum* – Chiron – Demetrius.'
MARCUS
What, what? The lustful sons of Tamora
Performers of this heinous, bloody deed?
TITUS
Magni dominator poli,   80
Tam lentus audis scelera, tam lentus vides?
MARCUS
O, calm thee, gentle lord, although I know
There is enough written upon this earth
To stir a mutiny in the mildest thoughts,
And arm the minds of infants to exclaims.
My lord, kneel down with me; Lavinia, kneel;
And kneel, sweet boy, the Roman Hector's hope;
> *They kneel*

63

And swear with me – as, with the woeful fere
And father of that chaste dishonoured dame,
90   Lord Junius Brutus swore for Lucrece' rape –
That we will prosecute by good advice
Mortal revenge upon these traitorous Goths,
And see their blood, or die with this reproach.
    They rise

TITUS

'Tis sure enough, and you knew how.
But if you hunt these bear-whelps, then beware:
The dam will wake, and if she wind ye once.
She's with the lion deeply still in league,
And lulls him whilst she playeth on her back,
And, when he sleeps, will she do what she list.
100   You are a young huntsman, Marcus. Let alone,
And come, I will go get a leaf of brass,
And with a gad of steel will write these words,
And lay it by. The angry northern wind
Will blow these sands like Sibyl's leaves abroad,
And where's our lesson then? Boy, what say you?

YOUNG LUCIUS

I say, my lord, that if I were a man
Their mother's bedchamber should not be safe
For these base bondmen to the yoke of Rome.

MARCUS

Ay, that's my boy! Thy father hath full oft
110   For his ungrateful country done the like.

YOUNG LUCIUS

And, uncle, so will I, and if I live.

TITUS

Come, go with me into mine armoury.
Lucius, I'll fit thee, and withal my boy
Shall carry from me to the Empress' sons
Presents that I intend to send them both.

Come, come, thou'lt do my message, wilt thou
    not?
YOUNG LUCIUS
  Ay, with my dagger in their bosoms, grandsire.
TITUS
  No, boy, not so. I'll teach thee another course.
  Lavinia, come. Marcus, look to my house;
  Lucius and I'll go brave it at the court.   120
  Ay, marry, will we, sir, and we'll be waited on.
                  Exeunt Titus, Lavinia, and boy
MARCUS
  O heavens, can you hear a good man groan
  And not relent, or not compassion him?
  Marcus, attend him in his ecstasy,
  That hath more scars of sorrow in his heart
  Than foemen's marks upon his battered shield,
  But yet so just that he will not revenge.
  Revenge the heavens for old Andronicus!   *Exit*

Enter Aaron, Chiron, and Demetrius at one door; and IV.2
at the other door young Lucius and another with a
bundle of weapons and verses writ upon them
CHIRON
  Demetrius, here's the son of Lucius;
  He hath some message to deliver us.
AARON
  Ay, some mad message from his mad grandfather.
YOUNG LUCIUS
  My lords, with all the humbleness I may,
  I greet your honours from Andronicus –
  (*Aside*) And pray the Roman gods confound you both.
DEMETRIUS
  Gramercy, lovely Lucius, what's the news?

IV.2

YOUNG LUCIUS (*aside*)

That you are both deciphered, that's the news,
For villains marked with rape. (*To all*) May it please
you,

10   My grandsire, well advised, hath sent by me
The goodliest weapons of his armoury
To gratify your honourable youth,
The hope of Rome, for so he bid me say.

Attendants give weapons

And so I do, and with his gifts present
Your lordships, that, whenever you have need,
You may be armèd and appointed well.
And so I leave you both – (*aside*) like bloody villains.

Exit with attendant

DEMETRIUS

What's here? A scroll, and written round about?
Let's see:

20   '*Integer vitae scelerisque purus,*
Non eget Mauri iaculis, nec arcu.'

CHIRON

O, 'tis a verse in Horace, I know it well;
I read it in the grammar long ago.

AARON

Ay, just – a verse in Horace, right you have it.
(*Aside*) Now what a thing it is to be an ass!
Here's no sound jest. The old man hath found their
guilt,
And sends them weapons wrapped about with lines
That wound beyond their feeling to the quick.
But were our witty Empress well afoot,

30   She would applaud Andronicus' conceit.
But let her rest in her unrest awhile.
(*To Chiron and Demetrius*)
And now, young lords, was't not a happy star

66

Led us to Rome, strangers, and more than so,
Captives, to be advancèd to this height?
It did me good before the palace gate
To brave the tribune in his brother's hearing.

DEMETRIUS

But me more good to see so great a lord
Basely insinuate and send us gifts.

AARON

Had he not reason, Lord Demetrius?
Did you not use his daughter very friendly?   40

DEMETRIUS

I would we had a thousand Roman dames
At such a bay, by turn to serve our lust.

CHIRON

A charitable wish, and full of love.

AARON

Here lacks but your mother for to say amen.

CHIRON

And that would she, for twenty thousand more.

DEMETRIUS

Come, let us go and pray to all the gods
For our belovèd mother in her pains.

AARON (*aside*)

Pray to the devils; the gods have given us over.
                    Trumpets sound

DEMETRIUS

Why do the Emperor's trumpets flourish thus?

CHIRON

Belike for joy the Emperor hath a son.   50

DEMETRIUS

Soft, who comes here?
                    Enter Nurse with a blackamoor child

NURSE   Good morrow, lords.
O, tell me, did you see Aaron the Moor?

67

AARON

Well, more or less, or ne'er a whit at all.

Here Aaron is, and what with Aaron now?

NURSE

O, gentle Aaron, we are all undone.

Now help, or woe betide thee evermore!

AARON

Why, what a caterwauling dost thou keep.

What dost thou wrap and fumble in thy arms?

NURSE

O, that which I would hide from heaven's eye,

60 Our Empress' shame and stately Rome's disgrace:

She is delivered, lords, she is delivered.

AARON

To whom?

NURSE   I mean she is brought abed.

AARON

Well, God give her good rest. What hath he sent her?

NURSE

A devil.

AARON   Why then, she is the devil's dam:

A joyful issue.

NURSE

A joyless, dismal, black, and sorrowful issue.

Here is the babe, as loathsome as a toad

Amongst the fair-faced breeders of our clime.

The Empress sends it thee, thy stamp, thy seal,

70 And bids thee christen it with thy dagger's point.

AARON

Zounds, ye whore, is black so base a hue?

(*To the baby*)

Sweete blowze, you are a beauteous blossom, sure.

DEMETRIUS

Villain, what hast thou done?

68

AARON

That which thou canst not undo.

CHIRON

Thou hast undone our mother.

AARON

Villain, I have done thy mother.

DEMETRIUS

And therein, hellish dog, thou hast undone her.
Woe to her chance, and damned her loathèd choice!
Accursed the offspring of so foul a fiend!

CHIRON

It shall not live.

AARON   It shall not die.   80

NURSE

Aaron, it must, the mother wills it so.

AARON

What, must it, nurse? Then let no man but I
Do execution on my flesh and blood.

DEMETRIUS

I'll broach the tadpole on my rapier's point.
Nurse, give it me; my sword shall soon dispatch it.

AARON (*taking the child and drawing his sword*)

Sooner this sword shall plough thy bowels up!
Stay, murderous villains, will you kill your brother?
Now, by the burning tapers of the sky
That shone so brightly when this boy was got,
He dies upon my scimitar's sharp point   90
That touches this, my first-born son and heir.
I tell you, younglings, not Enceladus
With all his threat'ning band of Typhon's brood,
Nor great Alcides, nor the god of war,
Shall seize this prey out of his father's hands.
What, what, ye sanguine shallow-hearted boys,
Ye white-limed walls, ye alehouse painted signs!

Coal-black is better than another hue,
In that it scorns to bear another hue:
100   For all the water in the ocean
Can never turn the swan's black legs to white,
Although she lave them hourly in the flood.
(*To Nurse*) Tell the Empress from me I am of age
To keep mine own, excuse it how she can.

DEMETRIUS

Wilt thou betray thy noble mistress thus?

AARON

My mistress is my mistress, this myself,
The vigour and the picture of my youth.
This before all the world do I prefer;
This maugre all the world will I keep safe,
110   Or some of you shall smoke for it in Rome.

DEMETRIUS

By this our mother is for ever shamed.

CHIRON

Rome will despise her for this foul escape.

NURSE

The Emperor in his rage will doom her death.

CHIRON

I blush to think upon this ignomy.

AARON

Why, there's the privilege your beauty bears.
Fie, treacherous hue, that will betray with
    blushing
The close enacts and counsels of thy heart.
Here's a young lad framed of another leer.
Look how the black slave smiles upon the father,
120   As who should say, 'Old lad, I am thine own.'
He is your brother, lords, sensibly fed
Of that self blood that first gave life to you,
And from that womb where you imprisoned were

70

He is enfranchisèd and come to light.
Nay, he is your brother by the surer side,
Although my seal be stampèd in his face.
NURSE
Aaron, what shall I say unto the Empress?
DEMETRIUS
Advise thee, Aaron, what is to be done,
And we will all subscribe to thy advice.
Save thou the child, so we may all be safe.   130
AARON
Then sit we down and let us all consult.
My son and I will have the wind of you.
Keep there. (*They sit*)
                    Now talk at pleasure of your safety.
DEMETRIUS (*to Nurse*)
How many women saw this child of his?
AARON
Why, so, brave lords, when we join in league
I am a lamb, but if you brave the Moor,
The chafèd boar, the mountain lioness,
The ocean, swells not so as Aaron storms.
(*To Nurse*) But say again, how many saw the child?
NURSE
Cornelia the midwife, and myself,   140
And no one else but the delivered Empress.
AARON
The Empress, the midwife, and yourself.
Two may keep counsel when the third's away.
Go to the Empress, tell her this I said:
        He kills her
'Wheak, wheak!' – so cries a pig prepared to the spit.
        All stand up
DEMETRIUS
What mean'st thou, Aaron? Wherefore didst thou this?

AARON

 O Lord, sir, 'tis a deed of policy.
 Shall she live to betray this guilt of ours?
 A long-tongued, babbling gossip? No, lords, no.
150 And now be it known to you my full intent.
 Not far, one Muly lives, my countryman:
 His wife but yesternight was brought to bed;
 His child is like to her, fair as you are.
 Go pack with him and give the mother gold,
 And tell them both the circumstance of all,
 And how by this their child shall be advanced,
 And be receivèd for the Emperor's heir,
 And substituted in the place of mine
 To calm this tempest whirling in the court,
160 And let the Emperor dandle him for his own.
 Hark ye, lords, (*pointing to the Nurse*)
      you see I have given her physic,
 And you must needs bestow her funeral.
 The fields are near, and you are gallant grooms.
 This done, see that you take no longer days,
 But send the midwife presently to me.
 The midwife and the Nurse well made away,
 Then let the ladies tattle what they please.

CHIRON

 Aaron, I see thou wilt not trust the air
 With secrets.

DEMETRIUS For this care of Tamora,
170 Herself and hers are highly bound to thee.
    Exeunt Chiron and Demetrius with the Nurse's body

AARON

 Now to the Goths, as swift as swallow flies,
 There to dispose this treasure in mine arms,
 And secretly to greet the Empress' friends.
 Come on, you thick-lipped slave, I'll bear you hence,

For it is you that puts us to our shifts.
I'll make you feed on berries and on roots,
And feed on curds and whey, and suck the goat,
And cabin in a cave, and bring you up
To be a warrior and command a camp.   *Exit*

Enter Titus, old Marcus, his son Publius, young IV.3
Lucius, and other gentlemen (Caius, Sempronius)
with bows, and Titus bears the arrows with letters on
the ends of them

TITUS

Come, Marcus, come; kinsmen, this is the way.
Sir boy, let me see your archery.
Look ye draw home enough, and 'tis there straight.
Terras Astraea reliquit: be you remembered, Marcus,
She's gone, she's fled. Sirs, take you to your tools.
You, cousins, shall go sound the ocean,
And cast your nets:
Happily you may catch her in the sea,
Yet there's as little justice as at land.
No, Publius and Sempronius, you must do it.   10
'Tis you must dig with mattock and with spade,
And pierce the inmost centre of the earth.
Then, when you come to Pluto's region,
I pray you deliver him this petition.
Tell him it is for justice and for aid,
And that it comes from old Andronicus,
Shaken with sorrows in ungrateful Rome.
Ah, Rome! Well, well, I made thee miserable
What time I threw the people's suffrages
On him that thus doth tyrannize o'er me.   20
Go, get you gone, and pray be careful all,
And leave you not a man-of-war unsearched.

73

This wicked Emperor may have shipped her hence,
And, kinsmen, then we may go pipe for justice.

MARCUS

O Publius, is not this a heavy case,
To see thy noble uncle thus distract?

PUBLIUS

Therefore, my lords, it highly us concerns
By day and night t'attend him carefully
And feed his humour kindly as we may,
30   Till time beget some careful remedy.

MARCUS

Kinsmen, his sorrows are past remedy.
But [   ]
Join with the Goths, and with revengeful war
Take wreak on Rome for this ingratitude,
And vengeance on the traitor Saturnine.

TITUS

Publius, how now? How now, my masters?
What, have you met with her?

PUBLIUS

No, my good lord, but Pluto sends you word
If you will have Revenge from hell, you shall.
40   Marry, for Justice, she is so employed,
He thinks with Jove in heaven, or somewhere else,
So that perforce you must needs stay a time.

TITUS

He doth me wrong to feed me with delays.
I'll dive into the burning lake below
And pull her out of Acheron by the heels.
Marcus, we are but shrubs, no cedars we,
No big-boned men framed of the Cyclops' size,
But metal, Marcus, steel to the very back,
Yet wrung with wrongs more than our backs can bear.
50   And sith there's no justice in earth nor hell,

We will solicit heaven and move the gods
To send down Justice for to wreak our wrongs.
Come, to this gear. You are a good archer, Marcus.
    He gives them the arrows
'*Ad Jovem*', that's for you. Here, '*Ad Apollinem*';
'*Ad Martem*', that's for myself.
Here, boy, 'To Pallas'. Here, 'To Mercury'.
'To Saturn', Caius, not to Saturnine!
You were as good to shoot against the wind.
To it, boy! Marcus, loose when I bid.
Of my word, I have written to effect: 60
There's not a god left unsolicited.

MARCUS (*aside*)
Kinsmen, shoot all your shafts into the court;
We will afflict the Emperor in his pride.

TITUS
Now, masters, draw. (*They shoot*)
                O, well said, Lucius!
Good boy, in Virgo's lap! Give it Pallas!

MARCUS
My lord, I aimed a mile beyond the moon:
Your letter is with Jupiter by this.

TITUS
Ha, ha! Publius, Publius, what hast thou done?
See, see, thou hast shot off one of Taurus' horns.

MARCUS
This was the sport, my lord! When Publius shot,   70
The Bull, being galled, gave Aries such a knock
That down fell both the Ram's horns in the court,
And who should find them but the Empress' villain!
She laughed, and told the Moor he should not choose
But give them to his master for a present.

TITUS
Why, there it goes. God give his lordship joy.

Enter the Clown with a basket and two pigeons in it
News, news from heaven! Marcus, the post is come.
Sirrah, what tidings? Have you any letters?
Shall I have justice? What says Jupiter?

80 CLOWN Ho, the gibbet-maker? He says that he hath taken
them down again, for the man must not be hanged till
the next week.

TITUS

But what says Jupiter, I ask thee?

CLOWN Alas sir, I know not Jubiter. I never drank with
him in all my life.

TITUS

Why, villain, art not thou the carrier?

CLOWN Ay, of my pigeons, sir, nothing else.

TITUS

Why, didst thou not come from heaven?

CLOWN From heaven? Alas, sir, I never came there. God
90 forbid I should be so bold to press to heaven in my
young days. Why, I am going with my pigeons to the
tribunal plebs to take up a matter of brawl betwixt my
uncle and one of the Emperal's men.

MARCUS (*to Titus*) Why, sir, that is as fit as can be to serve
for your oration, and let him deliver the pigeons to the
Emperor from you.

TITUS Tell me, can you deliver an oration to the Emperor
with a grace?

CLOWN Nay, truly sir, I could never say grace in all my
100 life.

TITUS

Sirrah, come hither; make no more ado,
But give your pigeons to the Emperor.
By me thou shalt have justice at his hands.
Hold, hold. (*Gives him money*)
　　　　　Meanwhile, here's money for thy charges.

76

Give me pen and ink. (*Writes*)

Sirrah, can you with a grace deliver up a supplication?

CLOWN Ay, sir.

TITUS (*gives letter*) Then here is a supplication for you,
and when you come to him, at the first approach you
must kneel, then kiss his foot, then deliver up your 110
pigeons, and then look for your reward. I'll be at hand,
sir; see you do it bravely.

CLOWN I warrant you, sir. Let me alone.

TITUS

Sirrah, hast thou a knife? Come, let me see it.
    Takes a knife and gives it to Marcus
Here, Marcus, fold it in the oration;
(*To the Clown*)
For thou must hold it like an humble suppliant,
And when thou hast given it to the Emperor,
Knock at my door, and tell me what he says.

CLOWN

God be with you sir. I will.   *Exit*

TITUS

Come, Marcus, let us go. Publius, follow me.   *Exeunt* 120

Enter Emperor and Empress and her two sons, Chiron IV.4
and Demetrius, and attendants. The Emperor brings
the arrows in his hand that Titus shot at him

SATURNINUS

Why, lords, what wrongs are these! Was ever seen
An emperor in Rome thus overborne,
Troubled, confronted thus, and for the extent
Of egall justice, used in such contempt?
My lords, you know, as know the mightful gods,
However these disturbers of our peace
Buzz in the people's ears, there naught hath past

77

But even with law against the wilful sons
Of old Andronicus. And what and if
His sorrows have so overwhelmed his wits?
Shall we be thus afflicted in his wreaks,
His fits, his frenzy, and his bitterness?
And now he writes to heaven for his redress.
See here's 'To Jove', and this 'To Mercury',
This 'To Apollo', this 'To the god of war' –
Sweet scrolls to fly about the streets of Rome!
What's this but libelling against the Senate,
And blazoning our unjustice everywhere?
A goodly humour, is it not, my lords? –
As who would say, in Rome no justice were.
But if I live, his feignèd ecstasies
Shall be no shelter to these outrages,
But he and his shall know that justice lives
In Saturninus' health, whom, if he sleep,
He'll so awake as he in fury shall
Cut off the proud'st conspirator that lives.

TAMORA

My gracious lord, my lovely Saturnine,
Lord of my life, commander of my thoughts,
Calm thee and bear the faults of Titus' age,
Th'effects of sorrow for his valiant sons,
Whose loss hath pierced him deep and scarred his
        heart;
And rather comfort his distressèd plight
Than prosecute the meanest or the best
For these contempts. (*Aside*) Why, thus it shall
        become
High-witted Tamora to gloze with all.
But, Titus, I have touched thee to the quick:
Thy life-blood out, if Aaron now be wise,
Then is all safe, the anchor in the port.

Enter Clown

How now, good fellow, wouldst thou speak with us?
CLOWN Yea, forsooth, an your mistress-ship be Emperial. 40
TAMORA Empress I am, but yonder sits the Emperor.
CLOWN 'Tis he. God and Saint Stephen give you good
e'en. I have brought you a letter and a couple of pigeons
here.

Saturninus reads the letter

SATURNINUS (*to attendants*)
Go, take him away and hang him presently.
CLOWN How much money must I have?
TAMORA Come, sirrah, you must be hanged.
CLOWN Hanged, by'Lady? Then I have brought up a neck
to a fair end. *Exit guarded*
SATURNINUS
Despiteful and intolerable wrongs! 50
Shall I endure this monstrous villainy?
I know from whence this same device proceeds.
May this be borne? As if his traitorous sons,
That died by law for murder of our brother,
Have by my means been butchered wrongfully.
Go, drag the villain hither by the hair.
Nor age nor honour shall shape privilege.
For this proud mock I'll be thy slaughterman,
Sly, frantic wretch, that holp'st to make me great,
In hope thyself should govern Rome and me. 60

Enter Aemilius, a messenger

What news with thee, Aemilius?
AEMILIUS
Arm, my lords! Rome never had more cause:
The Goths have gathered head, and with a power
Of high-resolvèd men, bent to the spoil,
They hither march amain, under conduct
Of Lucius, son to old Andronicus,

Who threats in course of this revenge to do
As much as ever Coriolanus did.

SATURNINUS

Is warlike Lucius general of the Goths?

70 These tidings nip me, and I hang the head
As flowers with frost, or grass beat down with storms.
Ay, now begins our sorrows to approach.
'Tis he the common people love so much;
Myself hath often heard them say,
When I have walkèd like a private man,
That Lucius' banishment was wrongfully,
And they have wished that Lucius were their emperor.

TAMORA

Why should you fear? Is not your city strong?

SATURNINUS

Ay, but the citizens favour Lucius,

80 And will revolt from me to succour him.

TAMORA

King, be thy thoughts imperious like thy name.
Is the sun dimmed, that gnats do fly in it?
The eagle suffers little birds to sing,
And is not careful what they mean thereby,
Knowing that with the shadow of his wings
He can at pleasure stint their melody:
Even so mayst thou the giddy men of Rome.
Then cheer thy spirit; for know thou, Emperor,
I will enchant the old Andronicus

90 With words more sweet and yet more dangerous
Than baits to fish, or honey-stalks to sheep,
When as the one is wounded with the bait,
The other rotted with delicious feed.

SATURNINUS

But he will not entreat his son for us.

TAMORA

    If Tamora entreat him, then he will,
    For I can smooth and fill his agèd ears
    With golden promises, that were his heart
    Almost impregnable, his old ears deaf,
    Yet should both ear and heart obey my tongue.
    (*To Aemilius*)
    Go thou before to be our ambassador: 100
    Say that the Emperor requests a parley
    Of warlike Lucius, and appoint the meeting
    Even at his father's house, the old Andronicus.

SATURNINUS

    Aemilius, do this message honourably,
    And if he stand in hostage for his safety,
    Bid him demand what pledge will please him best.

AEMILIUS

    Your bidding shall I do effectually.   *Exit*

TAMORA

    Now will I to that old Andronicus,
    And temper him with all the art I have
    To pluck proud Lucius from the warlike Goths.   110
    And now, sweet Emperor, be blithe again,
    And bury all thy fear in my devices.

SATURNINUS

    Then go incessantly, and plead to him.   *Exeunt*

    Flourish. Enter Lucius with an army of Goths with V.1
    drums and soldiers

LUCIUS

    Approvèd warriors and my faithful friends,
    I have receivèd letters from great Rome,

Which signifies what hate they bear their emperor,
And how desirous of our sight they are.
Therefore, great lords, be as your titles witness:
Imperious, and impatient of your wrongs,
And wherein Rome hath done you any scath
Let him make treble satisfaction.

FIRST GOTH

Brave slip, sprung from the great Andronicus,
Whose name was once our terror, now our comfort,
Whose high exploits and honourable deeds
Ingrateful Rome requites with foul contempt,
Be bold in us. We'll follow where thou lead'st,
Like stinging bees in hottest summer's day
Led by their master to the flowered fields,
And be avenged on cursèd Tamora.

ALL THE GOTHS

And as he saith, so say we all with him.

LUCIUS

I humbly thank him, and I thank you all.
But who comes here, led by a lusty Goth?

Enter a Goth leading Aaron with his child in his arms

SECOND GOTH

Renownèd Lucius, from our troops I strayed
To gaze upon a ruinous monastery,
And as I earnestly did fix mine eye
Upon the wasted building, suddenly
I heard a child cry underneath a wall.
I made unto the noise, when soon I heard
The crying babe controlled with this discourse:
'Peace, tawny slave, half me and half thy dam!
Did not thy hue bewray whose brat thou art,
Had nature lent thee but thy mother's look,
Villain, thou mightst have been an emperor.
But where the bull and cow are both milk-white,

82

They never do beget a coal-black calf.
Peace, villain, peace!' – even thus he rates the
    babe –
'For I must bear thee to a trusty Goth,
Who, when he knows thou art the Empress' babe,
Will hold thee dearly for thy mother's sake.'
With this my weapon drawn, I rushed upon him,
Surprised him suddenly, and brought him hither
To use as you think needful of the man.

LUCIUS

O worthy Goth! This is the incarnate devil   40
That robbed Andronicus of his good hand;
This is the pearl that pleased your Empress' eye,
And here's the base fruit of her burning lust.
(*To Aaron*)
Say, wall-eyed slave, whither wouldst thou convey
This growing image of thy fiend-like face?
Why dost not speak? What, deaf? Not a word?
A halter, soldiers. Hang him on this tree,
And by his side his fruit of bastardy.

AARON

Touch not the boy, he is of royal blood.

LUCIUS

Too like the sire for ever being good.   50
First hang the child, that he may see it sprawl:
A sight to vex the father's soul withal.
Get me a ladder.

    A ladder is brought, which Aaron is made to climb

AARON   Lucius, save the child,
And bear it from me to the Empress.
If thou do this, I'll show thee wondrous things,
That highly may advantage thee to hear.
If thou wilt not, befall what may befall,
I'll speak no more but 'Vengeance rot you all!'

LUCIUS

Say on, and if it please me which thou speak'st,
60   Thy child shall live, and I will see it nourished.

AARON

And if it please thee? Why, assure thee, Lucius,
'Twill vex thy soul to hear what I shall speak:
For I must talk of murders, rapes, and
    massacres,
Acts of black night, abominable deeds,
Complots of mischief, treason, villainies,
Ruthful to hear, yet piteously performed;
And this shall all be buried in my death,
Unless thou swear to me my child shall live.

LUCIUS

Tell on thy mind; I say thy child shall live.

AARON

70   Swear that he shall, and then I will begin.

LUCIUS

Who should I swear by? Thou believest no god.
That granted, how canst thou believe an oath?

AARON

What if I do not? As indeed I do not.
Yet for I know thou art religious
And hast a thing within thee callèd conscience,
With twenty popish tricks and ceremonies
Which I have seen thee careful to observe,
Therefore I urge thy oath. For that I know
An idiot holds his bauble for a god,
80   And keeps the oath which by that god he swears,
To that I'll urge him: therefore thou shalt vow,
By that same god, what god soe'er it be
That thou adorest and hast in reverence,
To save my boy, to nurse and bring him up,
Or else I will discover naught to thee.

LUCIUS

Even by my god I swear to thee I will.

AARON

First know thou, I begot him on the Empress.

LUCIUS

O most insatiate and luxurious woman!

AARON

Tut, Lucius, this was but a deed of charity
To that which thou shalt hear of me anon.   90
'Twas her two sons that murdered Bassianus;
They cut thy sister's tongue and ravished her,
And cut her hands and trimmed her as thou sawest.

LUCIUS

O detestable villain, call'st thou that trimming?

AARON

Why, she was washed and cut and trimmed, and
        'twas
Trim sport for them which had the doing of it.

LUCIUS

O barbarous, beastly villains, like thyself!

AARON

Indeed, I was their tutor to instruct them.
That codding spirit had they from their mother,
As sure a card as ever won the set.   100
That bloody mind I think they learned of me,
As true a dog as ever fought at head.
Well, let my deeds be witness of my worth:
I trained thy brethren to that guileful hole,
Where the dead corpse of Bassianus lay;
I wrote the letter that thy father found,
And hid the gold within that letter mentioned,
Confederate with the Queen and her two sons;
And what not done that thou hast cause to rue
Wherein I had no stroke of mischief in it?   110

V.1

I played the cheater for thy father's hand,
And when I had it drew myself apart,
And almost broke my heart with extreme laughter.
I pried me through the crevice of a wall
When for his hand he had his two sons' heads,
Beheld his tears and laughed so heartily
That both mine eyes were rainy like to his;
And when I told the Empress of this sport,
She sounded almost at my pleasing tale,
120 And for my tidings gave me twenty kisses.

A GOTH

What, canst thou say all this and never blush?

AARON

Ay, like a black dog, as the saying is.

LUCIUS

Art thou not sorry for these heinous deeds?

AARON

Ay, that I had not done a thousand more.
Even now I curse the day – and yet I think
Few come within the compass of my curse –
Wherein I did not some notorious ill,
As kill a man or else devise his death,
Ravish a maid or plot the way to do it,
130 Accuse some innocent and forswear myself,
Set deadly enmity between two friends,
Make poor men's cattle break their necks,
Set fire on barns and haystacks in the night,
And bid the owners quench them with their tears.
Oft have I digged up dead men from their graves
And set them upright at their dear friends' door,
Even when their sorrows almost was forgot,
And on their skins, as on the bark of trees,
Have with my knife carvèd in Roman letters,
140 'Let not your sorrow die though I am dead'.

86

But I have done a thousand dreadful things
As willingly as one would kill a fly,
And nothing grieves me heartily indeed
But that I cannot do ten thousand more.

LUCIUS

Bring down the devil, for he must not die
So sweet a death as hanging presently.

Aaron is brought down

AARON

If there be devils, would I were a devil
To live and burn in everlasting fire,
So I might have your company in hell
But to torment you with my bitter tongue.   150

LUCIUS

Sirs, stop his mouth and let him speak no more.

Aaron is gagged.
Enter Aemilius

A GOTH

My lord, there is a messenger from Rome
Desires to be admitted to your presence.

LUCIUS

Let him come near.
Welcome Aemilius. What's the news from Rome?

AEMILIUS

Lord Lucius, and you princes of the Goths,
The Roman Emperor greets you all by me,
And, for he understands you are in arms,
He craves a parley at your father's house,
Willing you to demand your hostages   160
And they shall be immediately delivered.

A GOTH

What says our general?

LUCIUS

Aemilius, let the Emperor give his pledges

Unto my father and my uncle Marcus,
And we will come. March away!   *Flourish. Exeunt*

V.2   *Enter Tamora disguised as Revenge, and her two sons,*
             Chiron as Rape and Demetrius as Murder

TAMORA

Thus, in this strange and sad habiliment,
I will encounter with Andronicus,
And say I am Revenge, sent from below
To join with him and right his heinous wrongs.
Knock at his study, where they say he keeps
To ruminate strange plots of dire revenge;
Tell him Revenge is come to join with him
And work confusion on his enemies.
             They knock and Titus opens his study door above

TITUS

Who doth molest my contemplation?
10 Is it your trick to make me ope the door,
That so my sad decrees may fly away,
And all my study be to no effect?
You are deceived, for what I mean to do
See here in bloody lines I have set down,
And what is written shall be executed.

TAMORA

Titus, I am come to talk with thee.

TITUS

No, not a word. How can I grace my talk,
Wanting a hand to give it action?
Thou hast the odds of me, therefore no more.

TAMORA

20 If thou didst know me, thou wouldst talk with me.

TITUS

I am not mad, I know thee well enough:

88

Witness this wretched stump, witness these crimson
    lines,
Witness these trenches made by grief and care,
Witness the tiring day and heavy night,
Witness all sorrow, that I know thee well
For our proud Empress, mighty Tamora.
Is not thy coming for my other hand?

TAMORA

Know, thou sad man, I am not Tamora.
She is thy enemy, and I thy friend.
I am Revenge, sent from th'infernal kingdom   30
To ease the gnawing vulture of thy mind
By working wreakful vengeance on thy foes.
Come down and welcome me to this world's light,
Confer with me of murder and of death.
There's not a hollow cave or lurking place,
No vast obscurity or misty vale
Where bloody murder or detested rape
Can couch for fear, but I will find them out,
And in their ears tell them my dreadful name,
Revenge, which makes the foul offender quake.   40

TITUS

Art thou Revenge? And art thou sent to me
To be a torment to mine enemies?

TAMORA

I am, therefore come down and welcome me.

TITUS

Do me some service ere I come to thee.
Lo by thy side where Rape and Murder stands.
Now give some surance that thou art Revenge:
Stab them, or tear them on thy chariot wheels,
And then I'll come and be thy waggoner,
And whirl along with thee about the globe,
Provide thee two proper palfreys, black as jet,   50

To hale thy vengeful waggon swift away,
And find out murderers in their guilty caves;
And when thy car is loaden with their heads,
I will dismount, and by thy waggon wheel
Trot like a servile footman all day long,
Even from Hyperion's rising in the east
Until his very downfall in the sea;
And day by day I'll do this heavy task,
So thou destroy Rapine and Murder there.

TAMORA

60   These are my ministers, and come with me.

TITUS

Are they thy ministers? What are they called?

TAMORA

Rape and Murder, therefore callèd so
'Cause they take vengeance of such kind of men.

TITUS

Good Lord, how like the Empress' sons they are,
And you the Empress. But we worldly men
Have miserable, mad, mistaking eyes.
O sweet Revenge, now do I come to thee,
And if one arm's embracement will content thee,
I will embrace thee in it by and by.   *Exit above*

TAMORA

70   This closing with him fits his lunacy.
Whate'er I forge to feed his brain-sick humours
Do you uphold and maintain in your speeches,
For now he firmly takes me for Revenge,
And being credulous in this mad thought,
I'll make him send for Lucius his son;
And whilst I at a banquet hold him sure,
I'll find some cunning practice out of hand
To scatter and disperse the giddy Goths,
Or at the least make them his enemies.

See, here he comes, and I must ply my theme.   80
    Enter Titus below

TITUS

Long have I been forlorn, and all for thee.
Welcome, dread Fury, to my woeful house;
Rapine and Murder, you are welcome too.
How like the Empress and her sons you are!
Well are you fitted, had you but a Moor.
Could not all hell afford you such a devil?
For well I wot the Empress never wags
But in her company there is a Moor,
And would you represent our Queen aright,
It were convenient you had such a devil.   90
But welcome as you are. What shall we do?

TAMORA

What wouldst thou have us do, Andronicus?

DEMETRIUS

Show me a murderer, I'll deal with him.

CHIRON

Show me a villain that hath done a rape,
And I am sent to be revenged on him.

TAMORA

Show me a thousand that hath done thee wrong,
And I will be revengèd on them all.

TITUS (*to Demetrius*)

Look round about the wicked streets of Rome,
And when thou find'st a man that's like thyself,
Good Murder, stab him: he's a murderer.   100
(*To Chiron*)
Go thou with him, and when it is thy hap
To find another that is like to thee,
Good Rapine, stab him: he is a ravisher.
(*To Tamora*)
Go thou with them, and in the Emperor's court

There is a queen attended by a Moor –
Well shalt thou know her by thine own proportion,
For up and down she doth resemble thee –
I pray thee, do on them some violent death:
They have been violent to me and mine.

TAMORA

110 Well hast thou lessoned us; this shall we do.
But would it please thee, good Andronicus,
To send for Lucius, thy thrice-valiant son,
Who leads towards Rome a band of warlike
    Goths,
And bid him come and banquet at thy house?
When he is here, even at thy solemn feast,
I will bring in the Empress and her sons,
The Emperor himself and all thy foes,
And at thy mercy shall they stoop and kneel,
And on them shalt thou ease thy angry heart.
120 What says Andronicus to this device?

TITUS

Marcus, my brother! 'Tis sad Titus calls.

    Enter Marcus

Go, gentle Marcus, to thy nephew Lucius.
Thou shalt enquire him out among the Goths.
Bid him repair to me and bring with him
Some of the chiefest princes of the Goths;
Bid him encamp his soldiers where they are.
Tell him the Emperor and the Empress too
Feast at my house, and he shall feast with them.
This do thou for my love, and so let him,
130 As he regards his agèd father's life.

MARCUS

This will I do, and soon return again.   *Exit*

TAMORA

Now will I hence about thy business,

And take my ministers along with me.

TITUS

Nay, nay, let Rape and Murder stay with me,
Or else I'll call my brother back again
And cleave to no revenge but Lucius.

TAMORA (*aside to her sons*)

What say you, boys? Will you abide with him
Whiles I go tell my lord the Emperor
How I have governed our determined jest?
Yield to his humour, smooth and speak him fair,   140
And tarry with him till I turn again.

TITUS (*aside*)

I knew them all, though they supposed me mad,
And will o'erreach them in their own devices,
A pair of cursèd hell-hounds and their dam.

DEMETRIUS

Madam, depart at pleasure, leave us here.

TAMORA

Farewell, Andronicus: Revenge now goes
To lay a complot to betray thy foes.

TITUS

I know thou dost, and sweet Revenge, farewell.

Exit Tamora

CHIRON

Tell us, old man, how shall we be employed?

TITUS

Tut, I have work enough for you to do.   150
Publius, come hither; Caius and Valentine.

Enter Publius, Caius and Valentine

PUBLIUS

What is your will?

TITUS   Know you these two?

PUBLIUS

The Empress' sons, I take them: Chiron, Demetrius.

V.2

TITUS

Fie, Publius, fie, thou art too much deceived:
The one is Murder and Rape is the other's name.
And therefore bind them, gentle Publius;
Caius and Valentine, lay hands on them.
Oft have you heard me wish for such an hour,
And now I find it; therefore bind them sure,
And stop their mouths, if they begin to cry.   *Exit*

160

CHIRON

Villains, forbear! We are the Empress' sons.

PUBLIUS

And therefore do we what we are commanded.
                *Publius, Caius and Valentine bind and gag Chiron
                and Demetrius*
Stop close their mouths, let them not speak a word.
Is he sure bound? Look that you bind them fast.
                *Enter Titus Andronicus with a knife, and Lavinia
                with a basin*

TITUS

Come, come, Lavinia; look, thy foes are bound.
Sirs, stop their mouths. Let them not speak to me,
But let them hear what fearful words I utter.
O villains, Chiron and Demetrius,
Here stands the spring whom you have stained with
          mud,
This goodly summer with your winter mixed.
You killed her husband, and for that vile fault
Two of her brothers were condemned to death,
My hand cut off and made a merry jest,
Both her sweet hands, her tongue, and that more dear
Than hands or tongue, her spotless chastity,
Inhuman traitors, you constrained and forced.
What would you say if I should let you speak?
Villains, for shame you could not beg for grace.

170

Hark, wretches, how I mean to martyr you:
This one hand yet is left to cut your throats,   180
Whiles that Lavinia 'tween her stumps doth hold
The basin that receives your guilty blood.
You know your mother means to feast with me,
And calls herself Revenge, and thinks me mad.
Hark, villains, I will grind your bones to dust,
And with your blood and it I'll make a paste,
And of the paste a coffin I will rear,
And make two pasties of your shameful heads,
And bid that strumpet, your unhallowed dam,
Like to the earth swallow her own increase.   190
This is the feast that I have bid her to,
And this the banquet she shall surfeit on:
For worse than Philomel you used my daughter,
And worse than Procne I will be revenged.
And now, prepare your throats. Lavinia, come,
Receive the blood, and when that they are dead,
Let me go grind their bones to powder small,
And with this hateful liquor temper it,
And in that paste let their vile heads be baked.
Come, come, be everyone officious   200
To make this banquet, which I wish may prove
More stern and bloody than the Centaurs' feast.
        He cuts their throats
So, now bring them in, for I'll play the cook,
And see them ready against their mother comes.
                                Exeunt with the bodies

Enter Lucius, Marcus, and the Goths with Aaron V.3
prisoner, and his child

LUCIUS
Uncle Marcus, since 'tis my father's mind

V.3

That I repair to Rome, I am content.

A GOTH

And ours with thine, befall what fortune will.

LUCIUS

Good uncle, take you in this barbarous Moor,
This ravenous tiger, this accursèd devil;
Let him receive no sust'nance, fetter him
Till he be brought unto the Empress' face
For testimony of her foul proceedings.
And see the ambush of our friends be strong:

10 I fear the Emperor means no good to us.

AARON

Some devil whisper curses in my ear,
And prompt me that my tongue may utter forth
The venomous malice of my swelling heart.

LUCIUS

Away, inhuman dog, unhallowed slave!
Sirs, help our uncle to convey him in.

Flourish

The trumpets show the Emperor is at hand.

Exeunt Goths with Aaron
Sound trumpets. Enter Emperor and Empress with
Aemilius, tribunes and others

SATURNINUS (*to Lucius*)

What, hath the firmament more suns than one?

LUCIUS

What boots it thee to call thyself a sun?

MARCUS

Rome's emperor and nephew, break the parle;

20 These quarrels must be quietly debated.
The feast is ready which the careful Titus
Hath ordained to an honourable end,
For peace, for love, for league and good to Rome;
Please you, therefore, draw nigh and take your places.

SATURNINUS

Marcus, we will.

Trumpets sounding. A table brought in. They sit. Enter
Titus like a cook, placing the dishes, and Lavinia with
a veil over her face, with young Lucius and others

TITUS

Welcome, my gracious lord; welcome dread Queen;
Welcome, ye warlike Goths; welcome, Lucius;
And welcome, all. Although the cheer be poor,
'Twill fill your stomachs. Please you eat of it.

SATURNINUS

Why art thou thus attired, Andronicus?   30

TITUS

Because I would be sure to have all well
To entertain your highness and your Empress.

TAMORA

We are beholden to you, good Andronicus.

TITUS

And if your highness knew my heart, you were.
My lord the Emperor, resolve me this:
Was it well done of rash Virginius
To slay his daughter with his own right hand
Because she was enforced, stained, and deflowered?

SATURNINUS

It was, Andronicus.

TITUS   Your reason, mighty lord?

SATURNINUS

Because the girl should not survive her shame,   40
And by her presence still renew his sorrows.

TITUS

A reason mighty, strong, and effectual;
A pattern, precedent, and lively warrant
For me, most wretched, to perform the like.
    Unveils Lavinia

Die, die, Lavinia, and thy shame with thee,
And with thy shame thy father's sorrow die.
        He kills her

SATURNINUS

What hast thou done, unnatural and unkind?

TITUS

Killed her for whom my tears have made me blind.
I am as woeful as Virginius was,
50   And have a thousand times more cause than he
To do this outrage, and it now is done.

SATURNINUS

What, was she ravished? Tell who did the deed.

TITUS

Will't please you eat? Will't please your highness
        feed?

TAMORA

Why hast thou slain thine only daughter thus?

TITUS

Not I, 'twas Chiron and Demetrius:
They ravished her and cut away her tongue,
And they, 'twas they, that did her all this wrong.

SATURNINUS

Go, fetch them hither to us presently.

TITUS

Why, there they are, both bakèd in this pie,
60   Whereof their mother daintily hath fed,
Eating the flesh that she herself hath bred.
'Tis true, 'tis true, witness my knife's sharp point.
        He stabs the Empress

SATURNINUS

Die, frantic wretch, for this accursèd deed.
        He kills Titus

LUCIUS

Can the son's eye behold his father bleed?

There's meed for meed, death for a deadly deed.
He kills Saturninus. Uproar on stage. Enter Goths to
protect the Andronici, who exit and go aloft
MARCUS (*aloft*)
You sad-faced men, people and sons of Rome,
By uproars severed, as a flight of fowl
Scattered by winds and high tempestuous gusts,
O, let me teach you how to knit again
This scattered corn into one mutual sheaf,   70
These broken limbs again into one body,
Lest Rome herself be bane unto herself,
And she whom mighty kingdoms curtsy to,
Like a forlorn and desperate castaway,
Do shameful execution on herself.
But if my frosty signs and chaps of age,
Grave witnesses of true experience,
Cannot induce you to attend my words,
(*To Lucius*) Speak, Rome's dear friend, as erst our
        ancestor
When with his solemn tongue he did discourse   80
To lovesick Dido's sad-attending ear
The story of that baleful burning night
When subtle Greeks surprised King Priam's Troy.
Tell us what Sinon hath bewitched our ears,
Or who hath brought the fatal engine in
That gives our Troy, our Rome, the civil wound.
My heart is not compact of flint nor steel,
Nor can I utter all our bitter grief,
But floods of tears will drown my oratory
And break my utt'rance even in the time   90
When it should move ye to attend me most,
And force you to commiseration.
Here's Rome's young captain: let him tell the tale,
While I stand by and weep to hear him speak.

V.3

LUCIUS

Then, gracious auditory, be it known to you
That Chiron and the damned Demetrius
Were they that murderèd our Emperor's brother,
And they it were that ravishèd our sister.
For their fell faults our brothers were beheaded,
Our father's tears despised and basely cozened
Of that true hand that fought Rome's quarrel out,
And sent her enemies unto the grave.
Lastly myself, unkindly banishèd,
The gates shut on me and turned weeping out,
To beg relief among Rome's enemies,
Who drowned their enmity in my true tears
And oped their arms to embrace me as a friend.
I am the turned-forth, be it known to you,
That have preserved her welfare in my blood,
And from her bosom took the enemy's point,
Sheathing the steel in my advent'rous body.
Alas, you know I am no vaunter, I;
My scars can witness, dumb although they are,
That my report is just and full of truth.
But soft, methinks I do digress too much,
Citing my worthless praise. O, pardon me,
For when no friends are by, men praise themselves.

MARCUS

Now is my turn to speak. (*pointing to Aaron's child*)
                                        Behold the child:
Of this was Tamora deliverèd,
The issue of an irreligious Moor,
Chief architect and plotter of these woes.
The villain is alive in Titus' house,
And as he is to witness this is true,
Now judge what cause had Titus to revenge
These wrongs unspeakable, past patience,

100

Or more than any living man could bear.
Now have you heard the truth, what say you, Romans?
Have we done aught amiss, show us wherein,
And from the place where you behold us pleading
The poor remainder of Andronici   130
Will hand in hand all headlong hurl ourselves,
And on the raggèd stones beat forth our souls,
And make a mutual closure of our house.
Speak, Romans, speak, and if you say we shall,
Lo, hand in hand, Lucius and I will fall.

AEMILIUS

Come, come, thou reverend man of Rome,
And bring our emperor gently in thy hand,
Lucius, our emperor – for well I know
The common voice do cry it shall be so.

ROMANS

Lucius, all hail, Rome's royal emperor!   140

MARCUS (*to attendants*)

Go, go into old Titus' sorrowful house,
And hither hale that misbelieving Moor
To be adjudged some direful slaught'ring death
As punishment for his most wicked life.

Exeunt Marcus, Lucius and attendants
A long flourish. Enter Marcus and Lucius below

ROMANS

Lucius, all hail, Rome's gracious governor!

LUCIUS

Thanks, gentle Romans. May I govern so,
To heal Rome's harms, and wipe away her woe.
But, gentle people, give me aim awhile,
For nature puts me to a heavy task.
Stand all aloof, but uncle, draw you near   150
To shed obsequious tears upon this trunk.
Kisses Titus

O, take this warm kiss on thy pale cold lips,
These sorrowful drops upon thy bloodstained face,
The last true duties of thy noble son.

MARCUS (*kissing Titus*)

Tear for tear and loving kiss for kiss,
Thy brother Marcus tenders on thy lips.
O, were the sum of these that I should pay
Countless and infinite, yet would I pay them.

LUCIUS (*to his son*)

Come hither, boy, come, come, and learn of us

160   To melt in showers. Thy grandsire loved thee well:
Many a time he danced thee on his knee,
Sung thee asleep, his loving breast thy pillow;
Many a story hath he told to thee,
And bid thee bear his pretty tales in mind,
And talk of them when he was dead and gone.

MARCUS

How many thousand times hath these poor lips,
When they were living, warmed themselves on thine!
O now, sweet boy, give them their latest kiss,
Bid him farewell, commit him to the grave,

170   Do them that kindness, and take leave of them.

YOUNG LUCIUS

O grandsire, grandsire, ev'n with all my heart
Would I were dead, so you did live again!
O Lord, I cannot speak to him for weeping;
My tears will choke me if I ope my mouth.

    Enter attendants with Aaron

A ROMAN

You sad Andronici, have done with woes.
Give sentence on this execrable wretch
That hath been breeder of these dire events.

LUCIUS

Set him breast-deep in earth and famish him;

There let him stand and rave and cry for food.
If anyone relieves or pities him, 180
For the offence he dies. This is our doom.
Some stay to see him fastened in the earth.

AARON

Ah, why should wrath be mute and fury dumb?
I am no baby, I, that with base prayers
I should repent the evils I have done.
Ten thousand worse than ever yet I did
Would I perform if I might have my will.
If one good deed in all my life I did
I do repent it from my very soul.

LUCIUS

Some loving friends convey the Emperor hence, 190
And give him burial in his father's grave;
My father and Lavinia shall forthwith
Be closèd in our household's monument;
As for that ravenous tiger, Tamora,
No funeral rite, nor man in mourning weed,
No mournful bell shall ring her burial,
But throw her forth to beasts and birds to prey.
Her life was beastly and devoid of pity,
And being dead, let birds on her take pity. *Exeunt*

Finis the Tragedy of Titus Andronicus

COMMENTARY

The abbreviations 'Q' and 'F' refer to readings common to all Quarto and Folio editions, unless otherwise specified. Quotations from other works by Shakespeare are followed by line reference to S. Wells and G. Taylor (eds.), *William Shakespeare: The Complete Works* (Oxford: Clarendon Press, 1986).

All relevant glosses have the support of the *Oxford English Dictionary*, M. P. Tilley's *A Dictionary of Proverbs in England in the Sixteenth and Seventeenth Centuries* (1950) and Gordon Williams's *A Glossary of Shakespeare's Sexual Language* (1997).

Title

The head-title in Q, *The Most Lamentable Romaine Tragedie of Titus Andronicus: As it was Plaide by the Right Honourable the Earle of Darbie, Earle of Pembrooke, and Earle of Sussex their Seruants*, is shortened in F to read, *The Lamentable Tragedy of Titus Andronicus*. There is no general consensus on whether the list of acting companies on the title-page in Q provides a chronological account of the early staging history of the play, or whether it simply implies that Sussex's Men hired actors who had previously worked for Derby (Lord Strange) or Pembroke for the short winter season of 1593–4.

I.1   The scene is located near the Temple of Jupiter or Capitol, which was the chief religious building of Rome. Even here, however, Shakespeare's Rome remains impressionistic, for he envisages the Capitol and the Senate House (or Curia) as adjacent buildings (see stage direction at line 66 below), or perhaps even as the same building. In fact they stood respectively on the Capitoline Hill, and in the Roman Forum below. The action is

divided into six major episodes: the dispute over the
succession (1–66); Titus's entry, the sacrifice of Alarbus
and the burial of his sons (67–159); the appointment of
Saturninus as Emperor with Lavinia as Empress (160–
278); the abduction of Lavinia, the killing of Mutius and
elevation of Tamora (279–340); the burial of Mutius
(341–401); and the formal reconciliation of the
Andronici with Saturninus (402–98).

0   (stage direction) *Flourish* a fanfare of trumpets, which
often marks an important entry or exit in F. The trum-
peters were usually placed in a curtained box called the
'music room' on part of the gallery above the stage.

tribunes constitutional officers elected to represent the ple-
beians in the state. The play, which blurs the distinctions
between Republican and Imperial Rome and has no specific historical location, disregards the fact that under the
emperors the function of the tribunes became nominal.

senators members of the ruling assembly of Rome, mostly
senior patricians, whose function became at best collaborative after the destruction of the Republic

aloft standard term in stage directions for the gallery,
also known as the balcony. The performances of the play
by the Earl of Sussex's Men recorded by Philip Henslowe
for 23 and 28 January and 6 February 1594 almost
certainly took place at the Rose Theatre. The recently
excavated foundations of the Rose show that Henslowe's
playhouse had a platform stage projecting into the auditorium from the wall of the tiring (or 'retiring') house.
The staging of the opening sequence of *Titus Andronicus*
requires two side doors, left and right in the wall, for the
entrance and exit of actors, perhaps a central opening
(see note to stage direction at line 92) and a gallery above
serving as an upper stage.

drums and colours drummers and standard-bearers

1–4   *Noble . . . swords.* Lines 1–2 are addressed to the senators
(patricians) in the gallery, lines 3–4 to those who have
entered with Saturninus below. Saturninus addresses the

senators because, as the representatives of the patricians, they are more likely to support his claim to the succession by right of primogeniture than the tribunes, who, as an elected body, champion the principle of 'pure election' (see note to line 16) and Bassianus's cause. Bassianus invokes their protection at line 66.

1   *patrons* defenders. See also note to line 68.

4   *successive title* title to the succession

5   *his . . . that* of him who

8   *age* seniority

      indignity lack of respect resulting from having his claim overlooked

10   *Caesar* title of Roman emperors

11   *Were gracious* found grace

12   *Keep . . . passage* guard . . . the route

      Capitol See head-note to I.1.

14   *consecrate* consecrated. The original punctuation in Q and F is altered because this participle clearly governs 'virtue' on line 14, as well as the three abstract nouns on line 15.

15   *continence* restraint (here both political and sexual). This implicitly corrects Saturninus's facile use of 'justice' at line 2.

16   *pure election* election only, unmixed with considerations of primogeniture. 'Pure', however, retains its connotations of 'virtue' (line 14). Bassianus implies (a) that his elder brother is given to a variety of vices, and (b) that the principle of free election is at risk (line 17).

17   (stage direction) The Quarto instructs Marcus to enter at the start of the scene with the tribunes and senators. This edition follows the Folio, where Marcus's delayed entrance is visually arresting and permits him to command the fray below.

19   *empery* imperial status

21   *special party* As a tribune of the people, Marcus represents an elective body, which was set by the Roman constitution above the contention of political parties.

22   *In election* as a candidate in the election

23   *Pius* the 'surname', or honorary title given to Aeneas, the legendary founder of Rome

27   *accited* summoned

28   *Goths* a generic name for the allegedly 'barbarian' Germanic tribes existing outside the pale of Roman rule. Shakespeare's depiction of Rome is composite, so that evidence for dating the action of the play remains uncertain. From the perspective of the Gothic wars, however, the action could be located at any time between the end of the second century AD, when the weaknesses of an overextended frontier became apparent, and 410 AD, when the Visigothic king, Alaric, sacked Rome.

30   *yoked* tamed

35–8   *at this day ... Goths.* See An Account of the Text, pp. 166–7.

36   *monument* the tomb. See also lines 353–4 and notes to lines 92 and 95.

41   *flourishing in arms* The two terms of this phrase enrich each other: 'arms' adds to 'flourishing', in its usual sense of 'thriving' and 'prospering', the further sense of 'waving a weapon'; 'flourishing' imparts to 'arms' the double sense of 'weapons' and 'limbs'.

42–3   *by honour ... succeed* out of respect for the reputation of him (the dead emperor) whom you wish to be succeeded decorously and meritoriously. The use of the word 'succeed' compacts two meanings: the princes should wish their father to 'be successful' in the only way a dead emperor can be, that is by being 'succeeded' worthily.

45   *pretend* claim

50   *so I do affy* I have such faith

58   (stage direction) Q and F provide an incomplete stage direction here – 'Exit soldiers' – and none at all at 62. It is, however, clear that whereas both Saturninus and Bassianus's soldiers leave to strengthen the massed entry at line 72, their followers remain on stage to make sense of the Captain's 'Roman, make way' at line 67.

64   *confident and kind* trusting and affectionate towards his kinsfolk

66   *competitor* candidate

68   *Patron* (a) defender; (b) pattern or model. This distinction hardened only in the latter part of the seventeenth century.

71   *circumscribèd* fenced in

72   (stage direction) The omission of Alarbus from the Quarto and Folio stage directions is not enough to establish that the incident of his sacrifice is a later addition. The error is sufficiently explained by the fact that he is a mute character. See An Account of the Text, pp. 166–7.

73   *mourning weeds* black apparel worn by widows

74   *his* its, as 'her' at line 76.

75   *lading* cargo. In Titus's metaphor, the dead sons brought back in exchange for the honour obtained.

77   *laurel* when woven into a crown, the emblem of victory

78   *tears* 'tears of grief', a meaning not obliterated by 'joy' of line 79. See also note to line 162.

80   *defender* Jove, also known as Jupiter Capitolinus. See head-note to I.1.

83   *Priam* The last king of Troy, whom Homer made the father of fifty sons.

86   *latest home* last home, the tomb. Proverbial.

87   The main clause of this line is 'let Rome reward', as suggested by the anaphora at lines 85–6.

89   *unkind* lacking in care and attention towards his kinsfolk. See note to line 64.

90–91   *Why . . . Styx* See Virgil, *Aeneid* VII.325–9: 'All this crowd thou seest is helpless and graveless . . . Nor may he [the grim ferryman, Charon] bear them o'er the dreadful banks and hoarse-voiced waters [of the river Styx] ere their bones have found a resting place. A hundred years they roam and flit about these shores.'

90   *suffer'st thou* do you allow, permit

92   *brethren* three syllables, also at lines 351 and 360
        (stage direction) The tomb of the Andronici is either

a building revealed through a central opening in the tiring-house wall, as indicated by lines 353–4, or a sepulchre suggested by raising the trap-door, as indicated by the phrase 'earthy prison' at line 102, or by the verb 'inter' at lines 149 and 378.

93   *greet* greet one another. The Roman family constituted a community of the living and the dead. See Introduction, p. xliv.

95   *receptacle* This noun combines the ideas of 'place of shelter' (for the bodies of Titus's sons) and of 'receiving vessel' (for Titus's 'joys').

101   *Ad manes fratrum* to the shades of our brothers. This may be an echo from Livy's account of the heroic beginnings of Rome. In the first book of his *History*, he cites Horatius's words as he is about to dispatch the last of the three Curatii: '*duos . . . fratrum manibus dedi*' ('I have given two men to the shades of my brothers').

103   *the shadows* the dead. The 'unappeased' shadows of the dead frequently come back to haunt the living as ghosts in Shakespeare and his contemporaries.

104   *prodigies* ominous portents. The sacrifice of a high-ranking captive to free the souls of the dead from entrapment in the places of their physical existence was not, it seems, current Roman practice. Yet the example of Seneca's *Troades*, in which Pyrrhus sacrifices the captive Trojan princess Polyxena to placate the ghost of his father Achilles, and of the funeral rites of Pallas in Virgil's *Aeneid* IX, where prisoners are sacrificed and their blood sprinkled on the pyre (lines 81–2), persuaded the Renaissance that the custom was a Roman one. Shakespeare, for instance, refers to it in the Roman portion of one of his last plays, *Cymbeline*, at V.5.70–78. See Introduction, pp. xlvi–xlvii.

107   (stage direction) That Tamora kneels is indicated by lines 457–8. That her sons should follow her example, however, is not required, despite the evidence of the Peacham drawing (from *c.* 1595, now in the library at

Longleat), which is generally supposed to depict Tamora
and her sons kneeling to Titus and his sons, with a
defiant Aaron proudly erect.

109 *passion* violent grief

112 *Sufficeth not* is it not enough

113 *triumphs* triumphal processions

115 *in the streets* without ceremony. See also lines 457–8.

120–21 *Wilt thou . . . merciful* proverbial. That the Elizabethan
was meant to be responsive to this plea is shown by its
memorable amplification in Portia's address to Shylock
(*The Merchant of Venice*, IV.1.184–97) and Isabella's
plea to Angelo (*Measure for Measure*, II.2.60–65).

123 *Thrice-noble* 'Thrice' is a standard intensifier in Elizabethan English. See also 'thrice-valiant' at V.2.112.

125 *These . . . whom* these are the brothers of those whom

132 *clean* completely

133 *O cruel . . . piety* Tamora's remark is sharply ironic, as
she spurns both Titus's surname, 'Pius' (line 23), and
his perception of Alarbus's sacrifice as a religious and
pious deed.

134 *Scythia* a region east of the Danube described by the
Greek historian Herodotus as a land of bloodthirsty
tribesmen

135 *Oppose* compare. Demetrius implies that Rome outstrips
Scythia in barbarism.

139–41 *The selfsame gods . . . tent* in Ovid's *Metamorphoses*
XIII.533–75. Hecuba, wife of King Priam, survives the
sack and firing of Troy only to have her last remaining
son, Polydorus, murdered by the self-serving Polymes-
tor, the barbarian chief to whom she had entrusted him.
Failing to obtain justice from the victorious Greek leader,
Agamemnon, she receives the help of the gods in blinding
Polymestor, and in killing his sons with her own hands.
The extremity of her sufferings drives her into a 'mad-
ness' which ends by transforming her into a dog.

141 *Thracian* Thrace was an inland area west and north-west
of the Black Sea, populated with ferocious warlike tribes

regarded by antiquity as specially barbaric. Tereus, rapist of Philomela, was a Thracian. See Introduction, pp. xxvii, xlix.

144   *quit* requite

(stage direction) *with their swords bloody* This addition to the stage direction as it appears in Q and F is required by Lucius's call, 'See . . . how we have performed | Our Roman rites.'

146   *lopped* This participle echoes 'hew' in lines 100 and 132, and prepares a significant parallel with Lavinia's fate at II.4.17–18 ('lopped and hewed'), and subsequently.

148   *Whose smoke . . . sky.* See *Cymbeline*, V.5.476–8: 'Laud we the gods, | And let our crooked smokes climb to their nostrils | From our blest altars.'

150   *'larums* alarums. From the Italian *all' arma*, alarums were usually trumpet calls to arms.

154   *readiest* most eager. The elaborate alliteration, 'Rome's readiest' balanced by 'repose . . . rest', points up the antithesis.

155–8   *Secure . . . sleep.* A first draft of the famous dirge over the supposedly dead Imogen ('Fear no more the heat o' th' sun') in *Cymbeline* IV.2.258–80.

157   *drugs* plants from which poison may be extracted

162   *tributary* (a) offered in tribute, payment, bound as Lavinia is by ties of kinship to her brothers; (b) Lavinia's grief is flowing into and merging with her father's grief, like the waters of a tributary river into a larger one. Both Titus's and Lavinia's tears of grief (line 162) are mingled with tears of joy (line 164). See III.1.268 and note to line 79.

163   *obsequies* funeral ceremonies

169   *cordial* a potion invigorating the heart. Titus thanks Rome for having preserved ('reserved') Lavinia, as the distillation ('cordial') of Roman virtue, for his retirement. The name Cordelia in *King Lear* shares the same etymology.

171   *date* term of existence

173   *Gracious* finding favour

180   *Solon's happiness* According to Herodotus (*History* II, 82), Solon, hearing the fabulously wealthy Croesus boasting of his happiness, observed: 'Call no man happy till he be dead.' This remark became a classical commonplace and a Renaissance proverb.

185   *palliament* white robe. A neologism, probably compounded of two Latin words for 'robe': *pallium* and *paludamentum*. Its only other known occurrence is in George Peele's poem, 'The Honour of the Garter' (1593): 'A goodly king in robes most richly dight, | The upper like a Roman palliament'. This has been cited as evidence in favour of Peele's authorship of Act I of Shakespeare's play. See Introduction, p. xxvi.

186   *in election* See note to line 22.

188   *candidatus* chosen as candidate. A Latin word, from which 'candidate', that is 'clad in white', is derived. The Latin *candidus*, 'white', gives *candida*, 'toga', which signifies 'white robe' or 'palliament'.

192   *What* for what reason

195   *set abroad* set afoot

200   *In right and service* in service of the right

201–2   *Give . . . the world.* With this antithesis, Titus assumes, as Lear will, that symbols of honour can dispense with the reality of power.

204   *obtain and ask* obtain by asking. Proverbial: for Titus, to ask is to receive.

205   *canst thou tell?* can you anticipate the outcome (of the election)?

209   *shipped to hell* banished without possibility of recall

214   *wean . . . themselves* separate them from their immature preferences

219   *meed* reward

221   *ask your voices* ask that you put your votes at my disposal

224   *gratulate* salute

229–30   *Reflect . . . ripen justice* This remarkable expression of hope combines, in a single sentence, images of refulgence

('Reflect'), the sun-god ('Titan'), natural foison ('ripen') and integrity of rule ('justice'), that turn out to be comprehensively illusory.

233   *sort* social class. Marcus's formulation sounds facile, especially in view of Lavinia's remark at I.1.167.

236   (stage direction) F supplies a necessary stage direction here. The Romans must have left the upper-stage (the Senate) by the time Saturninus ascends again at line 301 as the newly elected emperor, accompanied by Tamora and her party, in order to emphasize the threatening presence of the Goths at the very heart of the main Roman political institution.

238   *us in our* Saturninus starts using the royal plural immediately after his election.

        election four syllables

239   *in part* as part

241   *onset* start

245   *Pantheon* Roman temple dedicated to all the gods

246   *motion* proposal

251   *consecrate* dedicate as to a sacred cause. Titus is not offering Saturninus literal gifts. There is no reason to assume, with some editors, that Titus has brought his chariot on stage.

253   *imperious* imperial

255   *ensigns* symbols

256   *father of my life* as Lavinia's father, hence future father-in-law, but also as Saturninus's deceased father, since his succession has been enabled by Titus's intercession. See also line 426.

259   *unspeakable* inexpressible

260   *fealty* loyalty

262   *for . . . state* for the sake of . . . status

264   *hue* appearance

267   *cheer* facial expression. The word alliterates with 'chance' and 'change'.

271–2   *he . . . | Can* he . . . who can

274   *sith* since

275   *Warrants* justifies

283   *Suum cuique* to each his own: proverbial and echoed in
      A Midsummer Night's Dream, III.2 458–9: 'And the
      country proverb known, | That every man should take
      his own'

285   (stage direction) The seven-line confrontation between
      Titus on the one hand, and Bassianus, Marcus and
      Lucius on the other, takes place in the vicinity of one of
      the stage doors, while the Goths, released by Saturninus
      at line 277 and the processional exit prompted by Satur-
      ninus at line 276 – 'Romans, let us go' – file through the
      other. In processional exits, the emperor would leave
      last, not first (see, for example, Mantegna's painting
      Triumph of Caesar at Hampton Court). Saturninus is
      therefore still on stage to reply to Titus's warning at line
      287: 'Treason, my lord! Lavinia is surprised.'

286   *avaunt* begone

287   *surprised* seized

289   (stage direction) Bassianus's assertion of prior right over
      Lavinia (lines 288–9) sounds very much like an exit
      line.

292   (stage direction) Saturninus is still close to his exit door:
      what Titus asks him to do is not to follow him, for the
      qualifying clause, 'and I'll soon bring her back', shows
      that Titus is going to deal with the kidnapping himself.
      Titus is rather asking Saturninus to follow the departed
      procession as if nothing had happened.

301   (stage direction) Saturninus's reappearance 'aloft' with
      Titus's former captives, as Titus remains below alone
      except for the body of the son he has killed 'for Rome',
      provides a powerful tableau of the catastrophic reversal
      of fortune that has occurred since Titus's triumphal
      entry.

304   *by leisure* hardly, only after careful and lengthy consider-
      ation, as opposed to 'never' in the next line

307   *stale* laughing-stock

312   *changing piece* fickle trollop. The term 'piece' is often

115

derogatory when applied to a woman, probably because
it implies that she can be bought and sold. See, for
example, *Twelfth Night*, I.5.24–6: 'If Sir Toby would
leave drinking thou wert as witty a piece of Eve's flesh
as any in Illyria.'

313 *flourished . . . sword* brandished (with overtones of 'swag-
gered') his sword in order to get her. See note to line 41.

315 *bandy* brawl, exchange blows

316 *ruffle* swagger

317 *words are razors* an intensification of the proverbial
'words cut like swords'

319 *Phoebe 'mongst her nymphs* Diana, goddess of chastity and
the hunt, but here principally of the moon, among her
maiden stars. Shakespeare may be remembering Phaer's
1558 translation of the *Aeneid* I.498–501:

> *Most like unto Diana bright when she to hunt goeth out*
> . . .
> *Whom thousands of the lady nymphs await to do her*
> *will,*
> *She on her arms her quiver bears, and all them over-*
> *shines.*

Only Saturninus's fatuous lubricity could associate
Tamora with the goddess of chastity.

323 *Empress* three syllables

326 *sith* since

328 *Hymenaeus* Hymen, the Roman god of marriage

330 *climb* climb up to (as the Imperial Palace was traditionally
on the Palatine Hill)

334 *handmaid* possibly an anticipation of the visual pun
implied by the horrific stage action at the end of Act III,
when Lavinia follows Titus off stage, carrying his hand
between her teeth

339 *Whose wisdom* The antecedent is 'bride'.

340 *consummate . . . rites* complete the marriage ceremony

341 *bid to wait upon* invited to accompany, as a mark of
respect

343   *challengèd* accused

350   *as becomes* as is fitting

351   *brethren* See note to line 92.

358   *impiety* echoes Tamora's charge at line 133

360   *brethren* See note to line 92.

363   *vouch it* maintain it (pronounced as if one syllable: 'vouch't')

367   *crest* (a) helmet, by association with the plume that embellished it; (b) heraldic device, placed above the shield and helmet of a coat of arms. Double metonymy for 'honour'.

369   *repute* reckon

375   *if . . . speed* if all the others are to prosper

379   *virtue's nest* an image of nurture. The tomb of the honoured dead is the birthplace of their virtue – an idea made explicit in line 393.

381   *be not barbarous* The deconstruction of the problematic opposition between Roman virtue and barbarous cruelty, which was initiated by Tamora at line 133, is developed further by Marcus at line 359 first and then here.

382   *upon advice* after deliberation

382–4   *Ajax . . . funerals* In a fit of madness this Homeric Greek warrior attacked and killed a flock of sheep imagining them to be the Greek generals who had slighted him. When he recovered his senses he committed suicide. Ulysses, the son of Laertes, persuaded the Greek *supremo*, Agamemnon, to grant Ajax honourable burial.

391   *trophies* honorific memorials

392   (speech prefix) The exclusion of Titus from this little ceremony by later editors, in contradiction of the explicit direction of the early editions, is not warranted. Lines 386–9 show Titus to have capitulated, albeit gracelessly. Indeed, by the beginning of the third act, he includes Mutius among the sons who have 'died in honour's lofty bed' (III.1.10–11).

394   *dumps* bouts of melancholy

395   *subtle* crafty, calculating

399   *the man* Titus himself

401   MARCUS . . . *remunerate.* This line is absent from Q and has no speech prefix in F. Although the line seems in keeping with Marcus's attempt to reassure Titus, its origins remain doubtful.

       (stage direction) The entrance of Titus's sons with the newly wed Bassianus and Lavinia balances the entrance, at the opposite door, of the newly wed Saturninus and Tamora, with her two sons and Aaron. In Q, the symmetry of this entrance is mirrored by the layout of the stage direction, thus:

Enter the Emperour, Tamora   *Enter at the other doore*
and her two sonnes, with the   *Bascianus and Lavinia*
Moore at one doore.   *with others.*

402   *played your prize* won your game. Usually used of fencing, Saturninus implies that Lavinia is some brawler's moll.

407   *rape* abduction

411   *that* that which

412–13   *You are . . . you* a pointed adaptation of a common proverb: 'all that is sharp is short'

419   *opinion* reputation

423   *controlled . . . gave* curbed in what he gave so freely; 'controlled' suggests 'rebuking' as well as 'reining in'

427   *leave . . . deeds* stop justifying my actions

436   *put it up* sheathe the weapon, put up with the insult. A distant echo of line 402: Bassianus has fought his bout successfully; Saturninus is not even allowed to begin his.

437   *forfend* forbid

438   *author to dishonour you* responsible for dishonouring you

439   *undertake* vouch

441   *not dissembled* that Titus is unable to control, and therefore conceal. Titus's 'fury' in killing his son is a true expression of his 'griefs' on behalf of his own and the Emperor's honour.

443   *vain suppose* empty supposition

446   *Dissemble . . . discontents.* In open contrast with line 441.

452   *at entreats* to entreaties

        let me alone leave the rest to me

460   *Take up* raise to his feet. Titus has been kneeling for 30 lines.

465   *incorporate in Rome* incorporated into the body of Rome

477   (stage direction) Bassianus may or may not kneel here. Tamora's lines at 471–3 seems to imply that she has already obtained Saturninus's pardon on his behalf. However, Tamora's failure to mention Bassianus as one of the kneeling petitioners at line 483 is no indication that Bassianus should therefore be standing, as Lavinia, who is explicitly invited to kneel at lines 474–5, is not mentioned either.

479   *Tend'ring* having regard for

489   *like a churl* 'as if I were a rustic', if referred to Saturninus himself, or 'selfishly, like a miser', if referred to Lavinia

490   *sure as death* proverbial

494   *love-day* (a) a day appointed by the Church for settling disputes and restoring amity (Saturninus has been cued by Tamora's declaration at line 468); (b) a day devoted to love

498   *gramercy* great thanks. Saturninus matches Titus's '*bon-jour*' at line 497 with more French *politesse.*

498   (stage direction) Q has no act-division so Aaron remains on stage and comes forward to break his silence. In F, which marks act breaks, Aaron leaves with the others to return immediately in order to open Act II. This procedure violates Elizabethan stage conventions, which discourage immediate returns. This edition retains F's act-division, as opposed to assimilating Act II, scene 1 into Act I, as has been recently proposed, in order to stress the transition to a new episode, but departs from F by keeping Aaron on stage.

II.1   The figure of Aaron is used to establish an unbroken continuity between Act I and II, but the form of his first speech (a soliloquy to the audience), its style (exotic hyperbole) and its content (Machiavellian naturalism) represent so unexpected a development that it effectively announces a new act by taking us into a new world. By the end of the speech, though we are still in Rome we have been distanced from the Capitol, and we are ready to accept that Demetrius and Chiron have been able to become rivals in their pursuit of Lavinia. The scene is divided into three parts: Aaron's soliloquy (1–25); Demetrius's and Chiron's rivalry for Lavinia (26–98); and Aaron's solution to their problems (99–135).

1   *Olympus* snow-capped mountain on the borders of Thessaly in northern Greece, regarded as the abode of the gods

3   *of* from

7   *Gallops the zodiac* gallops through the zodiac, a belt in the celestial sphere extending on each side of the circle traced in the heavens by the apparent orbit of the sun
         coach Phaeton or Helios, the sun-god, was thought to drive a golden chariot daily across the sky.

8   *overlooks* looks down on

14   *mount her pitch* ascend to the apex of her flight. 'Pitch' is a term in falconry denoting the position from which the falcon swoops down on his prey; but, given the insistent repetition of 'mount', erotic overtones become audible.

14–15   *triumph . . . prisoner* Aaron's rivalry with Titus surfaces explicitly here.

17   *Prometheus . . . Caucasus* Prometheus was the son of a Titan, who stole fire from the heaven for the use of mankind. Zeus punished him for his presumption by chaining him to a cliff face in the Caucasus, and by having an eagle or vulture devour his liver every day. The sado-masochism of the image here is not accidental.

18   *weeds* garments

22   *Semiramis* legendary Assyrian queen, who became a by-word for opulent voluptuousness and cruelty
          nymph lesser goddess, inhabitant of trees and rivers, but, more generally, sexually desirable woman

23   *siren* mythological temptress whose magic songs lured sailors to their death; hence 'charm' in this line and 'shipwreck' in the next

25   *storm* Aaron redirects the associations of 'shipwreck' by punningly alluding to the noisy entry of the brothers.
          (stage direction) *braving* defying each other. The quarrel between Demetrius and Chiron is a parody of the rivalry between Saturninus and Bassianus (see lines 31–2 and 73–4 below).

26   *edge* sharpness

27   *graced* shown favour

28   *affected* loved

29   *dost overween* are presumptuous

30   *to bear me down with braves* to overwhelm me with blustering threats

32   *gracious* worthy of favour, thus echoing the claim made at line 27

35   *approve* prove

36   *plead* demonstrate (a legal term)

37   *Clubs* truncheons. Aaron is parodying the call for officers to check a public brawl. Compare the Lord Mayor's 'I'll call for clubs, if you will not away', *1 Henry VI*, I.3.84.

39   *dancing-rapier* ornamental sword worn at social assemblies

40   *so . . . to* so . . . as to

41   *Go to* a phrase expressing derisive incredulity
          lath toy sword. Pun on Chiron's sexual inexperience.

46   *So near . . . draw* In Elizabethan times, acts of violence performed 'within the verge', that is a circle with a radius of twelve miles surrounding the person of the sovereign wherever she went, were regarded as especially transgressive and fell under the jurisdiction of her coroner, and not under that of the local authorities.

48	*wot* know
53	*put up* put away your weapons
60	*Away* stop it. A standard exclamation.
62	*brabble* brawl
64	*jet upon* encroach on
67	*broached* started
68	*controlment* imposition of authority
70	*discord's ground* (a) the cause of this quarrel; (b) the bass melody of this inharmonious music
71–2	*all the world:*	*... all the world* This repetition emphasizes Chiron's naïve eagerness, which Demetrius remarks upon at line 41.
73	*meaner* of lower rank
75	*in Rome* The play observes a notional distinction between Roman strictness and Gothic licence.
80	*propose* offer to face
81	*Why ... strange?* why do you think it so difficult? As in *Two Gentlemen of Verona*, I.2.99.
82–7	Demetrius off-loads a stock of proverbs. The proverbial expression at lines 82–3 is frequent in early Shakespeare, see, for example, *Richard III*, I.2.215–16: 'Was ever woman in this humour wooed?	Was ever woman in this humour won?'; *1 Henry VI*, V.3.78–9: 'She's beautiful, and therefore to be wooed;	She is a woman, therefore to be won'; and Sonnet 41: 'Gentle thou art, and therefore to be won;	Beauteous thou art, therefore to be assailed'.
89	*Vulcan's badge* the cuckold's horns. Vulcan, the lame god of fire and the master blacksmith, was married to Venus, the goddess of love, and became cuckolded by Mars, the god of war.
91	*to court it* how to play the suitor
94	*cleanly* neatly, as in 'he got clean away'. Demetrius is inadvertently sounding the first note of the motif of the 'hunting' of Lavinia, which Aaron will elaborate at lines 112–18.
95	*snatch* quick theft, but also quick copulation

96   *turns* purposes, but also 'copulation', from the common
        expression 'to serve a turn', meaning 'to copulate'

97   *hit it . . . hit it* Demetrius means 'understood the point';
        Aaron, punning brutally, means 'hit the target', that is
        'enjoyed Lavinia'.

100   *square* quarrel

101   *speed* succeed

103   *join for that you jar* unite to achieve what makes you clash

104   *policy* machination

105   *That you affect* what you desire

106–7   *what you . . . may* proverbial

108   *Lucrece* The wife of a Roman patrician, she was raped
        by the son of Tarquin, seventh king of Rome, and stabbed
        herself to death. As a result, Rome banished the Tar-
        quins, abolished the monarchy and became a republic.
        Shakespeare wrote *The Rape of Lucrece* (1594) soon after
        Titus Andronicus.

110   *than ling'ring languishment* decisive repudiation of courtly
        love's cultivation of service as romantic fulfilment

111   *path* solution, developing from 'speedier course' at line
        110

112   *solemn* formal, as befits a royal entertainment

115   *plots* places, pieces of land

116   *kind* nature

117   *Single* hunting term, for the picking out of a particular
        quarry

120   *sacred* deliberately blasphemous, as is the participle 'con-
        secrate' in the next line

123   *file our engines* sharpen our plots. This phrase brings to
        a climax the passage of Machiavellian diction introduced
        by 'policy' at line 104.

124   *square yourselves* quarrel with each other, and so foil your
        purposes

125   *wishes' height* This phrase echoes Aaron's plan to 'arm
        [his] heart' and 'mount' Tamora's 'pitch' in his soliloquy
        at the beginning of Act II.

126   *house of fame* The title of a well-known poem by Chaucer,

but Shakespeare probably alludes to Ovid's *Metamorphoses* XII.39–63, which evokes a house in which silence, privacy and secrecy do not exist, for it is honeycombed with a thousand apertures, and filled with a ceaseless murmur of gossip and report.

129   *strike . . . turns* See note to line 96.

131   *treasury* maidenhead

133   *Sit fas aut nefas* (Latin) be it right or wrong

134   *fits* seizures, convulsions

135   *Per Stygia, per manes vehor* (Latin) I am borne across the Styx, and through the shades of the dead, that is 'I remain in hell'. Both Latin phrases evoke the language of Phaedra's last speech in Seneca's *Hippolytus*. Thomas Kyd's *The Spanish Tragedie* popularized a fashion for quoting Latin tags in tragedies.

II.2   In contrast to the previous scene, this short scene set outside the imperial palace offers preparations for the day's bona fide hunting.

0   (stage direction) *noise with hounds and horns* Hounds were sometimes introduced on to the Elizabethan stage, as were hunting horns, but 'noise' suggests a group of instruments playing off stage.

1   *morn* The alternative reading 'moon' preserved in Q1–2 is normally discarded. It is, however, worth noting that 'moon' establishes a further link between the imagery of the love-chase introduced by Aaron in the previous scene and the royal hunt which is about to start here, as the moon was traditionally associated with Diana, the maiden goddess of hunting. See also II.3.57–65.

3   *uncouple* set the hounds free
     bay prolonged barking

5   *hunter's peal* horn-blowing to set the dogs barking. See also line 13.

9   *troubled in my sleep* Titus had premonitory dreams and is concerned about the Emperor's safety.

21   *chase* hunting ground
24   *run like swallows* The subject is 'horse' (collective). The
      phrase is proverbial. Compare Aaron at IV.2.171: 'Now
      to the Goths, as swift as swallow flies'.
26   *dainty doe* Lavinia. See II.1.117.

II.3   This scene is located in the royal forest or hunting
      park. It is divided into six episodes: Aaron's divulsion
      to Tamora of his plot against the Andronici (1–54);
      Tamora's taunting by Bassianus and Lavinia (55–88);
      the killing of Bassianus (89–117); Lavinia's vain pleas
      (118–91); the entrapment of Martius and Quintus (192–
      245); and their inculpation for Bassianus's death by
      Aaron and Tamora (246–306). The pit is the dominant
      image of this scene. It is not only a hunting trap, as at
      lines 193 or 224. It is associated with (a) hell: see note to
      line 98, and Martius's allusion to 'Cocytus' misty mouth'
      (236), one of the foggy rivers of the underworld; (b) the
      grave: see, for example, references to the 'loathsome pit'
      (176) invoked by Lavinia as a shelter from Chiron and
      Demetrius's 'worse-than-killing lust', the 'detested,
      dark, blood-drinking pit' (224), in which Bassianus lies,
      or the 'fell devouring receptacle' (235), which echoes
      Titus's description of the tomb of the Andronici as the
      'sacred receptacle of [his] joys' at I.1.95; and, more
      complexly, with (c) 'entrails' (230), the 'swallowing
      womb' (239) and female genitalia (198–201).
2   *under a tree* As Henslowe's *Diary* shows, property trees
      and 'moss banks' were used on the barren Elizabethan
      stage. The burying of gold to frame an innocent person
      occurs in Ovid's *Metamorphoses* XIII.58–60, where Ajax
      alleges that Ulysses, in revenge for having been
      unmasked as a malingerer by Palamedes, produces gold
      he has hidden himself to prove that his denouncer has
      taken bribes.
3   *inherit* possess

5   *coin* (a) fabricate; (b) by means of coins (referring to
     Aaron's use of a bag of gold coins to frame Titus)

8   *repose . . . unrest* A widespread Elizabethan paradox put
     into circulation by Kyd's *The Spanish Tragedie*, I.3.5:
     'Then rest we heere a while in our unrest.' See also *Titus*,
     IV.2.31.

9   *That . . . chest* the beneficiaries of Tamora's treasury,
     that is the Andronici, who are now dependent on Tamora

12–14 *The birds . . . wind* See Seneca's *Hippolytus*, 5088–9:
     'Wherein the complaining birds make music, and the
     ash-trees and ancient beeches quiver, moving gently in
     the breeze'.

13   *snakes lies* common Elizabethan concordance of a third
     person singular verb with a plural noun

19   *double hunt* Compare *Venus and Adonis*, 695–6: 'Echo
     replies, | As if another chase were in the skies.' In the
     play, this image is ironic, pointing to the two simul-
     taneous hunts.

20   *yellowing* yelping, an extension of 'yell'

22–4 *wand'ring prince . . . cave* See Virgil's *Aeneid* IV, where
     Aeneas, in the course of his wanderings between his
     escape from Troy and his foundation of Rome, sojourns
     in Carthage where its queen, Dido, falls in love with
     him. In Book IV.160–72, the royal couple, surprised by
     a storm during a day's hunting, find shelter and solace
     in a convenient cave.

28–9 *nurse's song . . . asleep* Compare *Venus and Adonis*, 973–
     4: 'By this, far off she hears some huntsman's hollo; | A
     nurse's song ne'er pleased her babe so well'. Following
     the previous parallel with *Venus and Adonis* (see line 19
     above), and Aaron's explicit identification of his mis-
     tress with the goddess of love at line 30, the play links
     Tamora with Venus, as it has associated Lavinia with
     Lucrece.

31   *Saturn* Roman version of the Greek god Kronos, father
     of time and devourer of his children in an attempt to foil
     a prediction that he would be deposed by one of them.

In his planetary form he renders those born under his sign vengeful and unforgiving.

34–6   *My fleece ... execution?* Aaron is associated with the serpent who tempted Eve, as he provokes Tamora to collaborate in his crimes.

37   *venereal* having the character of Venus

39   *Blood ... head.* This metaphor occurs four times in Thomas Lodge's *The Wounds of Civil War*, at II.1.84; II.1.187; III.4.63; V.1.42. See Introduction, pp. lii, lvi.

41   *never ... in thee* Aaron takes literally the courtly lover's hyperbole that his mistress promises paradise, a trope which Berowne calls 'pure, pure idolatry' in *Love's Labour's Lost*, IV.3.73.

43   *Philomel* Ovid's account of the rape of Philomela (*Metamorphoses* VI.424–674) is a central source, model and theme of the play. See note to IV.1.47–8 and Introduction, pp. xxvii–xxviii.

47   *fatal-plotted scroll* letter containing a death-dealing plot, implicating Titus's sons, Quintus and Mutius, as the killers of Bassianus. See line 294.

49   *parcel of our hopeful booty* part of our anticipated loot

56   *Unfurnished ... troop?* indecorously deprived of her attendants

57   *Dian, habited like her* As goddess of the chase, the virginal Diana wore a hunting garment of great simplicity. Bassianus, however, has seen Aaron with her (line 48), and he sarcastically implies that her resemblance to the goddess is confined to her habit.

60   *Saucy controller* impudent inspector

61–4   *Had I ... limbs* Ovid's *Metamorphoses* III.138–253 describes how a young prince, Actaeon, hunting in the woods surprised Diana and her maidens bathing, how the outraged goddess turned him into an antlered stag, and how he was run down and killed by his own hounds. Tamora's ferocious appropriation of Bassianus's gibe covertly assumes the very power she disclaims, and thus promises an enactment of the same inverted hunt.

64   *drive* rush

66   *Under your patience* ironically polite

67–71   *horning . . . stag* Cuckolded husbands were fancifully said to wear horns on the brow (by analogy with rutting stags frequently deprived of their does by stronger interlopers). This allows Lavinia to query Tamora's appropriation of the Actaeon myth, by converting Bassianus as quarry into Saturninus as cuckold.

68   *doubted* suspected

72   *Cimmerian* Homer placed the mythical Cimmerians beyond the sunset, in total darkness.

74   *Spotted* soiled

83   *joy* enjoy

86   *noted* notorious

91–108 *Have . . . miserable death* Tamora's description of the valley seems to be entirely unrelated to her previous account of it (10–29). The change is not merely the effect of a change in mood (incitement to crime instead of invitation to love): the description is as conventional in its iconography (it assembles the tropes of the landscape of hell) as was its predecessor (variations on the tropes of the *locus amoenus*).

92   *'ticed* enticed

95   *O'ercome* overgrown
        baleful mistletoe So-called by association with the legend that the Scandinavian god of peace, Balder, was slain by an arrow made of mistletoe.

97   *fatal raven* The croak of the raven was thought to presage death.

98   *this abhorrèd pit* The first of several references to the pit. Here the pit is associated with hell, as line 105 confirms. It would be represented on stage by the open trapdoor, perhaps partly covered with foliage. See II.3.199–200.

101   *urchins* hedgehogs

104   *straight* immediately

107   *dismal yew* (a) sombre, cheerless; (b) unpropitious

118   *Semiramis* See note to II.1.22.

120 *poniard* dagger

122 *here is more belongs to her* she owns something in addition
to her life (her chastity)

123 *First thrash the corn ... straw* proverbial; 'thresh corn'
was a common term for sexual intercourse.

126 *quaint* fastidious. The original reading in Q and F,
'painted', is obviously inappropriate as Demetrius and
Chiron must believe Lavinia to be chaste, since they plan
to spoil her chastity.

131 *honey* sexual sweets. This image prompts 'wasp' and
'sting' at line 132.

ye desire Recent editors sometimes retain the original
reading provided by Q and F1, that is 'we desire', since
Lavinia's defilement is something both Tamora and her
sons desire. This edition follows F2 in order to emphasize Tamora's wish to dispatch Lavinia immediately,
which is first expressed at lines 120–21 and reiterated at
line 132.

132 *Let ... outlive ... sting.* This is the only known instance
in Elizabethan English in which the verb 'outlive' (survive) is used intransitively, as a result of a necessary
emendation of the original punctuation. See Collation 4.

133 *warrant* one syllable

135 *nice-preservèd honesty* chastity fastidiously preserved

140–41 *be your heart ... rain* combination of two proverbial
expressions: 'a heart as hard as flint' and 'constant dropping wears a stone'

146 *not sons alike* children unlike their mother, as Chiron's
reply suggests. See next note.

148 *prove ... bastard* (a) show myself an undutiful son (by
failing to heed my mother's teaching); (b) show myself
genetically illegitimate (by possessing virtues incompat-
ible with hers)

149 *raven ... lark* proverbial. See also note to III.1.158.

151–2 *The lion ... all away.* In Aesop, a lion who paid court to
a farmer's daughter had his claws pared and his teeth

pulled because the girl was frightened of him. By Shake-speare's time, the fable had turned into a proverb.

153–4   *ravens . . . nests* Compare *The Winter's Tale*, II.3.186–7: 'Some powerful spirit instruct the kites and ravens | To be thy nurses!'

154   *birds* chicks

171–9   This exchange is coded in terms of begging and paying. Lavinia, describing herself as 'Poor I' (171), is a pitiful beggar (170) in that she is reduced to begging for death (170, 173). This 'compassion' threatens to turn Tamora into a 'charitable murderer' (178). Thus Lavinia, herself reduced to a paradox (begging for *nothingness*), seeks to convert Tamora into an oxymoron. Tamora repudiates this appeal at line 179 by trumping Lavinia's 'charity' with her sons' *fee*.

172   *fond* foolish

174   *denies* forbids

179   *fee* reward. Lavinia's defilement is Chiron and Demet-rius's recompense for carrying out Tamora's orders (114–15) by killing Bassianus.

181   *stayed* delayed

183   *our general name* the good name of women

187   *sure* secure, unable to cause harm

189   *made away* killed off

191   *spleenful* lustful. The spleen was regarded as the seat of passion.

       trull harlot

192   *better foot before* proverbial, 'put your best foot forward'. Quintus and Martius enter as if drugged. They fall into the pit partly because of Aaron's misdirection, but chiefly because of their weakness. Their condition may have been partly suggested by Thyestes's sensation of impot-ence in Seneca's play of that name. Shakespeare had *Thyestes* in mind as he wrote *Titus* (see note to V.2.193–4). As Thyestes approaches the longed-for Argos and the appalling fate it has prepared for him, his body and spirit falter: 'I want to go on, but my limbs are unsteady

130

with sluggish knees, and I am borne back helplessly from
where I seek to go' (lines 436–7). See Introduction, p. liii.

208   *made away* See note to line 189.

210   *unhallowed* unsanctified

211   *surprisèd . . . fear* bewildered by an uncanny terror

219   *by surmise* by mere imagining

222   *berayed* defiled

223   *on a heap* prostrate

227   *ring . . . hole* a reference to the belief that rubies and
garnets emitted their own light

228   This simile suggests that the pit is in ambiguous relationship with the tomb of the Andronici. This is reinforced
by the application of the term 'receptacle' to both: the
pit at line 235, and the tomb at I.1.89.

229   *earthy* earth-coloured

230   *ragged entrails* rough interior

231   *Pyramus* The story of Pyramus and Thisbe is derived
from Ovid's *Metamorphoses* (IV.55–156). Neighbouring
adolescents fall in love, but being forbidden to see each
other, make an assignation outside the city. The girl,
Thisbe, arrives first, but seeing a lioness with bloody
jaws, runs away, leaving her cloak which the animal tears
to pieces. The boy, Pyramus, discovers the garment
and drawing the too-obvious conclusion, kills himself. Thisbe returns, finds her dying lover and also
kills herself. The tale was regarded as a model of pathos,
not least by Nick Bottom in *A Midsummer Night's
Dream.*

238–9 *Or, wanting . . . plucked* or that, if I lack the strength to
hoist you out of the pit, I may be pulled down myself

239   *womb* 'stomach' as well as 'matrix'. Everything in the
immediate context, including the epithet 'swallowing',
suggests that the idea of 'stomach' remains present. The
pit, which has been presented as the lair of the panther,
consistently attracts images of ingestion: mouth (199),
blood (200), blood-stainèd (210), blood-drinking (224),
entrails (230), devouring (235), mouth (236), swallowing

(239), gaping (249). Moreover, the stage action requires the trapdoor to 'swallow' three men in rapid succession: Bassianus, Martius and Quintus. What presides over this scene is Nature the Devourer.

246   *Along* come along

255   *chase* See note to II.2.21.

258   *out* an all-purpose intensifier

262   *search* probe

264   *writ* the letter introduced at line 46

265   *complot . . . timeless* plot of this untimely

266   *fold* hide in smiles

268   *handsomely* readily at hand, conveniently

272   *elder tree* associated with Judas who hanged himself from an elder

275   *purchase* win

281   *kind* nature, but with a strong implication of 'family'. See note to I.1.64 and I.1.89

294   *Andronicus . . . up.* Tamora must have refined on Aaron's plan (see II.3.46–7) by dropping the letter opportunely for Titus to pick it up.

295   *bail* Titus offers himself as 'bail'. This pre-shadows the sacrifice of his hand as 'ransom' at III.1.150 ff.

298   *their suspicion* the allegations contained in the letter

305   *Fear not* do not be afraid for

II.4   In performance this scene would be continuous with its predecessor. In its response to Lavinia's mutilations, it exhibits two starkly contrasting kinds of verbal inventiveness at 1–10 and 11–57; a third kind is reserved for Titus in the next scene. For a detailed discussion of the subtext of Marcus's speech at 11–57, see Introduction, pp. 17–22.

3   *bewray* reveal

5   *scrawl* gesticulate, with a possible anticipation of the modern meaning, 'to write or draw carelessly'

6   *sweet* scented

8   *silent walks* paths for meditation, but also a vicious allusion to Lavinia's mutilated tongue

9   *cause* case

10   *knit* knot

12   *Cousin* generic term used for any family relation beyond immediate kinship

13   *would all . . . wake me* I would give all my wealth to be awake. See also III.1.251.

14   *strike* astrological term signifying 'blast by malign (stellar) influence'

22–5   *a crimson river . . . honey breath* Compare *The Rape of Lucrece*, lines 1734–41:

> *And from the purple fountain Brutus drew*
> *The murderous knife, and as it left the place,*
> *Her blood, in poor revenge, held it in chase;*
> *And bubbling from her breast, it doth divide*
> *In two slow rivers, that the crimson blood*
> *Circles her body in on every side,*
> *Who like a late-sack'd island vastly stood*
> *Bare and unpeopled in this fearful flood.*

Lavinia's mutilation is rendered in terms of pastoral spoilation: branches (18), shadows (19), river (22), fountain (23), Titan (31), cloud (32), lily (44) and aspen leaves (45). The imagery of this passage is in keeping with the larger dualism of park and wilderness introduced in II.2.12–20 and 93–104.

26   *Tereus* King of Thrace, who raped his sister-in-law, Philomela, in the woods, cutting out her tongue to secure his safety. See note to II.3.43.

27   *detect* expose

30   *a conduit . . . spouts* graphic description of Lavinia's mutilated, bleeding arms and mouth, in contrast with the register and the pastoral imagery used in Marcus's speech

31–2   *red as Titan . . . cloud* Compare *Richard II*, III.3.63–6:

> *As doth the blushing discontented sun*
> *From out the fiery portal of the east,*
> *When he perceives the envious clouds are bent*
> *To dim his glory . . .*

34   *heart* the seat of thoughts as well as feelings

36–7 *Sorrow . . . where it is* proverbial

38   *Philomela* See Introduction, pp. xxvii–xxviii.

39   *in a tedious . . . mind* in a laboriously sewn embroidery conveyed what was in her mind. See note to II.3.43.

43   *Philomel* See note to II.3.43.

44   *lily* lily-white

45   *aspen leaves* proverbial. Poplar leaves are responsive to the softest wind.

47   *for his life* for fear of being struck dead

51   *Thracian poet* Orpheus. He attempted to recover his dead wife, Euridice, from Pluto's realm by putting to sleep the three-headed dog Cerberus, guardian of the entrance to the underworld.

III.1   This scene takes place in a Roman street, paved with stones (lines 29 and 37). It is divided into six episodes: Titus's vain pleas for Quintus and Martius (1–26); his discovery that Lucius is exiled (27–58); his discovery of Lavinia's mutilations (59–149); his sacrifice of his hand to Aaron (150–232); his discovery that he has been tricked (233–86); and the Andronici's commitment to revenge (287–99). The recurrence of the motif of Titus's 'bitter tears' (line 6) emphasizes the crescendo of pathos and grief in this scene. Titus first compares the tears he sheds in vain for Quintus and Martius to the rain which improves the ever-intemperate seasons (16–22). At lines 122–9, Titus invites his family to weep with him over a fountain, which the copious amount of their 'bitter tears' turns into a 'brine pit'. Titus also associates his overflowing tears with the waters of the river Nile (a river,

134

as line 71 reminds us, that 'disdaineth bounds' in its annual flooding), and finally with the sea (224), before his outburst of laughter at line 263, which marks the lowest point of his despair and the realization that he has 'not another tear to shed' (265).

10 *two-and-twenty* Mutius, though initially disowned, has found his place in the tomb of the Andronici.

13 *languor* corrosive grief

14 *stanch* quench

16 *O earth* Titus's appeal to the earth is more than a one-off gesture; it prepares for the elemental outbursts later in the scene (lines 93–7, 123–9, 210–12 and 220–28).

22 *So* on condition that
    drink . . . blood possible reference to Quintus and Martius's fall into the 'blood-drinking' pit at II.3.224; also a distant echo of Abel's death in Genesis 4:11: 'the earth, which hath opened her mouth to receive thy brother's blood'

24 *reverse the doom of death* suspend the death sentence which is pending over Quintus and Martius's heads. See also lines 47 and 51 below, IV.2.113 and V.3.181.

36 *And . . . them* The Folio conflates this half-line with the next line to read, as in Q3: 'Therefore I tell my sorrowes bootles to the stones.' The Folio version, however, has none of the directness and poignancy of the first two Quartos, where the expected pentameter line, as if overcome by the futility it expresses, fails to complete itself.

40 *intercept* interrupt

43 *grave weeds* solemn dress

44 *afford* provide

45 *soft as wax* proverbial. See *The Rape of Lucrece*, 591–2, where Lucrece pleads with her ravisher to allow her tears to soften his heart 'with their continual motion, | For stones dissolved to water do convert'.

46 *stone is silent* proverbial: 'still as a stone'

54 *wilderness* a place of anarchic lawlessness. See *The Rape of Lucrece*, 543–4: 'a white hind under the gripe's sharp

claws, | Pleads in a wilderness where are no laws'. See also line 94 below.

63   *so she is* The compassionate Marcus has mourned the loss of the unmutilated niece; the realistic Titus asserts his daughter's continued existence in mutilation, as his reproof of Lucius at line 65 indicates.

64   *object* something presented to the sight, as lines 65 and 67 confirm

66–7   *accursèd hand . . . handless* Titus's pun ('accursèd hand' is a synecdoche, 'handless' a literalism) expresses the unnaturalness of what he perceives. He continues later on in this scene to exploit the various applications of the word 'hands', as a symbol of service (lines 73 and 80), and as an instrument of life and of prayer (lines 75–6), until Titus's sacrifice at line 192 reduces the wordplay to grotesque literalism.

68   *What fool . . . sea* proverbial, 'to cast water into the sea'

69   *bright-burning Troy* emblem of terminal conflagration in classical antiquity

70   *grief was at the height* The idea of what constitutes 'the worst' has to be revised three times in the course of this scene: here, then at lines 215–19 and finally at lines 265–86.

72   *I'll chop . . . too* With lines 77–8 and 130 below, this prepares for the actual deed at line 190.

76   *effectless use* useless use, an oxymoron

81   *martyred* mutilated, as at line 107

82   *engine . . . thoughts* Lavinia's tongue

83   *blabbed* prattled, spoke with innocent volubility

84   *pretty hollow cage* Lavinia's mouth

90   *unrecuring* incurable

91   The previous act's imagery of Lavinia as the 'dainty doe' is resumed here, where Titus appropriates Marcus's image of Lavinia as quarry.

93–7   The idea of being swallowed up by elemental nature (II.3.192–245) makes Titus's powerful simile more than a figure of misery: it suggests that as Titus loses faith in *romanitas*, his sense of identity begins to implode.

96   *Expecting ever when* waiting always for the time when *envious* malignant

97   *his* its

101   *spurn* blow

105   *lively* living

107   *martyred* See note to line 81.

109   *by this* by this time

112   *honey-dew* a sweet substance on leaves, originally thought to be distilled like dew

113   *gathered* contracted, and thus forming folds or wrinkles (not 'picked', given the presence of honey-dew). Possibly an attempt on Titus's part to repress the thought that Lavinia has been 'plucked', 'deflowered'.

123   *fountain* water-spring, as at line 127

130   See note to line 72.

131   *dumb shows* those parts of a play representing action without speech. The dramatic conceit is sustained by 'plot' and 'device' (line 134), by the implied audience (line 135), and even by the covert allusion to Kyd's *The Spanish Tragedie* (IV.4.220), where Hieronymo bites out his tongue before killing the Duke of Castile and himself.

140   *napkin* handkerchief

148   *sympathy* community of feeling

149   *limbo is from bliss* Limbo is a region on the border of hell reserved for virtuous pagans and unbaptized infants, debarred from 'bliss' or the joys of paradise (see also line 271). This line cues the entrance of Aaron, who announces 'help' from above (the semi-divine Emperor): but he is a black angel, and the 'ransom' he is about to bring converts 'limbo' into 'hell'. See also next note.

156   *ransom for their fault* This phrase, which traditionally refers to Christ's redeeming sacrifice, feeds Aaron's blasphemous satanism. See also lines 172 ('ransom') and 180 ('redeem').

158   *raven . . . lark* Echoes of Lavinia's proverbial line 'the

137

raven doth not hatch a lark' at II.3.149 suggest how misplaced Titus's trust in 'gentle Aaron' is.

168–9   *And reared . . . castle* By wielding the battle-axe against the enemy's castle, Titus and Lucius have in effect been 'writing' the public annals of their 'high desert' (line 170) on the stricken ramparts, unlike Marcus, whose hand in this sense has been 'idle' (line 171).

177   *withered herbs* Titus's old hands. Titus has recently used a similar metaphor in relation to Lavinia ('lily almost witherèd', line 113). This time, however, the metaphor prompts the 'plucking up' (line 178) for which his hands are 'meet', that is 'fit'. See note to line 113.

179   *shall* am to

186   *Lend me . . . mine* The word-play is sardonic, not only because of the figurative-literal equivocation on 'hand' (as at line 160), but because of the contrast between the provisional 'lending' and the irrevocable 'giving'.

187   *If . . . honest* If deceit does good, then honesty must be presumed to do evil; thus, if Aaron is to be true to his evil nature, he must be honest. Compare Iago's paradoxical reasoning in *Othello*, II.3.339–53.

189   *in another sort* Aaron discloses his plan at line 201.

190   (stage direction) *left hand* as inferred from a later reference to Titus's right hand (III.2.7)

191   *what shall be is dispatched* what was to be decided (whose hand should be cut off) has already been settled

193   *warded* guarded

195   *that* i.e. burial

200   *Look . . . to* expect

202   *fat* feed succulently

206   *ruin* a body decayed as well as mutilated

210   *breathe . . . dim* obscure the sky, as a glass is misted by breath

213   *with* within the bounds of. Marcus's rational resistance to hyperbole prepares for the shock of his about-turn at line 240.

215   *Is . . . sorrows* See note to II.3.13.

219   *bind* confine

220   *o'erflow* become flooded

221   *sea wax mad* proverbial, 'as mad as the troubled sea'

222   *welkin* sky

223   *coil* commotion

224–5 *I am . . . earth* Lavinia with her sighs and tears is the sky
       with its wind and rain; Titus in his responsiveness to
       her is the flooded earth and the tempestuous sea. The
       chiasmus (an AB:BA sequence) is obscured, but not
       abolished, by the stop after 'sea'.

229–32 *For why . . . tongues.* The modulation of the simile from
       flooding (through too much rain) to vomiting (through
       too much drinking) displays the convulsive, uncontrol-
       lable interdependence of Titus's grief and its expression.

231–2 *losers . . . tongues* proverbial, 'give losers leave to speak'.
       Compare *2 Henry VI*, III.1.182: 'But I can give the loser
       leave to chide.'

237–9 *Thy grief . . . death.* The messenger's sympathetic
       response to Titus's plight represents the first indication
       that popular feeling in Rome will turn against the
       Emperor and his allies.

240   *hot Etna* an active volcano in Sicily

243   *To weep . . . weep* biblical: 'Weep with them that weep'
       (Romans 12:15)

244   *flouted at* mocked

247   *bear his name* still be called life

250   *starvèd* numbed through cold, and certainly not to be
       revived by 'frozen water'. In *2 Henry VI*, III.1.343, York
       warns the nobles not to 'warm the starvèd snake'.

251   *When . . . end?* See also II.4.13–15.

252   *flatt'ry* illusory comfort

255   *dear* grievous

258   *control* restrain

259–60 *thy other hand . . . teeth* This prepares for line 281.

261   *The closing . . . eyes* let this sight be the last thing we see

263   *Ha, ha, ha!* Laughter as a symptom of crazed grief is
       anticipated in Kyd's *The Spanish Tragedie*, III.11.77–8.

268   *tributary* See note to I.1.162.

269   *cave* The lair of Revenge, like that of other personifications of primitive instinct, is placed beyond the frontiers of human society.

271   *bliss* See note to line 149.

272   *returned again* avenged

275   *heavy* sorrowing

280–81 *Lavinia . . . thy teeth* Possibly prompted by lines 259–60. See Introduction, p. lxiii.

284   *Hie* go quickly

290   *pledges* his promises, but also his family, the persons to whom he is pledged by kinship and whose love will guarantee his return

292   *tofore* formerly

297   *Tarquin and his queen* See note to II.1.108.

III.2   This scene is first found in the First Folio, and is believed to represent a later addition to the original play as preserved by the First Quarto. See An Account of the Text, p. 166. The location is Titus's house.

4   *sorrow-wreathen knot* arms folded out of sorrow

6   *passionate* express passion fittingly

12   *map* model, or emblem

15   *Wound . . . groans* Sighing and groaning were thought to drain the heart of blood.

16–17   *little knife . . . hole* Compare *Richard II*, III.2.169–70: 'with a little pin | Bores through his castle wall, and farewell, king!'

19   *sink* receptacle for liquid

20   *fool* a term of compassionate tenderness

23   *dote* talk like a madman

25   *What . . . life?* Titus's punning continues the regression from metaphor to literalism which started in the previous scene. See note to III.1.66–7.

27–8   *Aeneas . . . miserable* In Virgil's *Aeneid* II.2, Aeneas begins his narration of the fall of Troy with the words:

'O Queen, you require me to revive unutterable grief.'

29 *handle . . . hands* Titus's obsessive punning shows that *he* cannot forget his and Lavinia's mutilations, as he himself goes on to recognize at lines 32–3.

31 *square* shape

35–6 *Here . . . signs* Titus, who has to help her to eat, finds her goblet empty, but is informed by her, maybe by a shake of the head, that she does not want to drink.

38 *mashed* fermented, a technical term from beer-making, developing 'brewed'. This metaphor reminds us that in the polluted Elizabethan cities a 'drink' was not water but beer.

40 *perfect* as in 'word-perfect'

41 *begging hermits* religious mendicants

45 *still* continuous

55 *cloyed* satiated with excess

62 *lamenting doings* helpless meanderings

66 *ill-favoured* ugly

71 *insult on* triumph over

72 *Flattering . . . as if* deceiving myself with the thought that

80 *shadows for true substances* proverbial

81 *take away* clear the table

82 *closet* private room

82–3 *read . . . of old* For the nostalgia of impotence, compare *Richard II*, III.2.155–6: 'let us sit upon the ground | And tell sad stories of the death of kings', or *King Lear*, V.3.8–19.

85 *dazzle* lose the faculty of distinct and steady vision, usually from ageing

IV.1 The location of this scene is the atrium, or inner court, of Titus's house. The action is divided into two episodes: the identification of Lavinia's assailants (1–79) and the diverse reactions to the discovery (80–130).

9 *somewhat* something

10–15   The First Quarto gives to Titus lines 9–15. Some of
        these lines must be attributed to Marcus, for lines 18–
        19 indicate that Young Lucius is answering his uncle,
        not his grandfather. The question is where to restore the
        dropped speech prefix MARCUS. Line 10 commends itself
        because of the repetition of 'Lucius' from line 9.

12   *Cornelia* Daughter of Scipio Africanus, Roman con-
        queror of Carthage, and mother of the Gracchi brothers,
        she is probably the most famous of the Roman matrons.

13   *Read to* instructed

14   *Sweet poetry* Possibly this is Ovid's poetry, should Shake-
        speare have the Grammar School curriculum in mind.
        Tully's Orator Marcus Tullius Cicero was formally
        known in the Renaissance as Tully. The book referred
        to could be either his *Orator ad M. Brutum*, a sketch of
        the ideal orator, or his *De Oratore*, a treatise on rhetoric.

15   *plies* importunes

20   *Hecuba of Troy* See note to I.1.139–41.

24   *but in fury* except in a fit of frenzy

26   *Causeless* without good reason

27   *go* go with me

28   *attend* wait upon

39   *fact* crime

41   *tosseth* throws to and fro

42   *Ovid's Metamorphoses* This most famous of compilations,
        perhaps the most influential classical text on the art and
        literature of the Renaissance, was available to Shake-
        speare in Arthur Golding's 1585–7 translation, as well
        as in the original Latin.

44   *culled* picked out

47–8   *Philomel . . . rape* Tereus is guilty of 'treason' because he
        betrays the trust not only of Pandion, the King of Athens
        and his father-in-law, but also of Procne his wife, and
        most of all of Philomela, his sister-in-law.

49   *annoy* grievous injury

50   *quotes* scrutinizes

51   *surprised* seized suddenly, as at I.1.287

53   *forced* raped

56   *Patterned by that* Titus implies that Nature is imitating
        Art and that because Lavinia's 'actual' rape possesses
        the completeness of Ovid's 'artistic' representation of
        Philomela's rape, her plight belongs to the realm of the
        tragic.

59   *tragedies* human suffering (but also a metadramatic allu-
        sion to the delight audiences take in watching tragedies)

62–3   *Tarquin . . . Lucrece* See note to II.1.108.

65   *Apollo, Pallas, Jove or Mercury* Apollo was the divinity
        of law, Pallas Athene was the goddess of wisdom and
        war, Jove was the guardian of justice and virtue, and
        Mercury was the god of cunning and prudence. These
        attributes all bear upon the crime about to be revealed.

68   *plain* level

71   *shift* expedient

73   *will have discovered for revenge* wishes to have revealed
        so that it may be avenged. The pious Marcus anachronis-
        tically seeks to reconcile the divine injunction against
        revenge – 'Vengeance is mine; I will repay, saith the
        Lord' (Romans, 12:19) – with the secular need for retri-
        bution. See also lines 127–8 below.

74   *plain* legibly

77   *Stuprum* (Latin) rape

80–81   *Magni . . . vides?* (Latin) 'master of the great heavens
        [i.e. Jove or Zeus], do you so calmly [*tam lentus*] hear
        crimes, so calmly see them?', from Seneca's *Hippolytus*,
        671–2

85   *exclaims* outcries

87   *Roman Hector* Lucius, champion of Rome, as Hector was
        champion of Troy.

88   *fere* husband

90   *Junius Brutus* the Roman patriot who persuaded
        Collatine, Lucrece's husband, to avenge her, and who
        led the revolt against the Tarquins. See *The Rape of
        Lucrece*, 1807–34.

91   *good advice* careful deliberation

143

93   *reproach* dishonour

94   *and* if

95   *bear-whelps* Chiron and Demetrius. Similarly 'dam' at line 96 is Tamora and 'lion' at line 97 Saturninus.

96   *wind* scent

98–9   *And lulls . . . list* By yielding to Saturninus sexually ('playeth on her back') Tamora gets him to yield to her politically ('do what she list'). The contrast is between a sleeping lion, and a wakeful she-bear who has Rome at her mercy.

100   *young huntsman* inexperienced as a hunter
        Let alone leave it alone

101   *leaf* sheet, but also 'foliage', thus anticipating line 107

102   *gad* spike used for engraving
        these words the words written by Lavinia

104   *Sybil's leaves* The prophecies of the Sybil at Cuma were written on leaves that sometimes blew away before they could be collected. See Virgil, *Aeneid* VI.74–5: 'Only trust not thy verses to leaves, lest they fly in disorder, the sport of rushing winds.' Like the leaves, the 'sands' contain a supreme but very vulnerable 'lesson' (line 105).

110   *done the like* defended Rome from foreign invaders

113   *fit* equip. An echo of Hieronymo's famous phrase, 'Why then Ile fit you', which launches his revenge, in Kyd's *The Spanish Tragedie*, IV.1.68.

120   *brave it* swagger

121   *waited on* not ignored, as they have been up to now

123   *compassion* take pity on

124   *ecstasy* mad fits

128   *Revenge the heavens* let the heavens take revenge

IV.2   The setting is a room in the Imperial Palace. The action comprises the reception of Titus's gifts (1–31); the reaction to the news that Tamora has a son (32–50); the Nurse's presentation of his black son to Aaron for dispatching (51–82); Aaron's protection of his child from

Demetrius and Chiron (83–126); Aaron's arrangements to secure the child's survival and to protect the Empress's good name, which involve the brutal murder of the Nurse (127–70); and his decision to entrust the child to the Goths (171–9).

0   (stage direction) *another* An attendant is required to carry the 'presents' referred to in IV.1.113–15.

6   *confound* destroy. Young Lucius's three asides, here and at lines 8–9 and 17, sustain the boyish bravado that surfaced at IV.1.106–8.

7   *Gramercy* thank you. The tone is patronizingly courtly.

8   *deciphered* detected, by means of reading

10   *well advised* acting rationally. Lucius is contradicting Aaron at line 3, but without betraying himself.

16   *appointed* equipped with weapons

18   *round about* all round

20–21   *Integer ... arcu* (Latin) from Horace, *Odes*, I.22.1–2: '[The man] upright of life and unstained by crime does not need the javelins or the bow of the Moor.'

23   *grammar* Lily's *Latin Grammar*, the prescribed textbook in late sixteenth-century grammar schools, quotes these lines twice.

24   *just* precisely. Aaron spots at once the ironic applicability of the quotation to Lavinia's rapists.

25   *ass* the standard epithet for the class-room dunce

26   *no sound jest* no honest joke. Aaron understands the real meaning of Titus's gesture, which is far from conciliatory.

28   *wound ... quick* proverbial, 'to wound to the quick', the 'quick' being acutely sensitive parts of the body

30   *conceit* clever idea, i.e. Titus's jest at line 26

31   *let her ... awhile* Tamora is in labour, as anticipated at line 29 and confirmed at line 47. For the phrasing, see note to II.3.8. This birth is an early example of Shakespearean double-time: the momentum of the play's events makes improbable the nine months required since Tamora's marriage to Saturninus, whom Rome believes

to be the father of the child; yet the required period is rendered plausible by the slow maturing of Titus's madness and revenge, and of Lucius's ascendancy over the Gothic army.

32–6   *And now . . . hearing* Aaron's defiance of Marcus in the hearing of Titus has not been shown.

38   *insinuate* curry favour

40   *friendly* This prompts a running blaspheming gag – 'charitable' (43), 'full of love' (43), 'amen' (44), 'pray' (46), 'belovèd' (47) – which is nailed by Aaron at line 48.

42   *At such a bay* so brought to bay, a resumption of the hunting analogy first introduced in Act II
     by turn in turn, but also by the sexual act. See note to II.1.96.

43   Chiron's blasphemous joke turns on the ambiguity of the word 'love', which can mean either 'charity' (in the Christian sense) or 'lust'.

45   *more* in addition to the 'thousand Roman dames' at line 41

46   *pray* The sons' cynicism seems to turn sentimental as soon as their mother is involved. Their inconsistency rightly earns Aaron's contempt at line 48.

50   *Belike* possibly

53   *more . . . whit* Aaron's sardonic puns on more/Moor and whit/white prepare for the Nurse's disclosure, when his name and skin-colour abruptly cease to be a joke.

62   *To whom* Aaron affects to take the Nurse's 'is delivered' to mean 'has been handed over' and not 'has given birth'.

63   *good rest* further wilful misunderstanding

67   *as . . . toad* proverbial

71   *Zounds* The Folio dilutes the expletive 'Zounds', derived from 'God's wounds', to 'Out you', because of the Profanity Act against blasphemy (1606).

72   *blowze* ruddy-faced girl, provocatively applied to Aaron's black baby

75   *undone* ruin the reputation of

76   *done* had sex with

82–3   *let ... blood* Aaron claims the same paternal privilege of life and death over his son as Titus does in Act I.

84   *broach* pierce, as with a spit
rapier light fencing sword

88–9   *burning ... was got* Here 'burning' suggests both the sexual fierceness of the occasion and the potency of the pagan divinities Aaron invokes.

92   *Enceladus* one of the legendary Titans who attacked the Olympians and ignited the volcano of Etna

93   *Typhon* monstrous giant who nearly destroyed Olympus

94   *Alcides* Hercules
god of war Mars

95   *seize this prey* The hunting metaphor is resumed again here. See note to line 42.

96   *sanguine* red-faced. Aaron introduces the motif of the superiority of black complexion over white (or ruddy), which he then develops at length at lines 97–102 and 115–18.
shallow-hearted superficially valiant

97   *white-limed* whitewashed, punning on 'white-limbed', as suggested by the original spelling in Q2–3 'white limbde' and F1–2 'white-limb'd'.
alehouse painted signs Public-house signs were notorious for the crudeness of the drawing. See, for example, *2 Henry VI*, III.2.80–81: 'Erect his statue and worship it, | And make my image but an alehouse sign.'

98–9   *Coal-black ... hue* proverbial, 'black will take no other hue'

100–101 *For ... white* proverbial, 'to wash a blackamoor (Ethiope) white'

102   *lave* wash

104   *excuse it* account for the baby's complexion

107   *vigour ... picture* life and form. Compare V.1.45, where Lucius captures both attributes in the phrase 'growing image'.

109   *maugre* in spite of

110   *smoke* burn

112   *escape* escapade

113   *doom* See note to III.1.24.

114   *ignomy* ignominy

117   *close enacts* secret resolutions

118   *leer* countenance

121   *sensibly* feelingly, perceptibly or made capable of sensation. Combined with 'fed', however, 'sensibly' is merely a reinforcement of 'gave life' in the next line, and should not be attributed with over-specific meanings other than 'nourished' or 'sustained'.

123   *womb . . . imprisoned* A distant echo of the 'loathsome pit' in II.3, described there as a 'swallowing womb' at line 239 and 'subtle hole' at line 198. See head-note to II.3.

124   *enfranchisèd* freed

125   *the surer side* proverbial

126   *seal* Aaron's complexion, hence his paternity

129   *subscribe to* acquiesce in

132   *have . . . you* a further development of the hunting metaphor resumed from lines 42 and 95

137   *chafèd* enraged

143   *Two . . . away* proverbial

145   *Wheak* mimetic term, the Elizabethan equivalent of 'squeak'

147   *policy* realistic statecraft, a term associated with the Machiavellian villain. See notes to II.1.104 and 123.

149   *babbling gossip* Compare with 'babbling fountain' at II.4.23.

151   *Muly lives* 'Muliteus', the alternative reading preserved in Q and F1 is likely to be a corruption of the reading adopted in this edition, as 'Muly', a well-known Moorish name, rather than a pseudo-Latin name, such as 'Muliteus', seems appropriate for Aaron's 'countryman'. Besides, 'Muliteus' is syntactically awkward in the context of lines 151–3 and 'leus' can be easily explained as a misreading of 'lives'.

154   *pack* come to an arrangement. The register is contemptuous.

155   *circumstance* details

159   *tempest* scandal, should the identity of Tamora's baby be discovered

161   *physic* medicine. The register is brutally ironic.

162   *bestow* provide. The funeral in question will be no more genuine than Aaron's 'physic'.

163   *grooms* manual servants

164   *days* time

165   *presently* at once

167   *tattle* chatter emptily, as gossip can do him no harm, once all witnesses have been dispatched

168   *trust the air* proverbial

171   *as swift . . . flies* proverbial. See note to II.2.24.

172   *dispose* put away safely

173   *secretly . . . friends* Aaron is unaware that the Goths are now supporting Lucius's cause.

175   *puts . . . shifts* proverbial, 'makes us devise stratagems'

176–7   *feed . . . curds* The First Quarto's repetition of 'feed' seems appropriate, indeed expressive. Aaron's unself-conscious paternal pride has, in the rhythm and syntax so preserved, a touching simplicity.

178   *cabin* lodge (verb)

IV.3   This scene is located outside the Imperial Palace. It consists of the lament for Justice (1–49), the allegorical archery-shoot (50–76), and the enrolment of the clown as messenger (77–119). It develops Titus's counterplot from the first section of the previous scene.

0   (stage direction) *his son Publius* For Publius's relation to Marcus, see line 26.

2   *your archery* arrows bearing a hostile note

3   *draw home enough* stretch the bow sufficiently to ensure that the arrow strikes home

4   *Terras Astraea reliquit* (Latin) from Ovid, *Metamorphoses* I.150: 'Astraea [the goddess of justice] has left the earth'. The departure of Justice announces the arrival of the age

of iron, the fourth and final stage of the world's decline from an original golden age.

8   *Happily* by good fortune

11   *mattock* heavy tool used for digging up hard ground. A famous precedent of the motif of digging the earth to find justice is in Thomas Kyd, *The Spanish Tragedie* (IV.12.71): 'Away, Ile rip the bowels of the earth, (*He diggeth with his Dagger.*)'

13   *Pluto* Roman god of the underworld, also at line 38

18–20   *Ah, Rome . . . o'er me* Titus accepts political responsibility for the disappearance of Justice in Rome.

19   *What time* when

22   *man-of-war* fighting ship, anticipating 'shipped' in the next line. Titus casts his kinsmen as customs officers.

24   *pipe* whistle for, thus completing the sequence of nautical images

29   *feed his humour* proverbial, 'co-operate with his whims'. Compare *Richard III*, IV.1.64: 'To feed my humour wish thyself no harm', and *King Lear*, IV.1.38–9: 'Bad is the trade that must play fool to sorrow, | Ang'ring itself and others.'

32   *But* The catchword at the foot of the page of the First Quarto ('But') is followed by a different word at the top of the next page ('Ioine'). It is possible that one line, or even two, may have been omitted.

34   *wreak* revenge

37   *her* Astraea. See note to line 4 above.

42   *stay a time* wait a while

43   *feed . . . delays* proverbial

44   *burning lake* standard name for Phlegethon, one of the four rivers of the underworld. It is anticipated by Kyd in *The Spanish Tragedie*, III.12.11: 'That leades unto the lake where hell doth stand.'

45   *her* Revenge or Justice. The ambiguity is significant.
        Acheron another underworld river, round which the shades of the dead hover, including the shade of Revenge

46   *shrubs . . . cedars* proverbial, 'high cedars fall when low shrubs remain'

47   *Cyclops* one-eyed giants who devoured human beings. See, for example, Homer, *Odyssey* IX.

48   *steel . . . back* proverbial, 'he is steel to the back'

53   *to this gear* to the business

54–5   *Ad Jovem . . . Ad Apollinem . . . Ad Martem* (Latin) to Jove . . . to Apollo . . . to Mars

58   *were as good* might as well

60   *Of* on

64   *well said* good shot

65   *Virgo* zodiacal constellation of the Virgin, identified with the figure of Justice. However, the obscene connotations reactivated at line 69 encourage an ironic association of Virgo with Tamora.

69   *Taurus* zodiacal constellation of the Bull. Horns are the signs of cuckoldry: in Titus's less-than-fantastic allegory, the misconduct of the Virgo (Tamora) is related to the horns of Taurus (Saturninus).

71   *Aries* zodiacal constellation of the Ram. Marcus elaborates Titus's allegory on the basis that the Ram and the Bull are neighbouring constellations, and that Saturninus has been cuckolded by Aaron.

76   *God . . . joy* traditional blessing for newly weds. This ends the vein of erotic mockery opened at line 65.

76   *News . . . come* line erroneously assigned to Clown in Q1

80   *gibbet-maker* The Quarto spells Jupiter 'Iubiter' at lines 67, 79, 83 and 84, perhaps to underline the pun for its readers. The Clown understands 'gibbeter' (= maker of gibbets), prompting the retention of the spelling 'Jubiter' at line 84 in this edition.

81   *them* the gallows

90   *press* hasten

92   *tribunal plebs* malapropism for *tribunus plebis*, or 'tribune of the people'

        take up settle

93   *Emperal* malapropism for 'Emperor'

95   *oration* petition
98   *with a grace* gracefully, but the Clown wilfully takes it to mean 'with a thanks to God for food'
106-13 *Sirrah ... Let me alone* See An Account of the Text, p. 231.
116   *For thou must hold it* This conjectural emendation is preferable to the original in Q and F ('For thou hast made it'), as Titus is more likely to be addressing the Clown, as suggested by the pronoun 'thou', which Titus never uses to address Marcus.

IV.4   This scene is located in the state-room of the Imperial Palace. It dramatizes the emperor's rage at Titus's provocative behaviour (lines 1–38); the summary execution of the clown (lines 39–60); and the news of Lucius's approach with an army of Goths, followed by Tamora's proposed counter to that threat (lines 61–112).
2   *overborne* oppressed
3   *extent* exercise
4   *egall* impartial, from 'equal to all', a legal term from Norman French. See also *The Merchant of Venice*, III.4.13: 'an egall yoke of love'.
6-7   *However ... ears* despite the accusations the Andronici have publicly levelled against him
8   *even* level, in accord
11   *wreaks* vindictive actions
16   *Sweet* ironic, in fact, most unwelcome
18   *blazoning* loudly proclaiming
19   *humour* caprice
21   *ecstasies* See note to IV.1.124.
23-6   *justice ... that lives* Compare *Measure for Measure*, II.2.90: 'The law hath not been dead, though it hath slept.'
35   *gloze with all* flatter everybody, notably Saturninus at lines 27–8, and Titus's supporters at lines 32–4. But Tamora's satisfaction at her own cleverness ('High-

witted') is misplaced. She is wrong in her claim that
Titus is helplessly deranged (line 31), and in her reliance
on Aaron's manipulations (lines 37–8).

36 *touched* wounded. See note to IV.2.28.

37 *out* having been drawn out

42 *Saint Stephen* the first martyr stoned to death outside
Jerusalem

48 *by'Lady* by our Lady (the Virgin Mary), but also 'by (the
command of) a lady'; hence the pun on 'fair end' and
'an end set by the fair sex'

57 *shape privilege* create immunity

58 *slaughterman* executioner

63 *gathered head* raised an army

64 *bent . . . spoil* intent on pillage

65 *amain* with all speed

68 *Coriolanus* The military defender of the early Roman
Republic who, having been banished, marched on
Rome at the head of her enemies, threatening to burn
her. Shakespeare dramatizes the story in *Coriolanus*,
the last of his plays to be based closely on Roman history.

70 *nip* to pinch off the buds or shoots of a plant; hence to
'hang the head', and the similes at line 71

75 *walkèd . . . man* This is a reference to the often dramatized practice, whereby the ruler visits his subjects in-
cognito in order to gather intelligence and unmask
corruption, as in Shakespeare's *Measure for Measure* or
Thomas Middleton's *The Phoenix*, and/or to strengthen
the bond with his people, as in Shakespeare's *Henry V*
or the anonymous *Fair Em* (*c.* 1590).

76 *wrongfully* wrongfully ordered

84 *is not careful* does not care

86 *stint* stop

87 *giddy* fickle, without principles

89 *enchant* bewitch

91 *honey-stalks* clover stalks, a surfeit of which can be fatal
to sheep

92   *When as* when
96   *smooth* flatter
105   *stand in* insist on
109   *temper* mould or shape
113   *incessantly* immediately

V.1   The location is in the country on the approaches to
            Rome. The scene, framed by two brief episodes of politi-
            cal action focusing on the Goths' support of Lucius (1–
            18) and on Lucius's acceptance of Saturninus's invitation
            to attend a parley in Rome (152–65), is taken up with
            the capture of Aaron and the 'irreligious' confession of
            his crimes against the Andronici (19–151).
1   *Approvèd* tested
7   *scath* injury
9   *slip* shoot or twig of a branch, hence heir
13   *bold* confident
15   *master* In Elizabethan times, the bee-hive was thought to
            be ruled by a king-bee. See *Henry V*, I.2.190: 'They
            [honey bees] have a king . . . of sorts'.
16   *cursèd Tamora* Tamora, sharing 'ingrateful' Rome's
            indifference (line 12) to Titus's military feats, is now
            considered an enemy by the 'warlike' Goth, who is aware
            of his own switch of allegiance (see line 10).
19   *lusty* strong, vigorous
21   *ruinous monastery* A reference to the state of the English
            monasteries after the Reformation, with their 'Bare
            ruined choirs' (Sonnet 73.4), would reinforce their
            attraction to fugitives like Aaron, and to 'earnest' con-
            templatives like the Goth.
22   *earnestly* steadfastly
26   *controlled* See note to III.1.258.
27   *tawny* black
28   *bewray* discover unintentionally
33   *rates* scolds
39   *use . . . of* deal . . . with

42   *pearl . . . eye* proverbial, 'a black man is a pearl in a fair woman's eye'

44   *wall-eyed* glaring-eyed. Compare *King John*, IV.3.49: 'wall-eyed wrath or staring rage'.

50   *sire* father

51   *sprawl* twitch limbs convulsively

55   *show* reveal to

60   *nourished* 'cared for', as well as 'fed'

65   *Complots* Aaron's self-fashioning as author of tragic (com)plots is suggestively metadramatic. See also note to IV.1.59.

66   *Ruthful . . . piteously performed* pitiful . . . performed in order to provoke pity

71–2   *Who . . . oath?* In his *Arte of War* (translated by Peter Whithorn: 2nd edn, 1588), Machiavelli raises this very dilemma when discussing mercenaries: 'By what God or by what saints may I make them to swear? By those that they worship, or by those that they blaspheme? Who they worship I know not any: but I know well they blaspheme all. How shall I believe that they will keep their promise to them, whom every hour they despise?' See Further Reading, Maxwell, p. xc.

74   *for* because

76   *popish . . . ceremonies* To a Protestant audience this should evoke 'superstitious ceremonies'; but given that a criminal atheist is speaking, audience response is likely to have been more complex.

79   *bauble* jester's baton

88   *luxurious* lustful

90   *To* compared with

93   *trimmed* tidied by removing overgrowth, but also copulated with

95   *washed . . . trimmed* as by a barber

96   *Trim sport* fine or excellent entertainment. Aaron's brutal punning proliferates.

99   *codding* lustful

100   *As sure . . . set* proverbial, 'without doubt'

102   *at head* The best bull-dogs attacked the bull head-on.

103   *worth* Aaron's merits as a tutor

104   *trained* enticed

110   *stroke of mischief* harmful part

113   *broke my heart* died. Aaron is referring to III.1.201–4.

114   *pried me* spied on me

119   *sounded* swooned

122   *like a black dog* proverbial, 'to blush like a black dog'.
        Compare with IV.2.115–17.

125–7   *Even . . . notorious ill* Compare *The Troublesome Reign of
        King John* (1591): 'How, what, when and where, have I
        bestow'd a day | That tended not to some notorious ill?'
        (Part II, 8. 85–6).

126   *Few* few days

128–40 *As kill . . . dead* This boastful catalogue is a variation of
        Barabas's list in Marlowe's *Jew of Malta*, II.3.176–202.

142   *kill a fly* This passing remark may have prompted the
        climax of III.2, the so-called 'fly killing scene', which
        was added later.

146   *presently* immediately

149   *So* as long as

160   *Willing you* bidding you

V.2   The location is the atrium of Titus's house, with his
        study represented by the upper stage. The scene com-
        prises Tamora's entrance into Titus's property (1–8);
        her success in persuading Titus to come down to her
        (9–69); her briefing of her sons about her intentions
        (70–80); her success in getting Titus and Marcus to
        invite Lucius and the Gothic chiefs to a feast with
        Saturninus and his entourage (91–131); her consent to
        her sons' remaining with Titus (132–48); their arrest by
        Titus's men (149–64); and Titus's statement of what
        will happen to them and why, ending with his cutting
        their throats (165–204).

1   *sad habiliment* dismal costume. Tamora is dressed as a

personification of Revenge, as indicated in the opening stage direction.

3   *from below* Compare with IV.3.11–14 and 44–5.

8   *confusion* ruin

9   *Who . . . contemplation?* J. C. Maxwell (see Further Reading, p. xc) points out that this famous entry-line is comically remembered by the clown at line 1963 in Thomas Dekker's *The Welsh Embassador* (Malone Society Reprints, ed. H. Littledale and W. W. Greg, 1921). This play provides further evidence of popular response to *Titus Andronicus*: line 976 repeats Shakespeare's 'leaf of brass' (IV.1.101). Given that *The Welsh Embassador* can safely be dated at 1623 (line 2162 refers to 'yeares 1621'), it bears witness to the remarkable longevity of Shakespeare's tragedy for the play-going public of the period.

11   *sad . . . away* solemn resolutions may be scattered by the wind. Titus continues to harp on the vulnerability of his vengeance, as at IV.1.103–5.

14   *bloody lines* written in blood. See also 'crimson lines' at line 22 below.

18   *Wanting . . . action?* lacking a hand with which to dramatize my speech. Conjectural emendation of the corrupt reading preserved in Q ('Wanting a hand to give it that accord'), supported by a detail in 'The Ant and the Nightingale', where Thomas Middleton has a mutilated soldier referring to 'my lamentable action of one arm, like old *Titus Andronicus*' (*The Works of Thomas Middleton*, 8 vols., London, 1885–6, ed. A. H. Bullen, vol. 8, p. 94).

19   *odds of* advantage over

22–5   *Witness* The cumulative repetition of this word is a forensic device much used in the drama that preceded *Titus*, such as *Locrine* (1591–5) V.1.11–12 and *Selimus* (*c.* 1591), lines 1476–86.

23   *trenches* deep wrinkles

30   *th'infernal kingdom* Hades, the underworld realm of Pluto

31   *gnawing vulture* The metaphor is from Prometheus's vulture. See note to II.1.17.

32	*wreakful vengeance* a pleonasm: 'revengeful revenge'
38	*couch* lie hidden, lurk
45	*Rape and Murder* Titus has identified their alleged identi- ties by means of the allegorical 'habiliments' noted in the opening stage direction.
	stands See note to II.3.13.
46	*surance* guarantee
47	*chariot wheels* Titus's reference to Revenge's chariot should not be regarded as an implied stage direction. For similar examples, see I.1.252.
50	*proper* handsome
51	hale *haul*
56	*Hyperion* the sun-god, who, like Revenge, girdles the globe, but in a golden chariot drawn by white steeds
59	*So* provided that
60	*ministers* administrators
65	*worldly* mortal, of this world
70	*closing* agreeing
71	*forge* invent
76	*sure* under control
77	*practice out of hand* improvised expedient
78	*giddy* See note to IV.4.87.
80	*ply my theme* work assiduously at my plan
82	*Fury* one of the Eumenides or avenging deities
85	*Well . . . fitted . . . Moor* you would be perfectly equipped were you supplied with a Moor
87	*wags* moves about
89	*represent* act as or depict
90	*convenient* in keeping
101	*hap* luck
107	*up and down* exactly, completely
112	*thrice-valiant* See note to I.1.123.
120	*device* contrivance. See also III.1.131.
124	*repair* return
129	*let him* let him do
136	*cleave* cling. Titus cunningly threatens to take his

revenge out of Tamora's hands and leave it to Lucius
and his army.

139   *governed . . . jest* handled the joke we have planned

140   *smooth . . . him fair* flatter and humour him

141   *turn again* return

143   *And will . . . devices* and will beat them at their own game.
See also III.1.131 and line 120.

147   *complot* covert design planned in concert. See also V.1.65
and note.

156   *therefore* for that reason, since their names describe their
deeds
gentle well-born

159   *sure* securely

160   *cry* cry out

162   (stage direction) *Publius . . . Demetrius* Aaron, Chiron
and Demetrius, the three characters who connived to
mutilate Lavinia's tongue, are now gagged. The brutal
logic of Titus's revenge starts to unfold.

169   *Here stands . . . mud* See *The Rape of Lucrece*, line 577:
'Mud not the fountain that gave drink to thee'.

179   *martyr* slay cruelly

187   *coffin* burial case for a corpse, but also mould of paste for
a pie

188   *pasties* meat-pies

190   *Like . . . increase.* The earth as devourer of its own
offspring is a recurrent motif in the play. See, for
example, III.1.16–22.

193–4   *Philomel . . . Procne* Compare Seneca's *Thyestes* (lines
272–8): 'Tereus' Thracian house saw an abominable
banquet. I concede, it was a monstrous crime; but it is
one that has already been performed. My anguish must
devise something better than that. Inspire my soul, O
Daulian mother and sister [namely, Procne and Philo-
mela]; my case is like yours; help and urge on my hand.
Let the joyful and greedy father tear his sons to pieces
and devour his own flesh.' For Shakespeare's use of his

main source in Ovid's *Metamorphoses*, see Introduction, pp. xxvii–xxviii.

198   *temper* mix

200   *officious* diligently busy

202   *Centaurs' feast* Perithous, King of the Lapiths, a mythical people from Thessaly, invited the Centaurs (creatures with the head, arms and torso of a man, and the body and legs of a horse) to his wedding feast, at which a bloody fight ensued.

204   *against* by the time that

V.3   The location is as for V.2. This scene is divided into two parts: the end of the old regime (1–65) and the birth of the new (66–198). The first part comprises the arrival and reception of Lucius and the Goths in Rome (1–25), Titus's presentation of his feast, with the killings of Lavinia, Tamora, Titus and Saturninus (26–65). The second part consists firstly of Marcus and Lucius's speeches of exculpation and explanation to the Roman people, and Lucius's election as Emperor (66–147). It then concludes with the contrasting treatments of the dead Romans (Lavinia, Titus and even Saturninus), and of the dead Tamora and still living Aaron (148–98).

3   *ours with thine* our mind is at one with yours, following 'my father's mind' in line 1.

4   *in* into Titus's house

9   *our friends* either the Gothic allies whom Lucius has brought into Rome with him, or Roman supporters. Lucius is not helplessly delivering himself into Saturninus's hands.

13   *venomous . . . swelling heart* See also *Arden of Feversham* (I.327): 'the rancorous venom of thy mis-swollen heart', George Peele's *The Battle of Alcazar* (II.3.3): 'The fatal poison of my swelling heart', and Shakespeare's near-contemporary *1 Henry VI* (III.1.26): 'From envious malice of thy swelling heart'.

14   *unhallowed* unblessed, profane

16   (stage direction) *Exeunt Goths* The 'chiefest princes of the Goths' remain (V.2.125).

17   *more suns than one* Saturninus recognizes Lucius as a rival to the throne. See IV.4.77.

18   *What boots it thee* what use is it to you

19   *break the parle* open the parley

21   *careful* painstaking, but also full of grief

28   *cheer be poor* the fare be simple. A pasty occupied a modest place in Elizabethan standards of hospitality.

35   *resolve me this* settle this (doubtful point) for me

36   *Virginius* The story of Virginius's killing of his daughter Virginia is told by Livy in his history of the foundation of Roman institutions, *History of Rome* III, 44–9 (see *The Early History of Rome, Books I–IV*, Penguin Classics, translated by Aubrey de Selincourt, 1997, pp. 215–21). Appius Claudius, the most powerful of the *decemviri* (a group of ten magistrates with supreme power to establish the legal codes of Rome in 450 BC), made plans to ravish Lavinia. To forestall this fate, her father, a humble but respected military officer, killed her. This principled outrage prompted a revolution against the *decemviri*, and when Appius was eventually summoned to appear before the Roman tribunal he took his own life.

43   *pattern* model
     lively warrant vivid, forcible authorization

47   *unkind* See note to I.1.89.

48   *tears . . . blind* This brings to a climax a paradox linking paternal grief and blindness introduced by Marcus at II.4.52–3 and developed by Titus at III.1.268.

58   *presently* at once

60   *daintily* fastidiously. Compare *Tamburlaine* Part I, IV.4.24–5: 'Are you so daintily brought up you cannot eat your own flesh?'

62   *witness . . . point* The proof that Tamora is guilty of eating her own sons is her execution for that crime.

65   *meed for meed* proverbial

67–8   *By uproars . . . gusts* the commotion on stage, but also the disintegration of civil life under Saturninus

70   *scattered . . . sheaf* a strewn harvest, reassembled into an ordered stook. This is an agrarian version of the idea of the 'body politic', which appears in the next line.

71–2   *body, | Lest* The first Quarto assigns lines 72–92 to a 'Roman Lord', the First Folio to a 'Goth'. Both begin this new speech with a variant sentence: 'Let Rome herself . . .' The Folio solution can be rejected with confidence: not even an incompetent playwright would assign lines 79–86 to a non-Roman. Yet the Folio intervention is significant, in that it registers dissatisfaction with the Quarto text. It is therefore reasonable to assume that the compositor of the Quarto introduced the speech prefix 'Roman Lord' on his own initiative, maybe on the basis of an unsatisfactory transition between line 71/72 – whether finding a full stop after 'body', or reading 'Let' in his copy, as opposed to 'Lest'. This edition follows the emendations proposed by the great eighteenth-century editor of Shakespeare, Edward Capell, which addresses the one vulnerable spot in the Quarto text, and removes the incoherence at every level: grammatically, it turns lines 72–5 into a dependent clause of lines 66–71 and, structurally, it restores to Marcus at the end of the play the conciliatory public role he established at its start.

72   *bane* destruction

76   *frosty . . . chaps* white hair and cold cracks in the skin

78   *Cannot . . . words* Perhaps another outburst of commotion prompts him to cede the podium to Lucius.

79   *erst* once

       our ancestor Aeneas, who related the fall of Troy to Dido in Virgil's *Aeneid* II

84   *Sinon* A relation of Ulysses, he allowed himself to be taken prisoner by the Trojans and persuaded them to accept the Wooden Horse – the 'fatal engine' of the next line – into the city.

86   *civil wound* the mutilation of the body politic, civil war.

Marcus implies that the insertion of Tamora into the heart of the state is analogous to the Trojans' acceptance of the Wooden Horse.

87   *compact* composed

89   *But* without

91   *ye* Marcus addressing Lucius, along with the Romans

92   *force ... commiseration* Marcus claims that the misfortunes of the Andronici as told by Lucius will inevitably evoke pity, as much as the story of the fall of Troy told by Aeneas.

100   *and basely cozened* and he was despicably cheated

101   *fought ... out* fought to the end

103–14 *Lastly ... truth.* In *Coriolanus* Shakespeare returns to the exile of an uncompromising field commander, who, eventually, was forced out of Rome.

103   *unkindly* unnaturally

108   *turned-forth* the turned-out, the castaway

109–11 *That have ... body.* Lucius reminds the Romans of his record of service in order to show that he has been ill-rewarded for it, and that his alliance with the Goths should not be taken as treachery.

111   *advent'rous* willing to incur risk

113–14 *My scars ... truth.* The custom of showing scars and wounds in order to secure popular suffrage is also pivotal in *Coriolanus* II.2.136–9.

120   *irreligious* godless

125   *patience* Titus's excesses need explaining, as Patience – as opposed to revenge – was the acceptable moral stance against injury and adversity.

128   *Have we* if we have

133   *mutual closure* shared extinction

139   *The common ... so.* This line is anticipated at IV.4. 69–77 and V.1.1–4.

148   *give me aim awhile* assist me for a while. This is an expression from archery where the archer is helped in target practice by an observer reporting where the previous shaft has landed.

149   *puts me to a heavy task* imposes on me the burden of mourning

150–73 This episode of intimate grief contrasts with the formal obsequies and Alarbus's ritual sacrifice in I.1.

151   *obsequious* dutiful, but also pertaining to obsequies
        trunk corpse

156   *tenders* tender kisses, but also repayment of a duty, an image prolonged into a conceit by 'sum', 'pay' and 'countless' in lines 157–8

164–8 See An Account of the Text, p. 165.

172   *so* provided that

179   *cry for food* This terrible sentence has been anticipated at V.3.6. Aaron is to be executed by starvation.

181   *doom* See note to III.1.24.

194   *ravenous* rapacious, insatiable

195–9 The Romans' failure to grant Tamora a decent burial sheds a negative light on the new regime, which has just attempted to distinguish itself from the old one by replacing sacrifice and ritual obsequies with pity and compassion. See note to 150–73 above.

197   *to prey* to prey upon. Aaron is excommunicated from the ranks of the living, while Tamora becomes the food he lacks.

AN ACCOUNT OF THE TEXT

Titus Andronicus was first published in 1594 in a quarto edition (Q1) printed by John Danter. This is almost certainly the 'booke intituled a Noble Roman Historye of Tytus Andronicus' entered in the Stationers' Register by Danter on 6 February 1594.

There is no reason to doubt that Danter's edition was based on an authorial manuscript. Several aspects of Q1 suggest a direct link with Shakespeare's foul papers, that is, the state of the text before it reached the theatre, where it would be transcribed, normalized and used as a prompt-book. Most prominently, the stage directions in Q1 are sketchy and sparse; alternative speech prefixes are used to refer to the same character; and three passages at I.1.35–8, III.1.36 and IV.3.94–106 are sometimes regarded as afterthoughts, which Shakespeare failed to integrate with the scene or sequence within which they are embedded.

The Second Quarto (Q2) was set from a copy of Q1 and published in 1600. The corrector of Q2 omitted the first of the three passages mentioned above, tampered with the second, but left the last one unaltered. The corrector of Q2 was also responsible for replacing five original lines at V.3.164–8 with five new, spurious lines, for modifying the very last line of the play and for adding four new lines to the original ending. It was only in 1904, when the only extant copy of Q1 was discovered in Sweden, that editors realized that the corrector of Q2 must have been forced to compensate for extensive damage to the last two leaves in his copy of Q1 (see the collation of V.3 in the 'Rejected Emendations' list printed below). All editions subsequent to Q2 until the discovery of Q1 inherited the tampered ending, along with some accurate corrections of obvious compositorial mistakes in Q1.

The third Quarto (Q3) was published in 1611 and is a fairly

straightforward reprint of Q2. Q3 was used as copy-text for the First Folio in 1623 (F1), but only after being heavily annotated by comparison with a theatrical document, most probably a prompt-book, as the number and quality of the new stage directions introduced in F1 make clear. Besides more detailed and more accurate stage directions, F1 introduces act-breaks, a theatrical practice which first came into use around 1608. F1 drops five sound Quarto lines at II.1.101, IV.2.8, IV.2.76, V.2.160 and V.3.51, it adds a dubious line at I.1.403 and a similarly awkward half-line at IV.1.36, and provides a whole new episode at III.2, known as the 'Fly scene'. Although editors cannot establish the exact date of this addition, a remarkable consistency of imagery and diction suggests that it is almost certainly authorial. Internal evidence supports the hypothesis of a later addition. The previous scene, for example, concludes with a strong statement of the revenge motif of the Andronici, which is at once developed in IV.1; without III.2 the play retains an unbroken narrative line. Titus, Marcus, Lavinia and young Lucius leave the stage at the end of III.2 to reappear immediately at the start of IV.1, but the practice of exiting-to-return is not Shakespearean. Only in III.2 does Tamora appear as 'Tamira', and Titus as *Andronicus* in the stage directions, and as *An.* in the speech prefixes. The lines in III.2 are metrically and rhythmically freer than in the rest of the play, which might suggest that they were composed at a later date.

Given its direct link with the author's foul papers, Q1 is generally adopted as copy-text for modern scholarly editions of this early tragedy. The present edition is based on Q1, except for III.2, which is based on F1. This edition endorses the three dubious Q1 passages mentioned above, because, despite their hypothetical status as afterthoughts, they cause no significant disruption to the pattern of meaning and the pace of the surrounding dialogue. In the first passage at I.1.35–8, for example, Marcus announces that Titus has already sacrificed the noblest prisoner of the Goths. Later on in the same scene, however, Lucius obtains Titus's permission to sacrifice Alarbus, Tamora's eldest son, who is promptly dispatched off stage. As former editors have suggested, the opening of the first passage – 'and at this day' – might be interpreted as an allusion not to Alarbus's sacrifice, but to a ritual which Titus performs 'on such days as this one', that is on the days of his triumphant return to Rome from the wars against the Goths. Line 33 tells us that there have been five such days. 'Done' at line 37 would then parallel 'Five times he hath returned' at line 33 and read 'Five times hath he done sacrifice'. Lines 99–104 and 125–9 confirm that this ritual is well-established. Similarly, the metric awkwardness of the half-line in Titus's complaint at III.1.33–40 – 'And bootlesse vnto them' – can be justified as a symptom of Titus's progressive decline into madness, as opposed to Shakespeare's failure to delete a false start. The last controversial passage at IV.3.94–106, which is often believed to represent undeleted first thoughts in the foul papers, mainly on the grounds of a repetition, as Titus asks the Clown the same question at lines 97–8 and at line 106, also makes powerful dramatic sense. The Clown's first answer is a witty disclaimer of his rhetorical skills: to Titus's request, 'Tell me, can you deliver an oration to the Emperor with a grace?' (IV.3.97–8), the Clown replies that he cannot even say grace before dinner, let alone speak an oration. When Titus encounters further resistance, he asks the Clown to stop ('Hold, hold', IV.3.104) and offers him money. What could be more natural, therefore, than that Titus, having written the oration, should repeat in modified form the request originally resisted, and that he should now receive an affirmative answer?

Q1 is followed very closely in the present edition, and emended only when the other early texts or subsequent scholarly editions correct obvious compositorial mistakes. The original spelling and punctuation have been modernized, and the stage directions improved by resorting to F1 or to later editions. Jonathan Bate's Arden edition of *Titus Andronicus* (third series) and the innovative edition of *Titus Andronicus* included in Stanley Wells and Gary Taylor's *William Shakespeare: Complete Works* have proved particularly useful as a source of extensive new directions, which have greatly improved the reader's perception of the theatrical qualities of this play.

The following collations list the main departures from Q1, rejected emendations from earlier editions, stage directions which derive from a source other than Q1 and substantial emendations of the original punctuation in Q1, which affect meaning and/or lineation. Q and F indicate readings common to all Quarto and the Folio editions.

COLLATIONS

I

The collation printed below lists all departures from the First Quarto (Q1), except for stage directions and substantive emendations of the original punctuation and lineation, which are treated separately below. This list ignores corrections of misprints and modernization of archaic and obsolete spelling in Q1. The readings listed at III.2 represent departures from the First Folio (F1), as this scene does not appear in the earlier Quarto editions of 1594, 1600 and 1611. Origin is noted only when the source is a later Quarto or Folio edition. Eighteenth-century editors first introduced most of the other emendations listed below.

THE CHARACTERS IN THE PLAY] *not in* Q, F
I.1
6   wore] Q (ware)
18 MARCUS] *not in* Q, F
36 the Andronici] that Andronicy Q1; *not in* Q2–3, F
44 Capitol] Q3, F; Capitall Q1–2
67 CAPTAIN] F, *not in* Q
74 freight] fraught Q, F
81 rites] Q3, F; rights Q1–2
101 *manes*] F3; *manus* Q, F1–2
144 these] the Q, F
146 rites] F2–4; rights Q1–3, F1
160 LAVINIA] *not in* Q1–2; Laui. Q3, F
229 Titan's] Q2–3, F (Tytans); Tytus Q1

245 Pantheon] F3–4; Pathan Q, F1; Panthaeon F2

267 chance] Q2–3, F; change Q1

283 *cuique*] F2–4; *cuiquam* Q1–2; *cuiquam* Q3, F1

319 Phoebe] F2–4; *Thebe* Q, F1

361 MARTIUS *and* QUINTUS] *Titus two sonnes speakes.*
Q, F1–2; *Titus two sonnes speak* F3–4

363 MARTIUS] *Titus sonne speakes.* Q, F

371 QUINTUS] *3. Sonne* Q; *1. Sonne* F

372 MARTIUS] *2. Sonne* Q, F

374 MARTIUS] *2. Sonne* Q, F

399 beholden] beholding Q, F

401 MARCUS] *not in* Q; F *continues to Titus*
Yes, and will nobly him remunerate.] F; *not in* Q

408 seize] F2–4; ceaze Q; cease F1

454 raze] F3–4; race Q1–3, F1–2

477 LUCIUS] *not in* Q; *Son.* F

II.1 26 years want] F2–4; yeares wants Q, F1

110 than] this Q, F

122 with all] withall Q1

II.2   1 morn] Q3, F; Moone Q1–2

24 run] F2–4; runnes Q1–3, F1

II.3 69 try experiments] Q2–3, F; trie thy experimens Q1

72 swart] swartie Q1–2; swarty Q3; swarth F
Cimmerian] F2–4; Cymerion Q, F1

85 note] notice Q, F

95 O'ercome] Q2–3, F (Orecome); Ouercome Q1

107 yew] F; Ewghe Q1; Ewgh Q2; Ewe Q3

110 Lascivious] Q3, F; Lauicious Q1–2

126 quaint] painted Q, F

131 ye] F2–4; we Q, F1

144 sucked'st] suckst Q, F

150 heard] Q2–3, F; hard Q1

160 ears] Q3, F1–4; yeares Q1–2

192 AARON] F; *not in* Q

210 unhallowed] F (vnhallow'd); vnhollow Q

222 berayed in blood] bereaud in blood Q1; embrewed
heere Q2–3, F; heere reav'd of lyfe *early MS*

169

		emendation in the margin of the sole surviving copy of Q1
	231	Pyramus] Q2–3, F (Piramus); Priamus Q1
	236	Cocytus] F2–4 (Cocitus); *Ocitus* Q, F1
	260	grieved] Q2–3, F (greeu'd | grieu'd); griude Q1
	291	proved] proud Q1
II.4	11	MARCUS] *not in* Q, F
	27	him] them Q, F
	30	three] their Q, F
	39	sewed] F3–4; sowed Q, F1–2
	43	sewed] F4; sowed Q, F1–3
III.1	9	are] F2–4; is Q, F1
	12	these two,] these, Q, F1; these, these F2–3; these, these, F4; these, good
	21	on thy] Q1 (outhy)
	67	handless] Q2–3, F; handles Q1
	146	his true] F4; her true Q, F1–3
	169	Writing] F; Wrighting Q
	215	sorrows] sorrow Q, F
	224	blow] F2–4; flow Q, F1
	280	employèd:] imployde in these Armes, Q; employd in these things: F
III.2	1–85	*This scene does not appear in* Q, *see An Account of the Text above.*
	1	TITUS] An. F *(throughout scene)*
	13	with outrageous] F2–4; without ragious F1
	39	complainer] complaynet F1; complaint F2–4
	52	thy knife] F2–4; knife F1
	53	fly] F2–4; Flys F1
	54	thee] F3–4; the F1–2
	55	are cloyed] F2–4; cloi'd F1
	72	myself] F2–4; my selfes F1
IV.1	1	YOUNG LUCIUS] Puer Q; Boy F *(throughout scene)*
	10	MARCUS] *not in* Q, F
	19	griefs] Q3, F; greeues Q1–2
	50	quotes] Q2–3, F; coats Q1
	53	Forced] Q2–3, F (Forc'd); Frocd Q1

77   TITUS] *not in* Q1–2; *at line* 78 *in* Q3, F

87   hope] Q2–3, F; h op Q1 (*slipped to the edge of the page*)

90   swore] sweare Q, F1–2; sware F3–4

122 good man] Q2–3, F; goodman Q1

IV.2   15   that,] *not in* Q, F

51   Good] Q3, F; God Q1–2

68   fair-faced] fairefast Q1–2; fairest Q3, F

94   Alcides] Q2–3, F; *Alciades* Q1

95   seize] F3–4; ceaze Q, F1–2

123 that] Q3, F; your Q1–2

151 Muly lives] *Muliteus* Q, F

IV.3   32   But [ ]] But *catchword* Q1; *omitted in* Q2–3, F. *A line or more may be missing here.*

45   Acheron] F2–4; Acaron Q, F1

54   *Apollinem*] *Apollonem* Q, F2–4; *Appollonem* F1

57   Saturn', Caius] *Saturnine, to Caius* Q, F

66   aimed] aim Q, F

67   Jupiter] Q2–3, F; *Iubiter* Q1; *also at lines* 79 *and* 83

77   News, ... come.] F; *2 lines in* Q1, *assigned to Clowne; 2 lines in* Q2–3, *assigned to Titus*

116 must hold] hast made Q, F

IV.4   5   know, as know] know Q, F

48   by'Lady] Q (be Lady), F (berLady)

93   feed] Q3; seede Q1–2; foode F

98   ears] F; yeares Q

113 incessantly] sucessantly Q1; successantly Q2–3, F

V.1   9   FIRST GOTH] *Goth* Q, F

17   ALL THE GOTHS] F2–4 (*Omn.*); Q, F1 *continue to Goth*

20   SECOND GOTH] *Goth* Q, F

27   dam] Q2–3, F; dame Q1

43   here's] Q2–3, F; her's Q1

53   Get me a ladder] *assigned to Aaron in* Q, F

84   nurse] nourish Q, F

133 haystacks] F (Haystackes); haystalks Q1; haystakes Q2–3

V.2   18   give it action] F; giue that accord Q1–3; give it that accord

38   them out] Q2–3, F; the mout Q1

49   globe] Globes Q, F

52   murderers] murder Q, F

        caves] F2–4; cares Q, F1

56   Hyperion's] F4 (*Hiperion's*); *Epeons* Q; *Eptons* F1; *Hiperions* F2; *Hiperious* F3

61   Are they] F2–4; Are them Q, F1

65   worldly] Q2–3, F; wordly Q1

V.3   26   gracious] Q2–3, F; *not in* Q

72–94   *continued to Marcus*] *attributed to* Romane Lord *in* Q, *and to* Goth *in* F; *in* F4, *lines 76–94 are spoken by Marcus*

93   Here's] Her's Q1; Heere is Q2–3, F

124   cause] F4; course Q, F1–3

140, 145   ROMANS] *attributed to Marcus in* Q, F

153   bloodstained] F3–4 (blood-stain'd); blood slaine Q1–2; bloud-slaine Q3, F

195   rite] Q3, F; right Q1–2

2

Rejected Emendations

The following list includes some of the more interesting and important variant readings and proposed emendations *not* accepted in the present edition. They derive from the early editions (the three Quartos of 1594, 1600 and 1611 and the four Folios of 1623, 1632, 1663 and 1685) and from scholarly editions from the eighteenth century to the present. Provenance is noted only when emendations derive from the early editions. This list ignores obvious misprints and compositorial mistakes and/or tampering with verse and syntax, which slipped into every new early edition, while old misprints and inaccuracies inherited from Q1 were being progressively emended and normalized.

I.1	5	am his] was the F
	5–6	that was the last | That] of him that last F4
	35–8	and at this day . . . of the Goths.] *not in* Q2–3, F
	43	succeed] succeeded
	74	his] her F4
	102	earthy] earthly F
	141	his] her
	157	drugs] grudgges Q3, grudges F
	220	people's] Noble F
	307	none] there none els F2–4
II.1	18	servile] idle Q3, F
	26	wits wants] wit wants Q2–3, F
	64	jet] set F
	73	meaner] better F3–4
	101	*not in* F
II.3	20	yellowing] yelping F
	88	Why, I have] Why I haue F1; Why haue I F2–4
	115	be ye not henceforth] be not henceforth; be ye not from henceforth; be ye not henceforward
	120	the] thy Q3, F
	229	earthy] earthly Q3, F
II.4	15	an] in Q2–3, F
	21	half] have
	38	Philomela] Philomel
III.1	17	ruins] urns
	34	if] or if Q2–3; oh if F
		did mark] did heare F
	35	They would . . . I must,] *not in* Q3
	35–6	yet plead . . . unto them.] *not in* F
	37	sorrows] sorrowes bootles Q3, F
	59	agèd] noble Q3, F
	125	like] in Q2–3, F
	169	castle] casque; cask; crest
	229	her] their
	281	thy teeth] thine arms
III.2	1–85	*This scene does not appear in Q, see An Account of the Text above.*

	60	a father and mother] a father and a mother; father, brother
	62	doings] dolings; dronings; dotings; dirges
IV.1	36	F *adds* 'What booke?' *as a separate line*
	45	so] see how
IV.2	8	*not in* F
	9–17	*continued to* Demetrius *in* F1; *attributed to* Boy *in* F2
	71	Zounds, ye] Out you F
	76	*not in* F
	177	feed] fat; feast
IV.3	8	catch] finde Q3, F
	40	so] now
IV.4	18	unjustice] injustice F
	67	this] his
	78	your] our F
	102	*not in* Q3, F
V.1	46	deaf? Not a word?] deaf? no! Not a word? F2–4; deaf? What, not a word?
	141	But] Tut Q2–3, F
V.2	22	witness these] these
	71	humours] Q1 (humors); fits Q2–3, F
	160	*not in* F
V.3	51	*not in* F
	92	And force you to] Lending your kind Q2–3; Lending your kind hand F
	93	Rome's young] a Q2–3, F
	94	While I stand by] Your harts will throb Q2–3, F
	95	Then, gracious] Then noble Q2–3; This Noble F
	96	Chiron and the damned] cursed Chiron and Q2–3, F
	129	pleading] now Q2–3, F
	131	hurl ourselves] cast vs downe Q2–3, F
	132	souls] braines Q2–3, F
	163	story] matter Q2–3, F
	164–8	And bid thee . . .	their latest kiss,] Meete and agreeing with thine infancie,	In that respect then,

like a louing child. (*comma in* Q3, F) | Shed yet
some small drops from thy tender spring, |
Because kind nature doth require it so, | Friends
should associate friends in griefe and woe. Q2–3,
F

175 A ROMAN] Romans F

199 dead . . . pity.] so, shall haue like want of pitty. |
See iustice done on Aron that damn'd Moore, |
By (From *in* F1, F3–4; For *in* F2) whom our
heauie haps had their beginning: | Than (Then *in*
Q3, F) afterwards to order well the state, | That
like euents may nere it ruinate. Q2–3, F

3

Stage Directions

The collation printed below lists substantive departures from the
stage directions as they appear in Q1. Stage directions in Q1 are
notoriously sparse and inadequate. Supplementary directions
have therefore been added to clarify the action. The origin of
additional directions is indicated only when their source is F.
The alterations listed at III.2 represent departures from the First
Folio (F1), as this scene does not appear in the earlier Quarto
editions of 1594, 1600 and 1611. Minor editorial interventions,
such as the addition of 'asides' or the name of the addressee of a
specific speech or specific lines within a longer speech, are not
noted. Q2–3 and F2–4 are not collated separately, unless their
stage directions are used in the present edition, as at I.1.294 or
II.3.208.

I.1   0   *Flourish. Enter the tribunes and senators aloft; and
then enter below Saturninus and his followers at one
door, and Bassianus and his followers at the other,
with drums and colours*] Enter the Tribunes *and*
Senatours *aloft: And then enter* Saturninus *and his
followers at one dore, and* Bassianus *and his followers,
with Drums and Trumpets.* Q1; *Flourish. Enter the*

I.1   0   *Tribunes and Senators aloft. And then enter Satur-*
              ninus and his Followers at one doore, and Bassianus
              and his Followers at the other, with Drum & Colours.
              F

     17   *Enter Marcus Andronicus aloft with the crown*] F;
         Marcus Andronicus with the Crowne. Q

     58   *Exeunt his soldiers; his other followers remain*] *Exit*
         Soldiers. Q, F

     62   *not in* Q, F

     66   *Flourish*] *not in* Q

     72   *three sons, Alarbus, Chiron and Demetrius,*] *two*
         sonnes Chiron *and* Demetrius, Q, F

   107   *not in* Q, F

   132   *Exeunt Titus's sons with Alarbus*] *Exit Titus sonnes*
         with Alarbus. Q; *Exit sonnes with Alarbus.* F

   133   *not in* Q, F

   144   *Enter the sons of Andronicus, with their swords bloody*]
         Enter the sonnes of Andronicus againe. Q,F

   164   *not in* Q, F

   171   *not in* Q, F

   172   *not in* Q, F

   205   *not in* Q, F

   215   *not in* Q, F

   223   *not in* Q, F

   236   *A long flourish till Marcus, Saturninus, Bassianus,*
         tribunes and senators come down. Marcus crowns
         Saturninus] *not in* Q; *A long Flourish till they come*
         downe. F

   278   *not in* Q, F

   279   *not in* Q, F

   285   *not in* Q, F

   289   *not in* Q, F

   291   *not in* Q, F

   292   *not in* Q, F

   294   *He attacks Mutius*] *not in* Q, F

   295   *Titus kills him*] *not in* Q1–2; *He kills him.* Q3, F

   301   *Exit*] *not in* Q, F

340 *Exeunt all but Titus] Exeunt omnes.* Q, F

386 *not in* Q, F

392 *kneeling] They all kneel and say,* Q, F

393 *They rise] not in* Q, F
   Exeunt all but Marcus and Titus] Exit all but Marcus and Titus. Q, F

401 *Flourish. Enter the Emperor, Tamora and her two sons, with the Moor, at one door. Enter at the other door Bassianus and Lavinia, with Lucius, Quintus and Martius] Enter the Emperour, Tamora and her two sonnes, with the Moore at one doore. Enter at the other doore Bascianus and Lauinia, with others.* Q; *Flourish. Enter the Emperor, Tamora, and her two sons, with the Moore at one doore. Enter at the other doore Bassianus and Lauinia with others.* F

429 *not in* Q, F

463 *not in* Q, F

476 *not in* Q, F

480 *not in* Q, F

488 *not in* Q, F

498 *Sound trumpets. Exeunt all but Aaron] Exeunt. Sound trumpets, manet* Moore. Q; *Exeunt. | Actus Secunda* F

II.1 o *Aaron is alone on stage] not in* Q; *Flourish. Enter Aaron alone.* F

II.2 o *Enter Marcus, Titus Andronicus and his three sons, Lucius, Quintus, and Martius, making a noise with hounds and horns] Enter* Titus Andronicus, *and his three sonnes. making a noise with hounds & hornes.* Q; *Enter Titus Andronicus and his three sonnes, making a noise with hounds and hornes, and Marcus.* F

II.3 o *with gold] not in* Q, F

    7 *not in* Q, F

   45 *not in* Q, F

   54 *not in* Q, F

  116 *He stabs Bassianus] stab him* Q, F

  117 *not in* Q, F

168 *not in* Q, F

184 *not in* Q, F

186 *not in* Q, F

187 *not in* Q, F1; *Exeunt* F2, *after* 186

191 *Exit*] F; *not in* Q
     Quintus and Martius] *not in* Q, F

197 *not in* Q, F

208 *Exit*] Q2–3; *after* 207 *in* Q1; *Exit Aron.* F

245 *He falls in*] *not in* Q; *Boths fall in* F
     with attendants] *not in* Q, F

268 SATURNINUS (*reads*)] *Saturninus reads the letter.* Q, F

285 *not in* Q, F

288 *not in* Q, F

299 *not in* Q, F

303 *not in* Q, F

306 *Exeunt with Martius and Quintus under guard, and attendants with the body of Bassianus*] *not in* Q; *Exeunt* F

II.4   10 *Wind horns. Enter Marcus from hunting to Lavinia*] F; *Enter Marcus from hunting.* Q

III.1   0 *tribunes as*] *not in* Q, F
     over] *on* Q, F

16 *Exeunt the judges and others with the prisoners*] *not in* Q; *Exeunt* F

52 *not in* Q, F

64 *not in* Q, F

65 *not in* Q, F

138 *not in* Q, F

190 *left hand*] *hand* Q, F

205 *not in* Q, F

208 *not in* Q, F

232 *Titus and Lavinia rise*] *not in* Q, F

239 *Exit, after setting down the heads and hand*] *not in* Q1; *Exit* Q2–3, F

248 *not in* Q, F

277 *not in* Q, F

286 *They kiss] not in* Q, F

Exeunt all but Lucius] Exeunt. Q; *Exeunt. Manet Lucius* F

III.2 1–85 *This scene does not appear in* Q. *See An Account of the Text, above.*

3 *not in* F

11 *not in* F

75 *not in* F

IV.1 0 *Young Lucius]* F; *Lucius sonne* Q

4 *not in* Q, F

29 *not in* Q, F

64 *not in* Q, F

69 *at 67 in* Q, F

87 *not in* Q, F

93 *not in* Q, F

IV.2 13 *not in* Q, F

17 *Exit with attendant] Exit.* Q, F

86 *not in* Q, F

133 *not in* Q, F

145 *not in* Q, F

161 *not in* Q, F

170 *Exeunt Chiron and Demetrius with the Nurse's body] Exeunt.* Q, F

IV.3 0 *Enter* Titus, *old Marcus, his son Publius, young Lucius, and other gentlemen (Caius, Sempronius) with bows, and Titus bears the arrows with letters on the ends of them] Enter* Titus, *olde* Marcus, *young* Lucius, *and other gentlemen with bowes, and* Titus *beares the arrowes with letters on the ends of them.* Q1; *Enter Titus, old Marcus, young Lucius, and other gentlemen with bowes, and Titus beares the arrowes with Letters on the end of them.* F

64 *not in* Q, F

104 *not in* Q, F

105 *not in* Q, F

108 *not in* Q, F

114 *not in* Q, F

IV.4 0 *Chiron . . . attendants.*] *not in* Q, F
       34 *(Aside)*] *not in* Q; *at end of line 35 in* F
       49 *Exit guarded*] *Exit* Q, F
       60 *Aemilius, a messenger*] *Nutius Emillius* Q
V.1   0 *Flourish*] F; *not in* Q
       19 *leading*] F2–4; *leading of* Q, F1
       53 *not in* Q, F
      146 *not in* Q, F
      151 *Aaron is gagged*] *not in* Q, F
      165 *Flourish*] *at the end of line 164 in* F; *not in* Q
            Exeunt] Q3, F; *not in* Q1–2
V.2   0 *Enter Tamora disguised as Revenge, and her two sons,
            Chiron as Rape and Demetrius as Murder*] *Enter
            Tamora and her two sonnes disguised.* Q, F
        8 *above*] *not in* Q, F
       69 *not in* Q, F
       80 *not in* Q, F
      121 *at the end of line 120 in* Q, F
      131 *not in* Q, F
      148 *not in* Q, F
      151 *not in* Q, F
      160 *not in* Q, F
      162 *not in* Q, F
      204 *with the bodies*] *not in* Q, F
V.3   0 *with Aaron prisoner, and his child*] *not in* Q, F
       15 *Flourish*] F; *not in* Q
       16 *Exeunt Goths with Aaron*] *not in* Q, F
            Aemilius] *not in* Q, F
       25 *Trumpets sounding. A table brought in. They sit. Enter
            Titus like a cook, placing the dishes, and Lavinia with
            a veil over her face, with young Lucius and others*]
            *Trumpets sounding. Enter Titus like a Cooke, placing
            the dishes, and Lauinia with a vaile ouer her face.* Q;
            *Hoboyes. A Table brought in. Enter Titus like a
            Cooke, placing the meat on the Table, and Lauinia
            with a vale ouer her face.* F
       44 *not in* Q, F

46 *He kills her*] Q3, F; *not in* Q1–2
63 *not in* Q, F
65 *not in* Q, F
66 *not in* Q, F
75 *not in* Q, F
118 *not in* Q, F
144 *not in* Q, F
151 *not in* Q, F
155 *not in* Q, F

4

Punctuation and Lineation

This collation lists substantive emendations of the original punctuation and lineation, but ignores incidental alterations in the punctuation which leave the original sense unaltered. The alterations listed at III.2 represent departures from the First Folio (F1), as this scene does not appear in the earlier Quarto editions of 1594, 1600 and 1611.

I.1   14 seat, to virtue consecrate,] seate to vertue, consecrate Q; seate to Vertue: consecrate F
      206 *2 lines in* Q, F
      288 *2 lines in* Q, F
   293–4 *What . . . Rome?*] *1 line in* Q, F
      336 queen, Pantheon. Lords, accompany] Queene: Panthean Lords accompany Q; Qeene, | Panthean Lords, accompany F
   488–9 *1 line in* Q, F
II.1   4–8 reach. . . . hills,] reach, . . . hills. Q; reach: . . . hills: F
       45 *2 lines in* Q, F
   79–80 Aaron . . . deaths | . . . propose to . . . love.] Aaron . . . deaths . . . propose, | To . . . loue. Q, F
       97 *2 lines in* Q, F
     102 *2 lines in* Q, F
II.2 16–17 I say no: . . . more] F; *1 line in* Q

	20	*2 lines in* Q, F
II.3	132	outlive, us] out liue us Q1; out-liue vs Q2–3, F
	184–5	Nay then . . . her husband.] F; *1 line in* Q
III.1	63	*2 lines in* Q, F
	176	*2 lines in* Q, F
	184	*2 lines in* Q, F
III.2	65	*2 lines in* F
	66	*2 lines in* F
	74–5	*1 line in* F
IV.1	95–9	beware: | The . . . once. | She's . . . league, | And . . . back, | And, . . . list.] beware, | The . . . once, | Shee's . . . league, | And . . . backe. | And . . . list. Q; beware | The . . . once, | Shee's . . . league. | And . . . backe, | And . . . list. F
IV.2	20–21	*1 line in* Q; *2 lines (prose) in* F
	51–2	Good morrow, lords. | . . . the Moor?] F; *1 line in* Q
	62	*2 lines in* Q, F
	64–5	*1 line in* Q, F
	80	*2 lines in* Q, F
	168–9	*Aaron . . . secrets.] 1 line in* Q, F
IV.3	7–8	*1 line in* Q, F
	77	News, . . . come.] F; *2 lines in* Q1, *assigned to* Clowne; *2 lines in* Q2–3, *assigned to Titus*
	84–5	Alas sir, . . . life.] *2 lines (verse) in* Q, F
	89	From . . . there.] *verse in* Q, F
IV.4	36–7	quick: . . . out,] quick, . . . out: Q, F
V.1	95–6	Why, . . . and 'twas | Trim . . . doing of it.] Why . . . trimd, | And twas trim . . . doing of it. Q, F
V.2	152	*2 lines in* Q, F
V.3	28	all. Although] *after* F (all: although); all although Q
	39	*2 lines in* Q, F
	71	body,] body. Q, F
	72	herself,] her selfe. Q, F
	124	revenge] F; reuenge. Q

PENGUIN SHAKESPEARE

THE MERCHANT OF VENICE
WILLIAM SHAKESPEARE

A noble but impoverished Venetian asks a friend, Antonio, for a loan to impress an heiress. His friend agrees, but is forced to borrow the sum from a cynical Jewish moneylender, Shylock, and signs a chilling contract to honour the debt with a pound of his own flesh. A complex and controversial comedy, *The Merchant of Venice* explores prejudice and the true nature of justice.

This book includes a general introduction to Shakespeare's life and the Elizabethan theatre, a separate introduction to *The Merchant of Venice*, a chronology of his works, suggestions for further reading, an essay discussing performance options on both stage and screen, and a commentary.

Edited by W. Moelwyn Merchant

With an introduction by Peter Holland

General Editor: Stanley Wells

PENGUIN SHAKESPEARE

RICHARD III
WILLIAM SHAKESPEARE

The bitter, deformed brother of the King is secretly plotting to seize the throne of England. Charming and duplicitous, powerfully eloquent and viciously cruel, he is prepared to go to any lengths to achieve his goal – and, in his skilful manipulation of events and people, Richard is a chilling incarnation of the lure of evil and the temptation of power.

This book includes a general introduction to Shakespeare's life and the Elizabethan theatre, a separate introduction to *Richard III*, a chronology of his works, suggestions for further reading, an essay discussing performance options on both stage and screen by Gillian Day, and a commentary.

Edited by E. A. J. Honigmann

With an introduction by Michael Taylor

General Editor: Stanley Wells

PENGUIN SHAKESPEARE

THE TWO GENTLEMEN OF VERONA
WILLIAM SHAKESPEARE

Leaving behind both home and beloved, a young man travels to Milan to meet his closest friend. Once there, however, he falls in love with his friend's new sweetheart and resolves to seduce her. Love-crazed and desperate, he is soon moved to commit cynical acts of betrayal. And comic scenes involving a servant and his dog enhance the play's exploration of how passion can prove more powerful than even the strongest loyalty owed to a friend.

This book includes a general introduction to Shakespeare's life and the Elizabethan theatre, a separate introduction to *The Two Gentlemen of Verona*, a chronology of his works, suggestions for further reading, an essay discussing performance options on both stage and screen, and a commentary.

Edited by Norman Sanders

With an introduction by Russell Jackson

General Editor: Stanley Wells

PENGUIN SHAKESPEARE

THE WINTER'S TALE
WILLIAM SHAKESPEARE

The jealous King of Sicily becomes convinced that his wife is carrying the child of his best friend. Imprisoned and put on trial, the Queen collapses when the King refuses to accept the divine confirmation of her innocence. The child is abandoned to die on the coast of Bohemia. But when she is found and raised by a shepherd, it seems redemption may be possible.

This book includes a general introduction to Shakespeare's life and the Elizabethan theatre, a separate introduction to *The Winter's Tale*, a chronology of his works, suggestions for further reading, an essay discussing performance options on both stage and screen by Paul Edmondson, and a commentary.

Edited by Ernest Schanzer

With an introduction by Russ McDonald

General Editor: Stanley Wells

PENGUIN SHAKESPEARE

HENRY IV, PART I
WILLIAM SHAKESPEARE

Prince Hal, the son of King Henry IV, spends his time in idle pleasure
with dissolute friends, among them the roguish Sir John Falstaff. But
when the kingdom is threatened by rebellious forces, the prince must
abandon his reckless ways. Taking arms against a heroic enemy, he
begins a great and compelling transformation – from irresponsible
reprobate to noble ruler of men.

This book includes a general introduction to Shakespeare's life and the
Elizabethan theatre, a separate introduction to *Henry IV, Part I*, a
chronology of his works, suggestions for further reading, an essay
discussing performance options on both stage and screen, and a
commentary.

Edited by: Peter Davison

With an introduction by Charles Edelman

General Editor: Stanley Wells

PENGUIN SHAKESPEARE

AS YOU LIKE IT
WILLIAM SHAKESPEARE

When Rosalind is banished by her uncle, who has usurped her father's throne, she flees to the Forest of Arden where her exiled father holds court. There, dressed as a boy to avoid discovery, she encounters the man she loves – now a fellow exile – and resolves to remain in disguise to test his feelings for her. A gloriously sunny comedy, *As You Like It* is an exuberant combination of concealed identities and verbal jousting, reconciliations and multiple weddings.

This book includes a general introduction to Shakespeare's life and the Elizabethan theatre, a separate introduction to *As You Like It*, a chronology of his works, suggestions for further reading, an essay discussing performance options on both stage and screen, and a commentary.

Edited by H. J. Oliver

With an introduction by Katherine Duncan-Jones

General Editor: Stanley Wells

PENGUIN SHAKESPEARE

ANTONY AND CLEOPATRA
WILLIAM SHAKESPEARE

A battle-hardened soldier, Antony is one of the three leaders of the
Roman world. But he is also a man in the grip of an all-consuming
passion for the exotic and tempestuous Queen of Egypt. And when
their life of pleasure together is threatened by the encroaching politics
of Rome, the conflict between love and duty has devastating
consequences.

This book includes a general introduction to Shakespeare's life and the
Elizabethan theatre, a separate introduction to *Antony and Cleopatra*,
a chronology of his works, suggestions for further reading, an essay
discussing performance options on both stage and screen, and a
commentary.

Edited by Emrys Jones

With an introduction by René Weis

General Editor: Stanley Wells

Penguin Shakespeare

KING LEAR
WILLIAM SHAKESPEARE

An ageing king makes a capricious decision to divide his realm among his three daughters according to the love they express for him. When the youngest daughter refuses to take part in this charade, she is banished, leaving the king dependent on her manipulative and untrustworthy sisters. In the scheming and recriminations that follow, not only does the king's own sanity crumble, but the stability of the realm itself is also threatened.

This book includes a general introduction to Shakespeare's life and the Elizabethan theatre, a separate introduction to *King Lear*, a chronology of his works, suggestions for further reading, an essay discussing performance options on both stage and screen, and a commentary.

Edited by George Hunter

With an introduction by Kiernan Ryan

General Editor: Stanley Wells

PENGUIN SHAKESPEARE

All's Well That Ends Well
Antony and Cleopatra
As You Like It
The Comedy of Errors
Coriolanus
Cymbeline
Hamlet
Henry IV, Part I
Henry IV, Part II
Henry V
Henry VI, Part I
Henry VI, Part II
Henry VI, Part III
Henry VIII
Julius Caesar
King John
King Lear
Love's Labour's Lost
Macbeth
Measure for Measure
The Merchant of Venice

The Merry Wives of
* Windsor*
A Midsummer Night's
* Dream*
Much Ado About Nothing
Othello
Pericles
Richard II
Richard III
Romeo and Juliet
The Sonnets and A Lover's
* Complaint*
The Taming of the Shrew
The Tempest
Timon of Athens
Titus Andronicus
Troilus and Cressida
Twelfth Night
The Two Gentlemen of
* Verona*
The Two Noble Kinsmen
The Winter's Tale